THE GIFT OF LOVE

Book of Love, Book Eight

Meara Platt

Text by Meara Platt
Cover by Dar Albert

Dragonblade Publishing, Inc. is an imprint of Kathryn Le Veque Novels, Inc.
P.O. Box 7968
La Verne CA 91750
ceo@dragonbladepublishing.com

Produced in the United States of America

First Edition September 2020
Print Edition

The characters and events portrayed in this book are fictitious. Any similarity to real persons, living or dead, is purely coincidental and not intended by the author.

ARE YOU SIGNED UP FOR DRAGONBLADE'S BLOG?

You'll get the latest news and information on exclusive giveaways, exclusive excerpts, coming releases, sales, free books, cover reveals and more.

Check out our complete list of authors, too!

No spam, no junk. That's a promise!

Sign Up Here

www.dragonbladepublishing.com

Dearest Reader;

Thank you for your support of a small press. At Dragonblade Publishing, we strive to bring you the highest quality Historical Romance from the some of the best authors in the business. Without your support, there is no 'us', so we sincerely hope you adore these stories and find some new favorite authors along the way.

Happy Reading!

CEO, Dragonblade Publishing

Additional Dragonblade books by Author Meara Platt

The Book of Love Series

The Look of Love
The Touch of Love
The Taste of Love
The Song of Love
The Scent of Love
The Kiss of Love
The Hope of Love
The Gift of Love
The Chance of Love

Dark Gardens Series

Garden of Shadows
Garden of Light
Garden of Dragons
Garden of Destiny

The Farthingale Series

If You Wished For Me (A Novella)

Also from Meara Platt

Aislin

Chapter One

London, England
December 1820

OF ALL THE *bad luck.*

Dahlia Farthingale forced a smile on her face as the guests at her sister's party crowded around her and cheered because she'd found the pea in her slice of Twelfth Night cake.

"Queen Pea! Queen Pea!"

Ugh! They were all still chanting as they closed in around her and Captain Ronan Brayden, forcing them up against each other. He had the misfortune to find the bean in his slice of cake, which meant he was now her King Bean.

"King Bean! King Bean! Kiss your queen!"

Dahlia's sister, Holly, had recently married Ronan's brother, Joshua, and this reception was to welcome family and friends to their elegant new home in Mayfair. It was still early December, too soon in the season for the traditional Yuletide cake to be served. But a fire crackled in every hearth throughout the house, and the scent of spiced wine and roasted chestnuts filled the air, so their guests were quickly drawn into the festive spirit.

To add to the effect, light snow had fallen overnight, leaving London in a beautiful coat of white.

Despite the bitter temperature outside, the house was filled with warmth, and everyone was imbibing quite a bit of the freely flowing champagne, mulled wine, and nog. Oh, and there was tea since this was supposed to be a tea party, but she didn't think anyone had actually bothered with that staid drink. This explained why they were all so raucously merry. But could they not have waited until Christmas to start these silly revels?

Ronan held out his hand to her. "Give me your pea, Dahlia."

She handed it over, wondering why he wanted it. She took no offense at his familiar use of her name since they were among close friends and family.

He held up the pea along with his bean, cheerfully playing to his ridiculous title of King Bean and earning the adoration of these revelers, many of whom were in their cups. Of course, adoration was nothing new to him. Several women were already swooning as he stood there in his Royal Navy uniform, looking too exquisite for words.

"Ready?" He grinned wickedly and turned her to face him, his dark emerald eyes gleaming with mirth.

"Don't you dare kiss me," she said between clenched teeth, the forced smile still on her face.

He leaned closer and whispered in her ear. "If your face were any stiffer, it would crack. Breathe, Dahlia. I am only going to give you a light kiss on your cheek, not eat you."

"It isn't only that. We also have to open the dancing, and it's to be a waltz. Oh, why did I have that slice of cake? Gerald won't like this at all."

"Gerald Wainscott?" Ronan's gaze shot to her beau. "Don't tell me you and that priggish lord are still an item? If he finds fault with this harmless bit of fun, then he's a humorless clot, and you are better off without him. If you want my opinion–"

"Which I *still* don't."

"I'll *still* give it anyway," he said, tucking a finger under her chin to draw her gaze up to his and rousing more cheers from the crowd. He leaned forward to continue whispering in her ear, knowing only she would hear him because of the surrounding noise. "He's a pompous, overstuffed peacock who cares more for outward appearances than for what is truly important in life. He'll crush your spirit."

"So, you like him then?" She cast Ronan an impish smirk, wanting to be irritated and take offense. But she could never be angry with him because he meant well and always looked out for her. Over the course of these past few months, he had assigned himself to be her guardian angel.

Only in small ways, of course.

Offering to dance with her if he ever saw her standing alone at an affair.

Suddenly appearing at her side if a gentleman he deemed unsuitable approached her.

Always finding a moment to sit beside her and ask about her day.

He was a typical Brayden. Ridiculously protective and forthright. Most of all, she always got an honest answer from him. Perhaps a little too honest, at times.

Being a typical Brayden also meant he was big and muscled. Built like a Roman gladiator. Handsome as sin in a rugged, manly way.

He laughed and put his arm around her waist to draw her closer. "I shall try to like him for your sake. Take another deep breath. Our kiss will be quite painless, I assure you. Close your eyes and tip your head to the side, just the littlest bit."

"Why must I tip my head?" She did not understand why her thoughts were suddenly so muddled. Perhaps it was the champagne she had been served, an excellent vintage, and she'd taken two glasses already.

Or was it three?

Cake, champagne, and being held in Ronan's arms were a heady combination.

"I need to get the correct angle to kiss you on the cheek. It may seem a simple matter, but it is actually a rather complex set of mathematical calculations required to–"

"Kiss your queen! Kiss your queen!"

"Ah, the crowd is getting restless," he joked and brought his head down to kiss her before she was ready so that his lips landed on her mouth. Her *open* mouth. Her fault, really. She should not have turned and looked up at him to ask another question at this precise moment.

And now that she had…holy crumpets!

His warm lips pressed down on hers…and pressed some more…and…warmth flooded her body. Suddenly, everything tingled, and she became acutely aware of *him*. The sandalwood scent of him. The gentleness of his embrace despite the strength of his arms.

The perfection of his kiss.

Oh, my heavens.

He abruptly drew his mouth off hers and stared down at her in confusion. He was looking at her so oddly, she knew she must have done something terribly wrong and had to apologize at once. "I'm so sorry! You caught me unprepared. I had more questions to ask and did not see your lips coming at me until it was too late."

She was not certain he heard any of her apology, for the enthusiastic crowd was cheering too loudly and now began to shove them in the direction of the music room to open the dance.

Ronan held her by the elbow to keep her from stumbling. This was always the Brayden way. If someone was in trouble, a Brayden rushed forward to help. Not that she was in any serious trouble, but she was not very big, and this crowd would have easily knocked her down in their enthusiasm.

Ronan was the size of an oak tree.

No one was going to push him over.

"Are you all right, Dahlia?" He appeared to be sincerely concerned, taking a moment to look her over as they stood alone on the dance floor.

"A little shaken up, I fear." Everyone was staring at them, still cheering in anticipation of the musicians striking the first notes. The musicians were a quartet consisting of a pianist, several violinists, and a harpist.

Ronan's arm went around her waist, and he placed the palm of his hand at the small of her back. With his other, he took her hand in his. "I've got you. You'll be fine."

She gave a stiff nod, just wanting this ordeal to end. First a kiss, and now a dance? She was still reeling over the touch of his mouth to hers. No man had ever kissed her before, certainly not like this. Gerald ought to have been the one to do it.

So why was she relieved Ronan had been the first? He wasn't her beau. It troubled her that she was still tingling. And dreading that Gerald would notice and find yet another reason to disapprove of her behavior.

"Bollocks, you're still wound in a tight coil. What is wrong with you today?"

"I don't know. I want to have fun, but Gerald is tossing daggers at me. How is it my fault that I got the pea? And don't you dare say anything to him once this dance is over. You've got that protective look in your eyes again. I do not want you fighting my battles."

"I am not doing any such thing."

She rolled her eyes. "Yes, you are. Stop it. He is my problem. Well, not my problem. He is my beau."

Ronan sighed. "Forget about him for the moment. You've done nothing wrong."

"But I am dancing in your arms, and he obviously does not like it."

"The music hasn't started yet. I'm just holding you."

"Which is even worse." They stood alone in the center of the room, the crowd still applauding them and tossing Ronan advice, which included shouts of *kiss her again* as if their first kiss hadn't been enough.

He arched an eyebrow. "Are you betrothed to the lunk?"

"No, not yet. I think we shall be soon."

"Then he has no claim on you. Enjoy the moment. Every man in the room wishes he were the one holding you in his arms. You are young and beautiful, Dahlia. It is impossible for you to look anything but enchanting no matter what you do."

This is why she treasured Ronan's friendship. He always made her feel good about herself, never awkward or inferior.

"However, one word of caution," he said with a glint in his eyes that warned he was about to tease her. "Whatever you do, *don't* smile."

Which had quite the opposite effect on her, as he knew it would. Her tension eased, and she cast him a heartfelt grin. He was right. It was just a dance. They were among friends and family. She did not owe Gerald an apology.

The music started up, and Ronan began to slowly twirl her around the room. The ladies clapped. The men cheered. Everyone was having a nice time.

They waltzed past Gerald, and she stiffened again.

Ronan frowned. "That man ties you up in knots. You must stop worrying about what he'll think."

"I'm trying. Perhaps if I were more polished. But how can I be when I am only in my first season? Lately, Gerald seems to be finding fault with everything I do, even down to the style of my hair and the fashion of my gowns."

His frown deepened. "How long has this been going on?"

"I don't know. Ever since I arrived in London. I always thought I had an elegant style, but apparently, he feels I am not up to London standards. Am I terribly out of step? Holly and Joshua's house decoration turned out quite splendidly, and I had a large part in that."

"You did a fine job. I'm quite impressed."

"Ronan, is he right about the way I look? You mentioned a moment ago that I was pretty. Did you mean it? Or were you just saying this to calm my nerves?"

"I believe I called you beautiful, which is what you are. If Wainscott does not appreciate you, then run from him. Do not marry him. You cannot pretend to be someone you're not and keep up the falsehood for the next forty years."

"Maybe I am making too much of it. Gerald knows who I am. He's known me for most of my life. We grew up together in York. He isn't as bad as you make him out to be." She glanced at her beau and noticed that he was still frowning at her. "Perhaps he wouldn't be quite so irritated if I were dancing with someone other than you."

The musicians had opened with one of Dahlia's favorites waltzes. She was relieved to be dancing with Ronan because if she wanted to be silly and take a few extra twirls to play up to the festive onlookers, he would go along with it.

Gerald never would.

In truth, it irked her that her beau often looked down his nose at such antics.

To her surprise, Ronan was a very good dancer and quickly got her back into the steady glides and spins of the waltz on the occasion or two that she missed a step. She did not know why she'd expected less. Perhaps because he was a captain in the Royal Navy, and she thought he'd be awkward on his sea legs. But he hadn't been out to sea in almost a year now, serving as the Admiralty liaison to Parliament.

"Why would he care who you danced with?"

She laughed and shook her head. "Surely, you must know how handsome you are. What man would not be jealous if he saw *you* dancing with his sweetheart?"

Indeed, he was perfection. Ebony-dark hair, dark emerald eyes, and a big muscled body. Who would not find him devastatingly attractive? He was no empty head, either. All these Braydens were highly intelligent and possessed a quick wit.

She might have fallen for Ronan if he weren't so daunting. Not that he had ever made her feel like a fumbling, inept debutante. But he had been out in the world, fought battles, was known and respected by the most powerful men in England because of his important role in Parliament.

Who was she?

No one yet.

Her greatest achievement in all of her almost twenty years was helping Holly decorate this house.

Other couples now joined them on the dance floor. Joshua and Holly, of course. This was their home, and they were the host and hostess. Dahlia's heart gave a little tug. They looked so happy together. Joshua was looking at Holly as though she were the only woman in existence. This is what she wanted for herself.

She craned her head to find Gerald now that there were so many people waltzing around her and blocking her view. She wasn't nearly as tall as Ronan, only on the small side of average height.

Then she saw him dance past her with a young woman in his arms. "Who is she?" she asked Ronan, who had followed her gaze and knew exactly where she was looking.

"Lady Alexandra Minton. She is a neighbor. Her parents own the house next door to this one. Her father is the Earl of Balliwick."

"I see." She took another peek at them, for there was something in the way Gerald held this young lady that sent an uneasy tingle up her spine.

Ronan drew her a little closer and gave her hand a squeeze. "She's a ninny."

Dahlia did not feel any better. "She's very pretty."

"She has an irritating laugh and is one of the dimmest girls I've ever met. I doubt Wainscott will bear to be in her company for more than five minutes. He'll come running back to you as soon as this waltz ends. I would, for certain."

She wished she could be as confident. In truth, what did she have to offer any man? What did Gerald see in her that made him want to court her? Lately, as she had just admitted to Ronan, he did not seem to like her very much.

If not for the ardent letters he'd been writing her over the course of the year, she would not think he liked her at all. In those dozen or so letters, he'd confided how much he missed her and how eager he was to escort her around London when she arrived.

Her stomach began to roil.

She had come to London believing Gerald would be offering for her at the start of the season or surely by the end of it. Now, she did not know what to think. She watched him as he twirled past her again with Lady Alexandra in his arms. Her father was a wealthy earl. How could she compete with that?

She couldn't.

"No, Ronan. He isn't coming back to me." She blinked away tears, not even certain why it hurt her so much. Perhaps she had forced herself into believing they could be as happy as Holly and Joshua were. She had only to look around the room to see how many of her Farthingale relatives had made love matches.

All of them.

Starlight shone in their eyes when they looked at their spouses.

Gerald had never displayed so much as a flicker for her. Thinking on it now, it was obvious he had never been in love with her despite his words to the contrary. Why had it taken her so long to realize it?

Their courtship, if it even was that, had been a pretense. She had been a fool to believe it would ever lead to a happy and loving marriage.

So had Gerald, perhaps.

Well, she wasn't certain what had been on Gerald's mind. Perhaps he had only meant to occupy his time with her until someone better came along.

"Dahlia," Ronan said, his voice deep and tender, "don't you dare shed a tear over that worthless bounder."

"It's all my fault. I should have refused to dance with you."

"You got the pea, and I got the bean. It was our sacred obligation to dance together. If Wainscott does not understand this and seeks to hurt you for indulging in a harmless Twelfth Night bit of fun, then I can only repeat, the clot does not deserve you."

The music had stopped, and couples were beginning to walk off the dance floor. Ronan was preparing to walk her back to her Aunt Sophie, but she shook her head. "No, I think I need a moment to myself."

She cast him a smile, hoping she did not appear as fragile as she now felt, and made her way out of the room. Although her back was to Ronan, she knew he was staring at her and worrying over her because this is what guardian angels did.

For this reason, she took her time strolling out and doing her best to hold herself together. She knew his protective instincts had to be flaring again and did not want him to follow her out.

It was odd how well she understood him. They had gotten to know each other over the past few months, especially while Holly and Joshua were falling in love and realizing they could not exist one without the other. It was quite a beautiful thing, and she was so happy for her sister.

Of course, she and Ronan held no such romantic notions about each other.

She caught sight of Gerald slipping into the library and called out to him, but he must not have heard her because he hurried in and shut the door behind him.

Dahlia wasn't certain what to do.

She stood in the hall and glanced around. The house was crowded, guests packed into the main rooms, and some were even spilling into the hall.

Why had Gerald felt the urgent need to disappear into the library? Perhaps she ought to wait for him to come out.

She doubted he'd gone in to read a book in the middle of this party. Gerald was not particularly introspective and enjoyed being the center of attention.

Sighing, she decided not to overthink the matter. Knocking lightly, she waited to the count of three and walked in. "Gerald, I–"

She blinked taking a moment to understand what she was looking at. Gerald was up against the shelves, his body pressed against Lady Alexandra, his pants down about his ankles, and her gown pushed up around her waist. "I…" The breath rushed out of her. Her madly pounding heart shot into her throat.

She felt ill.

The pair scrambled to put themselves in order. "Bloody hell," Gerald muttered with a snarl.

She turned to run out and slammed straight into Ronan's solid chest. He caught her before she could bounce off him and tumble backward. "What's going on here?"

Of course, being no dullard, he quickly realized what had just occurred. He curled his hands into fists at his sides. "I'm going to hit him."

"Don't you dare!" Dahlia tipped her chin up in the air. "I will handle this."

Ronan eyed her dubiously. "You are out of your depth here. Let me–"

"No." She stepped in front of him. "Captain Brayden, I will not have you interfering."

He clenched his jaw, obviously wanting to take charge of the situation. After a moment, he gave a curt nod. "But I'm not leaving."

"Dahlia has only herself to blame for this." Gerald immediately went on the offensive, which might have been more effective had he not been doing up the last buttons on his trousers as he feigned outrage.

What gall!

Ronan growled.

She cast him a warning glance.

But Gerald seemed to have a death wish, for he would not keep his mouth shut. "Her conduct these past few months has been unbecoming of a lady, and I will no longer tolerate it."

"Mine? Are you jesting?" she sputtered. "Don't be ridiculous. That Queen Pea silliness is a harmless holiday tradition. Over and done with now. Is this all you wish to say to me after all the years of our acquaintance?"

"No, there is one more thing." He cast her an imperious look, seeming not to care that they were now starting to draw a crowd. More importantly, he seemed not to notice that Ronan had gone deathly still. But she had and was now worried about it. Ronan was not patiently listening to Gerald. He was an uncaged beast about to pounce on him and rip out his throat.

Ronan's simmering rage was a palpable thing. She could feel his tension in the sudden crackle to the air. *Oh, dear.* Could she hold him back if he decided to take matters into his own hands? She did not think so.

His jaw was still clenched, and now his hands were curled into fists. It did not escape her notice that when fisted, they were the size of boulders.

"I had hoped your coming to London would give you some polish," Gerald continued, his manner snide and condescending, "but I realize this will never happen. You will never be elegant or sophisticated. My parents warned me that you would prove an endless source of embarrassment. I see now they were right. I wish you well, Dahlia. But do not expect me ever to call on you again."

Dahlia felt like a fool as more guests began to gather in the hall and were now elbowing each other out of the way to peer into the library and watch the bloodbath going on. Her blood. And Gerald was thoroughly dunking her in that bath.

Ronan turned to the onlookers and cast them a warning glance. He was not going to let any of them in.

As for her, she stood there gaping like a fool, too stunned to respond.

Perhaps she ought to have allowed Ronan to handle the situation. She was just standing there like an idiot and taking Gerald's verbal barbs. She wanted to say something tremendously clever and cutting, but words failed her.

Gerald could have taken her aside privately to say this. But it seemed his pettiness knew no bounds. He was the one in the wrong. He'd been caught with another woman and was now insulting her in front of her entire family just to be hurtful.

Ronan placed his hand to the small of her back and wordlessly drew her behind him.

He strode toward Gerald. "Wainscott…" He smashed his fist into Gerald's face, then strode back to her side. "Sorry, Dahlia. I had to do it."

She groaned. "No, you didn't."

What had Ronan accomplished other than to make himself feel better? It wasn't helping her to see Gerald on his knees in the middle of the library with blood gushing from his nose. She drew out her handkerchief and handed it to him, not that she cared a whit for this man who had done nothing but belittle her since she'd arrived in London.

However, she did not want him dripping blood on the beautiful carpet she had helped pick out not two months ago.

Lady Alexandra rushed over and knelt by his side. "My darling!"

Her darling?

Could this get any worse?

Ronan's hand was at her waist again.

Comforting.

Protective.

"Miss Farthingale," Lady Alexandra said, "this is most awkward, but you may as well know the rest of it. There's no point in keeping it quiet now that we've been caught in this compromising situation. Lord Wainscott and I have been secretly betrothed for a month now. Unofficially, that is. We dared not make the official announcement before the betrothal contract was signed, which it was yesterday."

Her words were like a punch to Dahlia's face. "What?"

"I'm so sorry. I did not think it was fair to keep it from you. But Lord Wainscott insisted. You must realize he was never yours. He never considered marrying you. But I do apologize it had to come out this way. Come, Gerald. Father and I will take you home now."

Dahlia moved aside to allow Alexandra's father in. At the same time, she took Ronan's hand and drew him aside, purposely keeping her fingers entwined in his until Gerald and the Mintons quit the room. She did not want him doing anything else to the oaf while he was in a seething rage.

Let him think she was a meek flower in need of his support.

It was not very far off the mark.

She had never seen a man look as angry as Ronan looked now. His eyes were ablaze, and if he were a tea kettle, he would have had steam pouring from his ears. "Bollocks," he said with a heartfelt groan, pity for her situation etched in his handsome features. "I'm so sorry, Dahlia. I did not see that one coming."

"Nor did I." She shoved her way through the crowd and ran from the room in tears.

CHAPTER TWO

RONAN FOUND DAHLIA sobbing on the bed in one of the upstairs guest bedchambers.

Her sisters, Holly and Heather, had run up with him, as had a flurry of her cousins, but he shooed the cousins away. "Give her a moment to herself. Holly, this is your party. You ought to return to your guests. Heather and I will look after her." Of course, he was going to stay beside Dahlia because…well, because he was her King Bean and she was his Queen Pea, and therefore, he was responsible for her.

As everyone dutifully filed downstairs, he and Heather strode in and shut the door behind them. Heather rushed to her sister's side. "I'm so sorry Gerald hurt you, Dahlia."

Dahlia responded by sobbing louder.

Now Heather looked ready to burst into tears herself. The sisters were close, not only in age but in their affection for each other. If one was hurting, then the other would hurt, too.

Ronan ran a hand through his hair, uncertain what to do or say.

These girls were both so young and innocent. Dahlia was not quite twenty years old. Heather had just turned eighteen.

Wainscott's betrayal had been a devastating blow.

Bollocks.

He knew how to handle a French army firing artillery at him, but he had never had to console two crying women before. He was lost.

Still, he had to say something. Didn't he? "Not all men are like him, Dahlia. You'll understand when the right one comes along."

"Go away, Ronan. Why did you have to hit him? It only made matters worse."

He did not see how that was possible.

Sighing, he drew up a chair beside the bed and sank onto it. "You must understand. I could not let him get away with speaking to you that way. He meant to humiliate you in front of your friends and family. That was a low thing to do even for a snake. Lady Alexandra ought to have been appalled by his behavior."

"Why? I am nobody to her. I will never be in her elevated circle."

"Your connections in society are just as good as hers, perhaps better. How many of your cousins have married dukes, earls, viscounts, barons? And what of my family? We have three earls among us, including my own brother, Tynan. Also my two cousins, Marcus and James. Westcliff, Kinross, and Exmoor, respectively."

"But I am no relation to you."

"Your sister is married to my brother. That is close enough."

She sniffled. "He made me feel so awful."

"I know." He took out his handkerchief and handed it to her. "Dry your eyes, Queen Pea. He isn't worth another moment of your anguish."

"Ugh! Don't call me that. This stupid Twelfth Night cake is what started this mess."

He cleared his throat. "Wainscott started this mess months ago. Now that he's secured an earl's daughter, he was looking for any excuse to pick a fight with you and cut ties."

She looked up at him, her nose pink and tears streaming down her face. "He could have just told me."

Heather nodded. "He should have. Why did he lie to Dahlia?"

Ronan ran a hand across the nape of his neck, still feeling the discomfort of the situation. "I don't know. Perhaps he meant to return to

Dahlia if things did not work out with Lady Alexandra. But now, with the ink drying on his betrothal contract, he may have felt the need to cut ties fast. I think his aim was to provoke a fight and have you appear as the villain when you began to shout at him and cause a scene."

Heather looked confused. "Dahlia would never do such a thing."

"I know, but obviously, Gerald did not realize it. In his dim mind, he thought he had to make Dahlia out to be unreasonable or deluded because if she came forward and claimed he had made promises to her, it would have put his betrothal to Lady Alexandra in jeopardy. He needed to discredit Dahlia before Lady Alexandra's father publicly announced their betrothal."

Heather finally caught on. "Because if Dahlia sounded logical and reasonable, then everyone would know Gerald had been a disreputable snake, and it would have made him look bad."

"And given Balliwick a reason to rescind the betrothal."

Dahlia sat up and regarded him, her eyes so sad and filled with pain. "So he had to humiliate me?"

"It was stupidly done. A big blunder on his part. But he's pompous, thoughtless, and a coward. It wasn't hard to see what he was thinking."

Heather, who was seated on the bed beside Dahlia and hugging her, shook her head in confusion. "He did not appear to be thinking at all. How did the dreadful scene he caused help him in any way?"

"It didn't. But he came here with a plan in mind and was not quick-witted enough to change it after Dahlia unexpectedly walked into the library and…um, caught him in the act." He cleared his throat, unable to state aloud what Wainscott and Alexandra had been doing. Not that he needed to explain it to Dahlia.

She'd gotten an eyeful.

Dahlia heaved a sigh. "You said Lady Alexandra was a ninny. It seems she was the clever one in all this."

Ronan rolled his eyes. "She is a ninny. The last thing Wainscott wanted was for her to announce to one and all that he'd been secretly courting her for months. All his scheming blew up in his face. No matter what he says or does now, everyone will know he was the conniving weasel, and you were the–"

"What was I? The spurned fool? The clueless rustic?" She dried her tears and cast him a look of resolve. "Well, not anymore. I've had my cry, and I am determined never to shed another tear over him again."

Ronan did not believe her for a moment. She had an expressive face that revealed all, and she was obviously still in pain. Her lips were trembling, and her chin began to wobble. *Bollocks.* She was going to burst into tears again.

He did not know what to do.

She looked so hurt and vulnerable.

He reached out and gently stroked her hair. What he truly wanted to do was wrap her in his arms and kiss her brow, tell her she was worth a thousand Lady Alexandras. But Heather was with them and might get the wrong impression. So he did nothing but remain by Dahlia's side and continue to stroke her hair.

"I'm done with men. I will not attend any balls or elegant supper parties," Dahlia declared a moment later. "No more musicales or teas for me. I'm going to hide up in my room for the next ten years."

"Oh, Dahlia. You can't!" Her sister was once again distressed and absorbing all her hurt. The two of them were sniffling and threatening to turn once more into watering pots.

He was not prepared for this.

He was going to send Heather out of the room on a made-up errand if she burst into tears.

Perhaps he would have managed them better if he'd ever had sisters. But he was the youngest of four brothers. And youngest of the eight male cousins the family had affectionately dubbed as the wildebeests because they had been wild as beasts when growing up.

Wildebeests did not cry.

They were big and brawny and one step above jungle animals when it came to grabbing their share at mealtimes. They did not hesitate to protect their territory from interlopers, even if it meant getting bloodied from time to time. And if one of them was in trouble, the others would band together to help him out.

He would do the same for Dahlia.

How could he not protect this gentle doe?

He took her hand in his, relieved when she did not attempt to draw it away. "If you hide away, then that codswallop wins. Will you allow him the victory? No, you won't," he answered for her immediately because he was not certain how she would reply. "First of all, your sisters will not let you. Holly gave you *The Book of Love* for a reason. You were meant to have it for the purpose of finding love, and this is what you are going to do. Where is it now? What have you done with it?"

"It's on my night table. I was going to read it tonight, but I haven't the heart for it now." She sniffled as she turned toward her sister. "Why don't you take it, Heather?"

"Heather doesn't need it yet." Ronan knew he was interfering, but he'd be damned if he would let this innocent girl ruin her life over that undeserving wretch. He tossed a glance at Dahlia's sister, silently warning her not to contradict him. "Seems to me, this is precisely the reason why you must read it. You cannot let that bounder continue to control your life. You came here to find yourself a husband, so this is what you must do."

"Who will have me now? I am a laughingstock."

He growled. "You are not. Don't ever call yourself that."

"And was Gerald so wrong in telling me that I will never fit in among the cream of society? Look at me. I'm no typical English rose. You must admit my looks are…I don't even know how to describe myself. My hair's an unruly mess."

She put her hands to her hair and began to take out the last of the pins holding the upswept twist in place. Most of the pins had already fallen out since she'd been burrowing her head under the pillows and that fashionable twist no longer looked recognizable. "And how would you describe its color? Have you ever seen anyone with hair like this?"

Blessed saints.

No, he hadn't. He'd never seen a lovelier mane on a lass. Her hair was a splendid dark red with hints of brown and gold.

His fingers began to itch.

He wanted to bury his fingers in the long, silky strands and–

What was wrong with him?

"My eyes, too." She wiped away the last of her tears and opened her eyes wide while leaning closer to him. "What color would you say they were? You can't tell, can you? It is as though an artist tripped and splashed his paints everywhere on them."

They were a stunning mix of green and blue with an outer ring of violet, and flecks of gold tossed in for good measure.

"And," she said with a groan, collapsing back against the pillows, "I have *freckles* on my nose."

"Heavens! What a disaster," he teased, wanting to laugh at her utter innocence. But she was too fragile still and would not take kindly to his attempt to coax her out of her misery. The few freckles she had were adorable and endearing, as was everything else about her. This was why she would never meet the *ton* standards of beauty.

Nor could she carry off that proud, disdainful look so many considered sophisticated. There was nothing cold or haughty about Dahlia.

Quite the opposite, she was vibrant and compassionate. She would never come across as anything but charming.

No, she wasn't a *ton* beauty.

She was something far better. "Don't forget your dimples."

"What?" She sat up again looking kittenish and pouty with her hair in a tumble, and her slightly too wide mouth turned down at the corners.

She had no idea how incredibly beautiful she looked.

He ran a finger lightly along her cheek. "You have dimples in your cheeks when you smile."

Heather nodded. "It's true, Dahlia. You do."

"Then I won't ever smile again," she said with a huff.

Ronan arched his eyebrow. "Fine. Whatever you do, don't–"

She broke into a smile because she knew this is how he always teased her. Sweeter still, she laughed and shook her head. "You are a wicked fiend! I am not through wallowing in my misery, and you are determined to have me see the folly in it. Thank you, Ronan," she said softly, emitting a ragged breath. "I don't know how I can ever repay you for your kindness."

"It isn't necessary."

"Please, let me do something to acknowledge my appreciation. I was so out of my depth when confronting Gerald. He was eating me alive and would have utterly destroyed me if you hadn't been there to protect me. I won't take no for an answer."

"If you are determined…"

"I am."

"Well, there is a way. You know I've been wanting to read *The Book of Love*. Would you have any objection to our reading it together?"

"Why together? Just take the book, Ronan. You are welcome to it, not that you would ever need its help to find love for yourself. Women fall all over themselves to get in front of you. Aren't you already escorting one of the most beautiful debutantes around town? Your name often appears in the gossip rags along with hers. *Who was that handsome Royal Navy captain seen escorting Lady M to the theater?*"

Heather bobbed her head in agreement. "Holly believes you are courting Lady Melinda Ridley."

He eyed her curiously. "Why would she say that? You think I'm interested in Lady Melinda?"

"Aren't you?" Dahlia furrowed her brow as though confused. "How can you not be? It is said she is stunning, and you've been escorting her about town."

"And you believe what the gossip rags say?"

She nodded. "Aren't you courting her?"

"No. It is all stuff and nonsense." He hated all the lies and manipulations that seemed to be the normal course of business in polite society.

Dahlia still appeared confused. "Then why are you seen everywhere with her?"

He arched an eyebrow. "Have you ever seen me with her?"

"Well, no. But gentlemen are supposed to be discreet."

"Dahlia, it is all made up. Are you going to believe everything you read? I haven't been anywhere with her in months. But I expect Lady Melinda is telling everyone quite a different story. It is likely she is the one sending this false information to the newspapers."

Now Dahlia seemed quite shocked. Of course, she would be since it would never occur to her to lie about anything. "Why would she do such a thing?"

"To make a certain marquess jealous and prod him into offering for her hand in marriage. I'm just a captain in the Royal Navy. Lady Melinda is the only child of a duke. I can assure you, her father is not going to allow her anywhere near me. He wants a marquess or better for his treasured offspring."

"Then he is a fool." She shook her head in disbelief, her lovely curls cascading over her shoulders in breathtaking disarray. "You'd make an excellent husband for his daughter. Anyone can see you are a man of substance and ridiculously handsome, too."

He laughed, pleased that she was offended for his sake and thought so highly of him. He liked all these Farthingale women because honesty seemed to be a trait among them. It would not occur to any of them to lie or manipulate in order to advance their positions. "Thank you, Queen Pea. But it isn't going to happen."

She turned to him, her eyes rimmed red and glistening, but at least she was no longer bemoaning her situation. "Ronan, what if it could happen?"

"What do you mean?"

"This book has worked its magic on my cousins and their friends. Even on my own sister. Why can it not do the same for you? Isn't the point to reach for the moon? Who is to stop you from marrying the daughter of a duke?"

His heart was going to stop him.

Did Dahlia not realize what had happened when they'd kissed?

"Perhaps, but I will only do this with you, Queen Pea."

She rolled her eyes. "Very well, *King Bean*. I will read the book with you because you've always been kind and protective of me, especially today, and I am very grateful. But just as you have always looked out for me, it will now be my turn to look out for you. You will have your elegant, *ton* bride. However, please be patient with me. I may not be very good at this matchmaking venture at first. You must understand my own heart is still reeling."

"I know," he said gently. His greatest concern was that Wainscott had hurt her so deeply, she would never be able to trust again. "We shall take it slow. In the meanwhile, your family will expect you to attend the various social engagements, and you ought to go. I'll be there to watch over you whenever I can. If you want to sit in the wallflower corner or with the dowagers, that's fine, too. I won't force you to engage with potential suitors until you feel comfortable enough to do so. But it is important that you not hide away, or others will believe there was truth to that bounder's cruel words. How does this sound to you?"

"Perfect!" Heather clapped her hands. "You are going to make brilliant matches for yourselves."

Dahlia cast him a fragile smile and stuck her hand out. "Agreed."

He took her hand and brought it to his lips. "Shall we start tomorrow, Queen Pea?"

Chapter Three

RONAN HAD NEVER considered courtship a military objective requiring careful strategy, but he did now. It was that cursed kiss to blame. The one he'd given Dahlia, his Queen Pea, at yesterday's party. He'd only meant to give her an innocent buss on the cheek. But she'd turned her head and opened her mouth at that very instant. His lips had landed on her perfect mouth, and nothing had been the same for him ever since.

That kiss had struck him like a bolt of lightning.

Now, all he could think about was Dahlia.

Bollocks.

He did not like feeling out of control, but he was. Heart thumping, body aching. Blood on fire. Half crazed, because he wanted to kiss her again so badly. Of course, it was not going to happen any time soon.

He sighed, knowing he ought to return to bed. It was well after midnight, probably closer to dawn, and he hadn't managed a wink of sleep. He'd spent these past few hours alone in his bedchamber, sitting in a wing chair and watching the fire blaze in the hearth. He'd undressed, taken off all his clothes save for his breeches.

The fiery heat felt good against his bare arms and chest.

He'd been shot last year while battling pirates off the coast of Portugal, taking a ball in the arm and another in the thigh. The one to the thigh was merely a flesh wound, hardly anything at all. But the one to the arm had been more serious. He still felt the nasty twinges whenever the weather turned cold.

The warmth of the stoked fire was a soothing balm.

He rubbed his eyes, hoping the gesture alone could erase the sight of Dahlia crying on the bed, her hair gloriously undone and tumbling over her slight and slender shoulders.

Wainscott had completely shattered her innocent heart, leaving Ronan to pick up the pieces and try to mend it.

He would do his best, of course.

He brought his glass to his lips and drank his port before setting the empty glass back on the table beside him. Still unsettled, he refilled it from the half-empty bottle and then stared at the crimson liquid for the longest while.

Dahlia was as fragile as this crystal glass right now. Having been hurt, she did not want to think of love or marriage, nor would she trust men again any time soon.

It was up to him to restore her faith in those of his sex. How else would she ever fall in love with him? He'd given the problem several hours thought and now had a plan. Whether it would work was an entirely different matter.

But it was a plan.

He drained the last of his port, liking the warmth as it slid down his throat. When he was done, he set the glass aside, stuffed the cork back in the bottle, and made his way to bed.

Hopefully, his Machiavellian strategies would not blow up in his face as Wainscott's had. His were well-intentioned.

Dahlia had to know he would never hurt her.

He was eager to share his ideas with Robbie MacLauren and Joshua the following day. The three of them had offices in the Palace of Westminster, among the oldest of the Parliament buildings. Joshua was a captain in the King's First Dragoon Guards serving as the War Ministry's liaison to Parliament. Robbie was a captain in the Royal Scots Dragoons, working as the Scottish liaison to Parliament. Ronan was a captain in the Royal Navy, working as the Admiralty's liaison to Parliament.

The three of them had grown quite close over the course of their assignments and often tossed ideas back and forth among themselves.

They were now gathered in Ronan's office, Ronan seated behind his desk, while Joshua and Robbie had made themselves comfortable in the chairs in front of his desk. "What is this about?" Joshua asked, casually stretching his legs in front of him. "Does it have anything to do with yesterday's incident?"

"Och, sorry I missed it," Robbie said. "I had to attend a regimental function. A damned boring affair, but I could no' get out of it. I heard all about the excitement that went on at Joshua's place. How did the little pixie take her sister's humiliation?"

Ronan arched an eyebrow. "You mean Heather? Not well at all. She's very close with Dahlia and cried along with her every time Dahlia burst into tears. I spent the entire time trying to calm both of them down."

Joshua nodded. "Heather is very soft-hearted. She adores her sisters. It could not have been easy for her to see one of them suffering. She was supposed to make her come-out with Dahlia, but I think both of them just want to hide out in the Farthingale home until the season is over. Of course, Holly is completely overset by what happened. She cried all night, too."

Ronan was not surprised. Holly was the eldest of the three and extremely protective of her sisters.

"I think Holly expected everything to be right as roses once she gave that book to Dahlia." Joshua shook his head and sighed. "Instead, she saw her sister humiliated and spurned. She blames herself for not seeing Wainscott for the bastard he is. Now that the damage has been done, she doesn't know what to do to make things right."

"Holly doesn't need to do anything. I'm working on the problem." Ronan took a deep breath and leaned forward in his chair. "I've agreed to read *The Book of Love* with Dahlia."

Robbie shot out of his seat. "Are ye bloody insane? Och, ye looby. Ye know what's going to happen next. Ye may as well pick out a ring and stick it through yer nose, for she's going to be leading ye about by it before ye finish reading the first chapter."

Joshua's mouth was agape. "Good Lord, not you, too? Are you sure about this, Ronan? Robbie's right. Have you lost your sanity?"

He arched an eyebrow. "Did you?"

"No, of course not. Marrying Holly is the best thing I ever did." Joshua rolled back his head and groaned. "What is it about Brayden men and Farthingale women? First Romulus. Then Finn. Then me. Now you. I'm not one for superstition, but there is something about that book. If you read it with Dahlia, just know that you are done for. There is no turning back."

Ronan winced. "Josh, I know. I think it is already too late for me."

His brother's eyes widened, and he laughed in disbelief. "Blessed saints! You're serious?"

He nodded. "But Dahlia isn't ready for another suitor yet. Wainscott completely destroyed her confidence. Worse, he's destroyed her trust in men. So I'm not going to say anything to her until we finish reading that book. And I have another plan I'd like to discuss with both of you."

Robbie had crossed to the window to stare out at the Thames, taking a moment to watch the boats sailing along swiftly flowing waters. He now turned back to Ronan with a dazed look on his face. "This is a calamity. All my friends married. My own brother is married, and so's my cousin, Thad. All because of that damn book." He ran a hand roughly through his hair. "I want it next. Will ye give it to me when ye're done with it, Ronan?"

"You too, Robbie? But it isn't his to give away," Joshua said. "Heather is getting it next. You'll have to ask her permission for it."

"The pixie? Och, so be it. Let me know when ye're done with it,

Ronan. I'll approach Heather then."

"Fine." He shook his head. "Why do you refer to Heather as a pixie?"

Robbie settled back in his chair. "Have ye taken a good look at her? Did ye not notice her big eyes? Her little ears that stick out. The mischievous arch to her eyebrows. Her light step. The twinkle in those big eyes. A pixie."

"Well, now that's cleared up." Joshua turned to Ronan. "What's this other plan you mentioned?"

"I'm going to buy a house in town and ask Dahlia to decorate it."

He endured more groans and snorts of disbelief from Joshua and Robbie. Finally, his brother quieted and began to ask his questions. "Miranda is going to eat you alive for this. You're her baby boy. The youngest of her four sons and the only one still at home. She isn't going to let you go so easily. Then she'll be alone in that big, rambling house."

"She will manage. I'm not going to spend the rest of my life living with my mother. She's your mother, too, Josh. And Finn owns the house. Let her be his problem. Or Tynan's. He's the bloody earl. But you have to promise me you'll keep this quiet. No one can know my intentions toward Dahlia or the real reason I want to buy a house. I want your oath on this. Yours too, Robbie. This stays between the three of us."

Joshua sighed. "Fine. You have it. I give you my oath."

"Mine, too. Ye have my word."

"Are you going to take Dahlia on the house search?" Joshua asked.

"As you did with Holly? No, I was thinking of asking Miranda to help me out." This was how her four sons always referred to their mother, for she was tall and fierce, more resembling a warrior out of Norse mythology than a sweet, booties knitting, gray-haired matriarch. Miranda's hair was flame red, and she'd bring her broadsword down on anyone who dared suggest she used a henna dye to keep it that color. "I thought it might ease the transition to involve her in the search."

Joshua snorted. "Or she might set a torch to every house you visit just to make certain you will never leave her."

"She would, too." Ronan sighed. "I'll have to think about how to approach her. I don't want Dahlia searching with me. She'll begin to suspect my intentions if I bring her in on it. But the decorating? She loves that aspect, and she's very good at it. However, the bastard beat her down so hard, she no longer has faith in herself. Having her decorate my new home is the best way I can think of to restore her confidence. However, I'm not going to ask her straight out."

"Why, no'?" Robbie asked.

"I want her to offer to help me. I want her to think our working together on this project is her idea. And I'll be more than happy to accept her offer."

"And she'll never suspect the house purchase or the decorating is part of yer grand plan?" Robbie leaned back and clasped his hands behind his head. "Och, Ronan. Ye seem to have it all figured out."

He shrugged. "I hope so. I'm going to stop by the Farthingale house after work this evening to pay a call on her. I want to discuss details of where and when we'll meet to read that book. Obviously, we need to find somewhere private. But it has to be somewhere properly out in the open as well."

Joshua pursed his lips. "Why not here? It worked for Holly and me."

"No, that was during grouse hunting season, so nothing was going on in Parliament. We had the place to ourselves while the lords were up in Scotland shooting."

"They're all back now," Robbie said. "Pains in my arse, they are. I've been caught up in meetings all week long and have accomplished no' a damn thing."

"I wasn't thinking of here. Not your house either, Josh. That's where the bastard broke Dahlia's heart. Too bad, really. Your place would have been perfect. Holly could have chaperoned her sister and still been discreet enough to give us time alone to read that book together."

Joshua arched an eyebrow. "Do you have another place in mind?"

"Yes, I was thinking of asking Violet if we could meet at her house since she lives right next door to her aunt and uncle on Chipping Way. Dahlia and Heather are living with the aunt and uncle now, so I thought it would be convenient. With Romulus out of town, Violet isn't doing much entertaining. I think she would be more than happy to help out her cousin."

Joshua grinned. "Ah, I have fond memories of that house."

Ronan stared at him, wondering at his addlepated expression. "You do? Why?"

"Never mind, little brother. It isn't important."

"Fine." He shook his head. "I have no idea what you are talking about or why you have that cat-ate-the-canary grin on your face. What do you think of what I've proposed?"

Joshua and Robbie gave their approval.

Good.

Three excellent military brains in agreement on his tactics.

What could possibly go wrong?

Chapter Four

It was dark, and a chill wind had whipped up off the Thames by the time Ronan left his office and made his way to Number Three Chipping Way. The Farthingale butler showed him in, his face expressionless except for the slight twinkle in his eyes. "Welcome, Captain Brayden."

"Thank you, Pruitt." *Ah, yes.* He knew what the man was thinking, for he had been in service with the family for decades and seen the parade of hapless bachelors fall victim to these beautiful Farthingale women. *Welcome, indeed.*

What Pruitt really meant was: *Resistance is useless. You are already ensnared. No point in fighting the inevitable.*

If anyone were resistant, it would be Dahlia.

Pruitt led him into the elegant parlor decorated in shades of blue and then went to announce his presence to John Farthingale, the head of the household. Ronan looked around the room, noting the pale blue silk of the chairs and settee, and the darker blue velvet of the drapes. He noticed the floral pattern on the decorative pillows and other accents around the room. Not that he had ever bothered to look at such things in his entire life. But it was something important to Dahlia, so he did not want to overlook these details.

John greeted him with an outstretched hand, and John's wife, Sophie, bussed his cheek. "To what do we owe the pleasure?" John asked.

Sophie rolled her eyes and took a seat on the sofa. "Honestly, John. We all know why he has stopped by. Dahlia will be down in a moment, Captain Brayden. Thank you for what you did the other day. While I don't usually condone violence, in this case, it was warranted. Lord Wainscott deserved to be soundly thrashed."

John chuckled. "I had to hold my wife back. Her hands were curled into fists, and she was ready to take down that blackguard on her own. But I am relieved you got to him first. He is no gentleman. I would not put it beyond him to hit a lady."

"Oh, John. Let us speak no more of that wretched man. Poor Dahlia has been moping around the house all day because of him. He isn't worth all this attention."

"Indeed, he isn't, Mrs. Farthingale." But Ronan said no more as Dahlia, Heather, and their cousin, Violet, walked in just then.

It was a struggle to tear his gaze from Dahlia. Even when despondent, she looked incredibly beautiful. While she had complained about the color of her hair and eyes, it seemed to him these features were among her finest assets. They complemented whatever gown she chose to wear, no matter the color. She looked stunning. The gown she had on now was dark blue and had no adornment other than a white fichu held in place by a cameo brooch pinned to the fabric at her bosom.

Not that he meant to stare at her bosom, but it was impossible not to notice the magnificent swell of...

Violet was grinning at him.

So was Heather.

Sophie and John exchanged amused looks.

Blessed saints.

"Good evening, Captain Brayden." Violet was still grinning at him. "I hope you had a lovely day."

"I did," he said with a nod and settled in a chair beside the one Dahlia had chosen. This met with a nod of approval from Violet. *Oh, yes*. She was going to help him out. Her matchmaking instincts were on fire.

He could see why his cousin, Romulus, was wildly in love with her. She was a little bubble of champagne, charming and effervescent. Despite her striking beauty, she was genuinely warm and held no conceit. Violet also had one of the finest singing voices in all of England, but she never put on airs. In fact, she was ridiculously modest about her talents.

Heather was the shy one in the family, but obviously felt more comfortable around him after yesterday's incident when they'd both been trying to console Dahlia. "We had a quiet day at home," she said. "Dahlia did not want to go out."

He turned to Dahlia. "Why is that?"

She glanced out the window. "It was too cold."

"I see. Well, perhaps tomorrow then. I'll come around in the morning and take you for a walk in the park. Do you think you will feel up to it?"

She took a deep breath. "Of course. I am perfectly fine. Tomorrow will be perfect. Just perfect."

He turned to Violet and Heather. "Will you join us?"

They gave enthusiastic nods. Dahlia's maid would have served as chaperone otherwise, but these two were not about to pass up the opportunity to watch him and Dahlia together.

Despite Dahlia's protestations that she was fine, perfectly fine, he did not believe her at all. In truth, she looked quite sad. He had not expected her to be chirpy, but it rankled that she was still torn up about her old beau. "Then, it is settled."

He rose to leave, knowing he'd interrupted the family's evening and did not wish to impose on them further.

"Captain Brayden, do stay for supper," Sophie said. "You are most welcome."

He glanced at Dahlia, not wishing to impose if she was not yet ready to accept his company.

But Heather and Violet took the matter out of her hands with an echoing chorus of "Yes, please do."

He nodded. "Thank you, I will."

It would also give him the chance to quietly plan their next meetings. Since most of his days were taken up with work, and often his evenings were occupied with social engagements, they would not have many opportunities to get together to read the book.

He would have gladly refused the social engagements if it were possible. But most of them were important for his work. A large part of his role as liaison was to make the connections necessary to secure funds needed for the navy.

Dahlia was not likely to attend many of those affairs, so he had to set some time apart for her.

They sauntered over to the dining room, and Ronan was surprised to note only eight of them sat for supper. In addition to the six of them was John's brother, Rupert, and a maiden aunt.

Hortensia Farthingale, the aunt, was a permanent fixture in their home. She was a bit of a curmudgeon and had no sooner taken her seat at the table than she began to eye him warily. "Another Brayden," she muttered with a grunt and said nothing further.

"A pleasure to see you again, Hortensia. You are looking quite lovely this evening." He cast her a rakish grin, knowing he probably should not goad her, but the woman was a bit of a dragon, and he knew she would give back twice as good as she got. Her glance alone could cut any man down to size.

In any event, if he teased her, it would only be gentle teasing.

She believed all Brayden men were depraved, lusting hounds – *thank you Romulus, Finn, and Joshua* – but still enjoyed a clever wit and good conversation. He wanted her on his side as he courted Dahlia. Surely, his intentions had to be obvious to everyone, except for Dahlia, who had been kicked too hard to believe anyone would ever want her again.

Rupert, he learned, often joined them for supper. His travels around the world to find new fabrics and bring them back to the Farthingale mills in England made it difficult for him to maintain a proper household of his own, he explained. "Besides, there is no hostess better than Sophie. I know I shall always find a good meal and the best company right here."

The soup course was served by the footmen, a hearty onion soup. They next dug into the main course, an excellent repast consisting of smoked trout, quail stuffed with apricots, roasted potatoes, leeks, and turnips.

Ronan enjoyed hearing of Rupert's travels, listening intently as he spoke of his more dangerous jaunts.

"I often venture along the ancient Silk Road, or so it has been named, but it is too dangerous in certain spots to ever bring family or friends along. The mountains are quite rugged, bandits abound, and not all tribes are friendly to the merchant caravans that make their way along the road."

"Indeed," John said with a shake of his head. "Our nephew, William, got caught in the crossfire between two warring tribes and was quite badly injured during their battle. Fortunately, he survived. But his wounds were quite serious. He's George's son. I believe you know my brother."

Ronan nodded. "The doctor? Indeed, I do. He saved my cousin James. He is a hero to my family."

Sophie smiled. "We're very proud of him, even if Rupert and John are still miffed at him for not coming into the family business."

The two men laughed.

Rupert raised his glass in a toast. "George has saved our hides often enough that we long ago accepted his decision and have been very grateful to him for defying us. To George."

Everyone raised their glasses and gave a chorus of "Here, here."

Hortensia was once again eyeing him. "And you, Captain Brayden. Have you had many adventures? You seem a little young to have done much in the war."

"Hortensia! Honestly. Do behave." Sophie cast him an apologetic smile.

He took a sip of his wine and then set the glass down before he replied to her question. "Indeed, I served mainly toward the end of the war. But I did see a little action at sea battling Napoleon's naval forces off the Iberian Peninsula. I was given command of one of the smaller frigates, obviously being too young to be trusted with the finer ships of the line."

"How old were you at the time?" Dahlia asked.

"I had just turned one and twenty...almost. Our captain was killed early on during one of our engagements. I was second in command, so I took over. The Admiralty decided to leave me in charge despite my young age and promoted me to captain. Our task after the war was to patrol the Mediterranean Sea along the northern coast of Africa and as far as the Aegean Sea. It was quiet for the most part. Not many skirmishes to be had. We were used mainly as a show of force or to battle pirates. Earlier this year, I was called back home and assigned to Parliament."

"You do not look pleased about it," John muttered. "But it is obvious the Lord Admiral has faith in you, or he would not have placed you in this important position."

He shrugged. "In truth, meeting constantly with these politicians is like having a daily tooth extraction. Very different from commanding one's own vessel. I am used to giving orders and having them immediately obeyed. No questions asked. But in Parliament? No one listens unless it serves their purpose. It is often frustrating and thankless."

Violet nodded. "Romulus loves to be out at sea. I think that is his true home."

Ronan shook his head. "No, Violet. You are his home. You are his everything. Wherever you are, that's where he longs to be."

"Crumpets," Heather said in a whisper. "I hope I find that sort of love someday."

Violet dabbed at her eyes with her table linen. "Thank you, Ronan."

He turned to Dahlia, suddenly worried the conversation would turn her thoughts to Wainscott again. So he quickly resumed their earlier conversation and began to describe the ports of call he'd visited during his time at sea. "I've seen a bit of the world, at times under enemy fire. But it was interesting, nonetheless. Casablanca, Tripoli, Alexandria, Izmir, Thessalonica."

Heather's eyes widened in delight. "Oh, how marvelous!"

"But as I said, once the war was over, there was little for us to do but remind everyone of our presence. The most excitement we had was chasing down smugglers and pirates. Much as Romulus is doing now off the coast of Cornwall."

"Were you ever injured in battle?" Violet asked.

He clenched his jaw, for this was not something he particularly liked to talk about. "A time or two. Nothing serious."

John eyed him curiously, obviously understanding what the medals pinned on his chest meant.

"Sophie and I intend to travel someday," the Farthingale patriarch said pensively. "But with so much going on with the family, we haven't made any definitive plans. Do you have a favorite place of all the ones you've visited, Captain Brayden?"

"They all have a charm of their own, and I enjoyed everywhere we sailed. It is almost impossible to choose just one, but if I were pressed, I would have to say Naples. There is something quite spectacular about that coastline."

Rupert nodded. "I quite agree."

"I would love to travel to Italy someday," Dahlia admitted.

"Greece, too. I could lose myself for months exploring the artistry of their ancient civilizations. The buildings, the fashions, the sculptures, and paintings."

"The food," Ronan added. "Quite the best you'll ever eat, present company excepted, Mrs. Farthingale. This quail is delicious."

Sophie laughed. "Mrs. Mayhew is a wonder. She's been our cook ever since John and I were first married. I don't know what I'd do without her. Perhaps we shall take her with us on our travels. Imagine the wonderful dishes she could learn to make on such a trip."

"Indeed," Rupert said. "And I shall volunteer myself to test out every one of them when she returns. But in all seriousness, if you are ever to go anywhere outside of England, it ought to be to Italy."

He turned to Dahlia. "Their fabrics are quite splendid, too. The Italian velvets are magnificent, not only for their softness, shimmer, and warmth, but in the way the colors hold to them. The reds, blues, greens, all appear deeper and richer. The cloths themselves are made by hand by artisans in Florence and Verona. They weave on the same looms used back in the time of the Renaissance."

Dahlia was listening intently, drawn in by her uncle's discussion.

"The silks from China are also quite exquisite. Did you know the mulberry tree–"

Hortensia groaned. "Rupert, you will put us all to sleep if you do not stop talking right now. I've heard your lecture on the origins of silk a thousand times and do not wish to hear it again."

But Ronan could see that Dahlia's eyes were alight for the first time since his arrival. It was a bit of a blow to know that she found fabrics more fascinating than him. However, this was entirely the point of their reading that book together, wasn't it?

She had to learn to trust in love again.

Dahlia set down her fork and turned to her uncle. "Uncle Rupert, I would be interested in learning more. Perhaps we can chat later if that is all right with you."

"My dear," Hortensia intoned. "Do not encourage him. Once you get him started, he will never stop talking."

Ronan saw this as an opportunity to further engage Dahlia in conversation. "Have you had any formal training in art? You did quite a professional job decorating Holly and Joshua's house. How did you manage it?"

Ah, now she was smiling and radiant.

"No formal training, but I think I have an eye for putting colors together."

He nodded. "You do."

Hortensia was not impressed. "Forgive me, Captain Brayden. But you are hardly one to judge. You wear the same uniform day in and day out. One color. Blue."

Gad, she could be a dragon. Did she not see how happy Dahlia was? Why dash her hopes? "I am not in the habit of looking at what I wear. But I do enjoy looking at the ladies, and I know what pleases me."

Well, perhaps that was not the impression he meant to give. He was no leering hound. He merely looked, as anyone else would, and this was all he did when around innocent young women. As for those not so innocent…he cleared his throat. There would be no more of that from now on. "The point is, my eye is always drawn to Dahlia. She always looks lovely. Elegant. Never garish or overdressed. Yet, always noticed. There is an art to it, is there not?"

"There is." Heather nodded enthusiastically. "I always ask her advice on what I should wear. She knows how to put things together beautifully."

Dahlia blushed. "Heather, you are my sister. You have to be kind."

"And what of me?" Ronan asked. "I think I qualify as an impartial third party. It isn't mere flattery. It is a statement of fact. You have a talent for this."

Violet agreed. "Romulus and I have done little with our house. It is very much the way he first bought it from General Allworthy. I would have to speak to him about this, of course. But if he will allow me to make some changes, I would love your help, Dahlia."

"Any time, Violet. It would be my pleasure."

Ronan did not remain long after supper, but he was pleased and thought his visit went surprisingly well. Dahlia was smiling and chatting throughout, and obviously in better spirits. Of course, Rupert and his discussion of Italy and fabrics deserved the credit for that. The possibility of also helping Violet decorate her home put a sparkle in her eyes.

It was a good first step.

Dahlia walked him to the front door and remained beside him while Pruitt went to fetch his cloak. "Thank you, Ronan. I think I was a beast to Violet and my sister all day. I don't know how they put up with me. But your visit cheered us all. I promise to be much nicer company for you and them from now on."

"I enjoyed this evening, too. Your aunt and uncle are quite gracious." He noticed Pruitt approaching. "I'll come around at ten o'clock tomorrow morning to pick you up. Is that all right? I have most of the day free except for a Parliament function in the evening."

"Yes, that's perfect. We prefer to be up and about early in the day. I look forward to it."

"So do I." He tossed his cloak over his shoulders and strode out before he gave into the urge to kiss her. She had been looking up at him, her eyes big and trusting, and her lips beckoning.

She had him aching.

But he forced his mind to his next problem. His mother, Lady Miranda Grayfell.

What was she going to do to him when told he was moving out?

CHAPTER FIVE

"HOW CAN YOU leave me, Ronan?" his mother said in her most theatrical tone, placing a hand over her heart as she sank into her chair like a dying butterfly. They were in the parlor, and he'd caught her just coming back from the theater with friends.

Obviously, she was mimicking one of the actresses from that play. Even for Miranda, her performance was over the top. He waited patiently while she finished her scene, hoping she would calm down and listen to him once she realized he would not respond to her high drama.

Her friends had not stayed long, so he had taken the opportunity to draw her aside before she retired for the evening. "Am I to be abandoned in my dotage?"

He rolled his eyes. "I am not abandoning you, Miranda. Besides, you are decades away from your dotage. And do you seriously believe any of your sons will ever leave you to fend for yourself if you were to become ill? We will always look after you. But it is time for me to go. You know it is."

He tried to speak gently because he knew it was hard for her. Yes, all her sons were grown. But until a few months ago, Tynan was the only son married and set up in his own happy household with his wife, Abigail.

Then suddenly, Finn fell in love with Dahlia's cousin, Belle, and married her. They lived close by, but he knew it was not the same thing as having them under her own roof. Miranda had yet to adjust to Finn's departure when Joshua fell in love with Dahlia's sister, Holly, and bought his own home.

Now here he was, the only son left. "I want you to help me find a place. I don't mind if it's next door, but I need it to be my own."

"My baby boy." She dabbed at her eyes with her handkerchief, but he knew it was mostly for effect.

He rolled his eyes again. "Will you help me? I'm hoping we can start tomorrow afternoon."

She stopped dabbing her eyes, which were not tearing in the first place, and regarded him curiously. "Why the urgency? You are not thinking to bring your *women* into your own home, are you? Isn't that what your seedier gentlemen's clubs are for?"

"First of all, I have no *women*. Nor will I turn my house into a den of iniquity. Can I not have a place of my own simply for want of a little privacy? Will you help me search? Or must I turn elsewhere for assistance?"

She cast him a quelling glance, obviously not liking the idea of that. "Of course I'll help you. Just don't expect me to be happy about it. I love you, my dear boy. It does hurt to see the last of my chicks leaving the coop."

He gave her a kiss on the cheek. "I know. Nor am I taking this next step lightly. But I need you to help me, not undermine me."

She gave a reluctant nod. "I think it will be easier than you imagine."

"Truly?"

"I have a friend who has a lovely house just off Park Lane. It is too much for her to keep up. Her husband died last year and did not leave her quite as well set up as she'd hoped. Her sister lives in Bath, and since my friend prefers the quieter life anyway, she would like to join her sister there."

Ronan's heart beat a little faster in anticipation. "That sounds ideal,

Miranda. Thank you."

"Let me speak to my friend first and make certain she is serious about selling. I'm not sure she will be ready to show it to you tomorrow, but hopefully in a few days' time."

Ronan retired to his bedchamber feeling quite pleased with all he'd accomplished today. He undressed and handed his uniform and boots to his valet. "Thank you, Harrigan."

"Have a good evening, Captain Brayden. I'll have these clothes cleaned and boots polished before you rise tomorrow morning."

He and his brothers had shared Harrigan until one by one they'd all left home. The codger had been a sergeant in his cousin James's regiment and was more of a mother hen than a servant.

Ronan did not have much use for a valet to personally attend him since he was well able to bathe and dress on his own. He almost always wore his uniform even to the more formal functions. There was no fancy tie to drape into a perfect knot or awkward fastenings on his shirt that required the help of another person.

Still, no one had the heart to dismiss Harrigan. He suspected his mother would find a reason to keep him on even when there were no sons at home.

He watched the man leave, then debated whether to read for a while beside the fire or simply climb into bed.

He opted for the latter and was asleep before his head hit the pillow.

He awoke early the next morning feeling better than he had in a long while and climbed out of bed to peer out the window. The sun was shining, and the sky was a crisp blue which boded well for his walk with Dahlia. They would have a nice day if one did not mind the cold too much. In truth, he preferred this weather to the summer's stifling heat.

One could always bundle up in winter, although he rarely did. He liked that bracing chill against his face. He'd endured some pretty bad winter storms at sea, sleet and hail pouring down on them, and a howling wind strong enough to rip sails if one were foolish enough to leave them unfurled.

A little bite to the air as they strolled through the park would be nothing to him. However, he hoped it would not be too much for her.

Ladies were not used to such hardships.

Dahlia, Heather, and Violet were ready and waiting for him when he arrived at John and Sophie's home at the appointed hour. This was another thing he liked about the Farthingale women, they did not play the typical *ton* games taught to all debutantes. It would not occur to any of them to purposely keep their escorts waiting. "Good morning, ladies."

He was usually surly in the morning, as were his brothers. No conversations took place until after they'd had their coffee and perused the newspaper. But seeing these three and their smiling faces brought home how different the sexes were.

"Good morning," Heather said, looking up at him with big, expressive blue eyes. Robbie was right. She did look like a pixie.

Violet gave a little squeal. "I received a letter from Romulus. He'll be home next week."

He was genuinely happy for her. "That is excellent news. I'm eager to hear how he's doing with those pirates off the Cornwall coast."

"Innes will return with him. Do you remember him, Ronan?"

"Yes, certainly. The Duke of Buchan's son serving under Romulus." He shook his head and chuckled. "That boy will soon be Lord Admiral. We'll all be hopping to his commands soon enough."

Violet nodded. "He's a sweet child. Exceptionally clever, too. I'm glad he'll be with us for the holidays. He'd be miserable if forced to be with his father's present wife. But I know he'll miss his father. Just shows you how badly an unhappy marriage can affect everyone, not just the spouses. The duke knows Innes will be with us. I'm sure he'll stop by as often as he can."

Dahlia said nothing, but she had a beautiful smile for him.

Her manner turned pensive as they walked toward the park at this unfashionable hour. The main thoroughfares were already crowded, but the more elegant side streets and squares were much quieter. The Upper Crust did not stir until midday.

"You mentioned last night that you had a function to attend this evening," Heather said, as they entered Hyde Park through the main gate near Apsley House. "Is it the same one Joshua plans to attend?"

He nodded. "Yes, the Earl of Liverpool is meeting with the senior members of the House of Lords and has invited the military liaisons to join them. Joshua, Robbie, and I had to accept, of course. It is obviously important for us to be present whenever budgets are discussed."

Dahlia sighed.

He quirked an eyebrow. "What was that sigh about?"

"Nothing…well, it's just that you've led an interesting life and have done so much with it already. But I've done so little."

"Dahlia, first of all, you are still young. I was doing little more than swabbing decks at the age of nineteen."

"You were already a junior officer and had probably been in several battles." She paused and regarded him curiously. "Did you not go to university?"

"I spent a year at Oxford, but I left in my second term to join the Royal Navy. It's in my blood. I could not sit in a classroom while England was at war. I suppose if ours had been a family of bankers, I would have graduated and then moved on to become an officious clerk seated behind a counter with a prune-faced expression as I counted pound notes and stamped documents all day. But Braydens have always been in the military. So that's where most of us went for lack of knowing anything different."

Dahlia shook her head. "You make it sound as though it is nothing. But your family is extraordinary."

He laughed. "Considering all the Farthingale-Brayden matches occurring lately, I'd say you Farthingales are quite extraordinary, too. Although our families will have to stop marrying after this generation, or else we'll be as inbred as the old royal dynasties of Europe."

"Ugh!" Heather cried, "That is the most unromantic thing I've ever heard."

He laughed. "Sorry."

They walked along the Serpentine and then turned back to return to Chipping Way. Ronan considered mentioning his search for a new house but decided to put it off until later in the week. He wasn't certain Miranda's friend would accept to sell her house to him or that he would like it. He also wasn't certain whether having Miranda help him search was one of his brightest ideas. It could very easily turn into a disaster.

Since he and Dahlia were now walking a little behind Heather and Violet, he took the opportunity to ask about the book. "I have some time today. Do you want to start now or wait a few more days?" He'd managed a quick word with Violet during their walk and knew she was more than eager to lend them her library for privacy any time they wished.

But Romulus would return next week, and he did not want to impose on their time alone. He was eager to start this very day.

"If that book can help me get over Gerald, then I'd like us to read it as soon as possible."

"I'm glad, Dahlia. You deserve better than that weasel."

They returned to Violet's house, and Dahlia ran next door to retrieve it while they removed their cloaks and settled in the parlor for tea and a light repast.

Dahlia returned with the book shortly, her cheeks pink from the outdoors. She sank onto the chair beside his and handed it over. "Here, Ronan. I hope you have more luck with it than I've had."

He tucked it on the seat between them. "Why do you say that?"

"Seriously? When was the last time you were humiliated in front of all your friends and family by a sweetheart caught…um…that…way? I'm sure it has never happened to you, nor will it ever."

He saw that she was getting overwrought again and wanted to reach out to take her hand. But they were not alone, and Heather and Violet were hanging upon his every word. "I'm not suggesting it was well done, but it did get rid of the man who was clearly wrong for you. And there is no doubt he was wrong for you."

"What are you suggesting? That this book brought it about?" She stared at the book's faded, red leather cover and spoke to it. "Next time, try to be a little more subtle, will you?"

None of them found it strange she was talking to a book.

The ladies believed it held magical properties.

Ronan knew a little about *The Book of Love* since Joshua had tried to read bits of it to him and Robbie several months ago. Of course, at the time, he and Robbie had wanted no part of it. Too bad. He wished he had been paying closer attention. "Have you finished your tea, Dahlia?" he asked a short while later.

She nodded.

He extended his arm to her. "Come on then. Time to embark on the journey of love."

She rolled her eyes and made a face, obviously uncomfortable with the notion. "I suppose it is important to learn how not to make a complete ninny of oneself while the man you thought intended to marry you was carrying on right under your nose and then told you that you were worthless."

He cleared his throat. "Right, looks like we have our work cut out for us."

They settled in the library, but he kept the door open for the sake of propriety. He knew Violet and Heather were going to put their ear to the wall to listen in on whatever he and Dahlia were saying.

It did not bother him very much. Right now, he and Dahlia were only going to read. He'd get her alone easily enough when the time was right. "Shall I read to you, or do you want to sit side by side and just read silently?"

Her hands were now clasped on her lap. "You read it aloud. My head is in a jumble, and we haven't even started yet."

"Very well." He took a deep breath and commenced. "Love does not come from the heart but from the brain. It is the brain that sends signals throughout the body, telling us what to feel." He paused a moment, for the next few sentences were devoted to a man's arousal response, and he did not think this was appropriate material for Dahlia so soon after her beloved had been caught with his pants down about his ankles as he drove himself into another woman.

He cleared his throat. "This is how our senses are stimulated. By touch, taste, sight, smell, and hearing."

He glanced at Dahlia.

Her cheeks were a gentle pink and her eyes, as she looked at him, were curious and trusting. "Joshua read this part to me and Robbie a few months ago," he said. "So I'm familiar with it. This opening chapter deals primarily with male responses, but I think the same would apply in reverse. For a man to win the heart of a woman, he would have to please her senses as well."

She nodded. "We know what can happen when the affection is all one-sided."

This is why he was glad they were reading the book together. She was doing exactly what he feared, berating herself and judging herself too harshly. As though any of what Wainscott did to her was her fault. The wretch had purposely duped and manipulated this guileless girl.

Ronan did not respond to her remark and read on. "A man's sense receptacles do not operate in quite the same way as the female's. Nor does a man's brain. It is very different from the female brain."

She snorted. "I'll say. I would never have treated Gerald the way he treated me."

"Because you are a far better person, Dahlia." He returned his gaze to the book and read on about the differences but took the liberty of condensing it to a more palatable form. "What the author is saying is that men are guided by their brains to procreate in order to sire offspring. Unchecked, they will simply go about siring as many offspring as possible. A woman's brain is guided by her need to protect herself and the offspring she delivers into the world. For this, she requires the male to remain by her side while she is at her most vulnerable."

He paused again to glance at Dahlia. "A man will look at any and all women to make a quick assessment regarding her ability to bear his children. Is she too old? Too young? Too sickly or frail? And while a man will ultimately peruse a woman's entire body, his first gaze is on her…"

Breasts.

He cleared his throat.

"Ronan, you are blushing."

"Am I?"

"Yes, you know you are. What does a man look at first?" She cast him a mirthless smile. "No need to spare my delicate sensibilities. I have already seen my supposed beloved with his pants down as he…well, you know what he was doing with Lady Alexandra. I don't think you can say anything that would shock me worse."

He placed his hand over hers. "I know. I'm so sorry you had to witness that."

"Do read on. Please."

"Where was I? Oh, yes. Here." He picked up where he left off. "When a man looks at a woman, he is making a series of quick assessments regarding her ability to bear his children. Is she too old? Too young? Too sickly or frail? And while a man will ultimately peruse a woman's entire body, his first gaze is on her breasts."

"I suppose it makes sense," she said. "The female has to feed her newborn infant, so the man would want to know that she can do it or else risk the infant starving. Unless they found a wet nurse, of course. What else does the book say?"

"Yes, that is exactly right, Dahlia. While a man will ultimately peruse a woman's entire body, his first gaze is…there…because they are the source of life, the source of milk for his newborn children. So, if he does not like the look of them, he will pass her over as a suitable mate."

He paused again to gaze at her. "Wainscott did not pass you over for that reason. Your body is spectacular, if you want my opinion. And I am not saying this to flatter you. I am saying it because it is a fact. That weasel behaved abominably toward you because he is greedy and ambitious. He would have married a cow if she came with a title and a pot of gold."

She laughed softly. "So, you still like him, then?"

He laughed along with her, for this was their private jest. He'd detested the man from the first, and Dahlia knew it. "So we've learned the man's need is to spread his seed. But he also has to protect the children he sires, or they will die."

She nodded. "How does a man reconcile these two urges?"

"The author states that a man's brain functions on two levels. In effect, he has two brains. One is simple or low, and the other is a higher brain allowing for more complex thought. When a man's brain is at its lowest function, he is only thinking of–"

He groaned and shook his head. "He is only thinking of *sex*. Sorry, Dahlia. Just let me know if you find this too offensive, and I'll stop."

"Heavens, no. These are the good bits, aren't they?"

He grinned. "It is his simple brain at work, the one formed thousands of years ago at the dawn of Creation when men first walked the primeval earth. Very little thought occurs when the man's sexual urges are aroused. Perhaps no thought at all."

She was staring at him now, studying him quite intently as she took in his features. "I cannot imagine you ever behaving so crudely, Ronan."

"I don't know. This book is not far off the mark. You see a better side of me because that is how I am when I'm around you. A better man. Not that I am a fiend by any means whenever I am not around you, but neither am I a saint."

"Oh, I see." She pursed her lips in thought. "But I cannot imagine you doing what Gerald–"

"Never! There is no excuse for what he did. It was low and venal. As I said, I am not a saint, but to hurt someone as he did you? Wouldn't ever happen."

"That's because Braydens are protective by nature. You are no exception."

He knew it was true. He couldn't be around Dahlia without wanting to take her in his arms and shield her from the ills of the world. Yet, he also liked that she wanted something more in life and was determined to make a mark for herself. "So, we now know that very little thought occurs when a man is using his low brain." He read on. "But that is good. It is evidence of his compelling need to breed heirs with any fertile female he comes across."

"Wait, is this condoning Gerald's behavior?"

"Hell, no. He wasn't in a lustful frenzy over Lady Alexandra. What he was doing was cold and calculated."

"What about you, Ronan?" She no longer appeared stiff and tense, but had propped one elbow on the reading table and was resting her cheek on her hand.

"What about me?"

"Have you ever felt this way about a woman? So wild for her, you could not control yourself?"

"Perhaps when I was an idiot boy of fourteen. Women were new and fascinating creatures for me back then."

"But the fascination quickly wore off?"

He laughed softly. "No, women remain a fascinating puzzle to me. But it did not take me long to move beyond the desire for a quick tumble. In any event, it is not in my nature to chase every woman I see."

"Of course not. Why would you need to when they all come to you?"

"I assure you, they do not. Nor do I encourage them. At one time, I was content with meaningless dalliances, but I am well beyond that now. It is a natural progression, I think. To move beyond that low brain thinking and desire something more permanent. When I marry, I will be faithful to my wife. It is the Brayden way. It is *my* way."

She shook her head and sighed. "Oh, Ronan. If only there were more men like you."

"There are, Dahlia. Most are decent. You have only to look at the men in your family and mine to know good men exist."

"What else does this book say?" She leaned over and read the next few lines aloud. "Love is a higher function of the brain. The important function that makes a man feel the need to protect his family. Wife and offspring. Otherwise, he'd merely spill his seed and then move on, leaving them to be eaten by wolves."

She looked at him and laughed. "The author wrote this just for you. I've never met any man more ridiculously protective than you. Well, perhaps your brothers and cousins. But you aren't smothering or unbearably jealous. Your natural instinct is to step in and shield those weaker than you whenever you sense danger. Your wife will be a very lucky woman. I know you will make her an excellent husband. I hope she appreciates you."

Ronan said nothing, just read on. "The author explained the man's low brain, that unthinking organ designed purely for the task of mating. But his high brain is what enables him to select the right mate for a lifetime. He was given a higher brain to enable him to love. That ability to love is why he stays loyal to his wife and offspring, in turn enhancing their chances of survival. However, before he reaches that upper function of intelligence, the man must first be attracted to the female on the simple brain level."

He set the book aside a moment. "So we have gone in a circle. Low brain to high brain and back to the low brain again. I think this is a good point to pause and consider what we've learned so far."

She groaned. "Are you going to test me on this?"

"In a way. I think we should discuss what traits we find attractive in each other."

"Well, that's easy enough. I can list a dozen of your attractive qualities off the top of my head. I'm the problem, aren't I? What traits do I possess that would interest any man?"

"Stop beating yourself up, Dahlia. You are jesting, aren't you? I can assure you, I will have no problem listing a dozen of your fine qualities."

She rolled her eyes. "You do not need to be gentle with me, Ronan. I'll learn nothing if you shield me from the truth."

"I am not shielding you. Nor am I one to cajole or flatter. So, go ahead and list my attributes. Then I will have my turn and list yours. All right?"

"All right." She took a long moment to study him. "You are handsome. You are intelligent. You are brave. You are protective. You are strong. You are patient, especially with me. Honestly, I don't know why you've appointed yourself as my guardian angel, but I do appreciate it, especially after *the incident*. You are an excellent guardian angel. I'm glad you punched Gerald's face. Does that count as a fine quality? I think it should."

He nodded. "If you want it to count, then it counts."

She shook her head and cast him a genuinely warm smile. "I like your rules. Let's see, where was I? You have beautiful eyes. And a beautiful smile. And a beautiful face. Well, a handsome face. But it's beautiful, too. Have I said handsome twice? I think I said it at the beginning. How many is that?"

"Ten, I think."

"Very well, two more, and then it shall be your turn. You are a natural leader. You are noble. How's that? I will forgive you if you cannot come up with twelve for me."

"It won't be hard. First, you have beautiful eyes. A beautiful body. Beautiful lips. I enjoyed kissing them."

She gasped. "You did?"

"Yes, very much. Beautiful hair. Beautiful breasts. Don't hit me, we have to be completely honest here."

"Ronan!"

"Well, it is important to me. To any man. Isn't this what we've just spent the last half hour talking about? My low brain responds favorably to your face and body. Why are you so surprised?"

"Gerald–"

"Bloody hell. Not him again. I don't give a rat's arse what Wainscott thinks. He cares only for himself. You and Lady Alexandra are mere pawns to him. Shall I go on with my list? You are smart. You have a good sense of humor. You are gentle. You are creative. You are talented."

"Two more to go."

"Easy. You are tenderhearted. You are an independent thinker. I'm not nearly done, but I've reached my twelve. Shall we move on to the next chapter?"

She nodded. "Thank you, Ronan. I appreciate what you said about my qualities."

He placed his hand over hers. "It's all true, Dahlia."

She said nothing for a long moment, then her eyes began to tear up.

Bollocks. "Why are you crying?"

She emitted a ragged breath. "I don't know…well…yes, I do. Gerald made me feel like rubbish beneath his boots. But you make me feel quite wonderful and special."

"Because you are, Dahlia." His hand was still on hers, so he gave it a little squeeze. "You are going to accomplish great things, I can see it in you. That rat-bastard, on the other hand, is going to live a miserable, unworthy life, detested by all, and he'll probably die of the pox. Which will still be too gentle a punishment for him."

Despite her tears, she laughed. "So, you still like him then?"

He chuckled. "As much as I ever did."

Chapter Six

RONAN RETURNED HOME in the afternoon, curious whether his mother had spoken to her friend. He was satisfied with his progress on reading the book with Dahlia and was more certain than ever that he'd made the right decision by insisting they read it together. She was like a little bird, still learning how to fly and needing his help to soar. All she lacked was confidence in herself. For this reason, she dared not fly on her own for fear of suddenly plummeting.

They had arranged to meet tomorrow at Violet's. He was to stop by there after work. Even though he'd just left Dahlia, he was already impatient to see her again.

"Ronan, I'm glad you are home early. Do you have a moment to ride over to Lady Wellbrook's? She is quite excited about the prospect of your purchasing her house and most eager to see you. She has invited us to call on her at three o'clock today."

He smiled. "Perfect. But I cannot stay long. I'm required to attend Lord Liverpool's banquet this evening. I dare not arrive late."

"Of course. It's almost three now. I'll have my carriage brought around immediately."

Lady Wellbrook lived close by. Were it not for the snow on the ground, he would have suggested they walk. But he could not ask his mother to do so, especially not when she had dressed elegantly for the occasion. Her shoes were utterly impractical for walking in snow. He climbed in her carriage and settled across from her to make the trip that would take them less than five minutes, even if the roads were jammed with carts and carriages.

When they arrived, they were shown in by Lady Wellbrook's butler, a doddering and slightly deaf, old fellow who would likely be pensioned off by her as soon as she sold her home.

After the required greetings, they attended to the matter of touring the house. "I know how impatient young men are, so I thought I'd show you about first, and then we can sit down to tea. You may ask me any questions after the tour. How does that sound to you, Captain Brayden?"

"A very good plan, Lady Wellbrook."

As they walked through the rooms, Ronan took note of their size. He counted the number of bedchambers, considered the size of the garden, the condition of roof, and construction of the house. He did not know what else he ought to be looking for.

To him, the house appeared to be exactly what he needed.

In truth, he'd known this was the house for him before he'd ever stepped foot in it. The location was prime, on one of the loveliest squares in London. The other homes were well maintained, the street itself was quiet and yet convenient to everything.

Upon completion of the tour, he sat down to tea with Lady Wellbrook and his mother. He asked general questions about her memories and enjoyed learning of her time spent living here. He did not ask about roofs or foundations or load-bearing crossbeams, for he doubted the kindly dowager would know anything about those items.

He would engage an architect for that purpose and intended to ask Finn to help him out on the purchase. He and Lady Wellbrook's man of affairs would handle matters to see the sale accomplished.

Pleased with the results, he left the two ladies soon afterward and walked home to wash and dress for this evening's banquet. His thoughts were still on Dahlia, looking forward to the day he could bring her around to see the house that would soon be his.

Gad! It felt so strange to be thinking of such matters.

A week ago, he'd been quite comfortable with his bachelorhood and not intending to settle down. Marriage had not been on his mind.

However, he'd always felt something for Dahlia. The kiss they'd shared had merely stirred the desire quietly simmering in his heart from the moment he'd set eyes on her. He had tamped down the feeling, warning himself to forget her because she was meant for Wainscott.

If he had realized how badly the bounder was about to hurt her, he would have come forward.

But he hadn't, and now he ached for seeing her so badly hurt.

Joshua and Robbie were already in the Parliament banquet hall, each of them involved in conversations with the various lords who still needed to be swayed in their favor when their particular appropriations came up for a vote.

Ronan merely nodded to them, not wanting to interrupt their important discussions.

Instead, he joined the Lord Admiral, who was engaged in conversation with several prominent lords regarding the needs of the Royal Navy. Among them was Lady Melinda's father, the Duke of Stoke.

Ronan briefly wondered whether Lady Melinda had managed to lure her marquess into making her an offer of marriage. However, he was not going to ask her father. The gossip rags would report it soon enough. Nor did he want Stoke believing he had any interest in his daughter. The man had already made it clear he wanted his daughter to marry a marquess or better, that a mere captain in the Royal Navy would never do.

Ronan was worried.

These rumors recently being reported about him escorting Lady Melinda around town were going to destroy a full year's hard work if the duke actually believed them. The navy needed his support on their appropriations.

The Lord Admiral turned to him. "Captain Brayden, you've done most of the work on these matters. Why don't you give us your opinion?"

"Yes, of course." He momentarily set aside all thoughts of Dahlia, the book, the house search, and the gossip connecting him to the duke's impulsive daughter. "My lords, as our reach expands throughout the world, it is imperative that we have enough ships to protect our holdings and our trade routes wherever they may extend. You are aware that our merchant vessels are often at the mercy of pirates, some of whom command fleets as powerful as those of small countries."

One of the lords nodded. "I have holdings in Jamaica. I can attest to this scourge."

Ronan agreed. "They operate almost everywhere without restraint, their power spanning from the South China Sea to the Tasman Sea. Throughout the Indian Ocean from the eastern coast of Africa to Ceylon. Across the Caribbean. But let us not forget we must deal with our usual enemies, the other European powers who seek to dominate those trade routes and lay claim to vast territories in order to establish their governmental rule. The Dutch have maintained a formidable presence in the South China Sea for centuries. The Spanish along the Americas."

"The European nations will next be vying for the mineral riches in Africa, India, and China," the Lord Admiral interjected.

"For this reason," Ronan said, "we must maintain the most powerful naval force in the world. Our enemies need to know we will obliterate their fleets if they step out of line. History has taught us this. One of our strongest and best strategies is to blockade enemy ports and destroy their fleets. They cannot attack us if they can't get out."

His remarks and those of the Lord Admiral were met with enthusiastic approval.

"You see, gentlemen. This is why I have complete faith in Captain

Brayden. Do go on with the rest of it," the Lord Admiral urged.

"We need funds for research. Do not leave us with old vessels and outdated cannons. We need fast ships, longer-range cannons, and reinforced hulls. Sleeker ships to allow us entry into the shallow harbors. We also need to invest in these new, steam-powered vessels. We are also conducting some experiments on other ship designs that could change how we fight the next wars. Give us the funds, and we'll have those ships built."

He imagined Joshua and Robbie were explaining much the same thing with respect to their land forces. As everyone sat down to supper, the three of them found themselves together at the far end of the table. Since none of them were lords, they were as low as one could be in the order of preference, merely one step removed from the clerks who were shuttling in and out, delivering messages to Lord Liverpool and those in his high circle.

They were perhaps two steps removed from the servants who were bringing in their sumptuous meal on gleaming silver trays.

"Did ye have the chance to visit Dahlia today?" Robbie asked as they finished their soup course, a white soup made from veal stock, and waited for the next courses to be brought out.

He nodded. "We read a little of the book together. I'll meet her again tomorrow. I'd like to get through as much of it as I can before the week is out. Romulus returns soon, and I don't think he'll appreciate having others around when his time with Violet is so short."

Joshua joined in the conversation. "Perhaps by then, Dahlia will feel better about coming over to our home. Holly will gladly help out in any way she can."

Ronan nodded. "I appreciate it. I think that will work out."

Robbie waited for one of the footmen to refill his glass of wine before responding. "Have ye done anything with yer house search? Does Lady Miranda know ye mean to move out?"

"Yes, I told her last night. To my surprise, she's been most helpful."

Joshua laughed. "You mean she actually wants you out?"

"No, she did her abandoned mother act. Tears, the vapors, wailing, and moaning. But she has a friend who lives close by and happened to mention she wants to sell her London home. I went to see it this afternoon. I think it's perfect. Good bones. Great location. A little run down and in need of Dahlia's touch. Couldn't ask for anything better."

Robbie arched an eyebrow. "Impressive."

Joshua raised his glass in toast. "Here's to success on your mission."

"Cheers." Ronan drained his glass that had also been refilled.

The evening ended late, but he was pleased with all he had accomplished. He stripped out of his clothes, handed them to Harrigan to be freshened, and fell into bed. His last thought before sleep overcame him was to wonder what tomorrow would bring.

Unfortunately, it brought an angry summons from the Lord Admiral to meet him at the Admiralty that morning. Ronan had just settled in his office in the Parliament building when a messenger arrived with the urgent note. "Bollocks, what now?" he muttered, waving to Joshua and Robbie, who were just walking in as he hurried off.

The Lord Admiral had one of the local gossip rags open on his desk when Ronan arrived. "Brayden," he said, his face red as he motioned to the paper, "what the hell is this?"

"With all due respect, my lord. What are you talking about?"

"You and Lady Melinda? Stoke's daughter. I thought your affair was over and done. You were seen at the theater with her last night."

"The theater?" Ronan groaned inwardly. "If you will recall, I was with you and His Grace all evening. I went straight home afterward. Although we have made great scientific advances, I do not think we have advanced far enough to allow me to be in two places at once."

"Don't take that smart tone with me, Brayden. This is serious. If

Stoke withdraws his support, we'll lose our funding. You have to end this with his daughter."

"Happily, sir. But how am I to end something that does not exist? She and I were never having an *affair*. I am not courting his daughter. I am not interested in courting his daughter. I never was. However, I suspect she is the one sending this misinformation to the papers."

"Why would she do this?"

"To make a certain marquess jealous and get an offer of marriage out of him. I am being used as her pawn for this purpose. Over my strenuous objections, I might add. Lady Melinda does not particularly care. His Grace must realize what his daughter is doing. I can ask her to stop, but I doubt she will listen to me since she never has before. It seems more prudent for me to avoid all contact with her. If I'm seen talking to her, even if it is merely for the purpose of asking her to stop, the gossips will report it."

The Lord Admiral put his hands to his temples and groaned. "I believe you, Brayden. But I don't know that Stoke will. Oh, he might be persuaded that this theater nonsense was a mistake, but what if it happens again and you are not in his company? Unless his daughter confesses to him what she is doing, we are sunk."

"I can seek an audience with the Duke of Stoke. Explain to him what is going on with his daughter, assuming he isn't already aware."

"You know how stubborn that old goat can be. He won't see you. He'll think you are requesting to see him in order to offer for his daughter's hand in marriage. Even if she has told him what she's doing, he will still wonder why she's chosen you in particular and worry that something more is going on behind his back. No, I have a better idea."

Ronan's stomach twisted in a knot. "I'm certain a talk with the duke will be all that is required."

"Did you not hear what I just said? As long as your name is involved, the duke will suspect you…unless…"

The knot tightened in his stomach. "Unless what, my lord?"

"Unless you are seen courting another young woman. Then you will be of no use to Lady Melinda. She needs someone who is unattached in order to lure the marquess. So, attach yourself to a young lady. I'm sure it will be easy enough for you to find one who is willing. You only need to keep up the pretense for a fortnight. The House of Lords will vote on the budget just before Christmas. You can quietly end matters as soon as the vote has taken place."

Bollocks.

"That is a terrible idea. How is it all right for me to use an innocent girl and then drop her at Christmastide?"

The Lord Admiral pounded his fist on the table. "You will do it for the sake of England! Find a girl. Tell her your plans if it eases your conscience. But make certain she can keep her mouth shut. If she ruins this for us, it will be your hide I'll be flaying. Oh, and she has to be beautiful, clever, and from a good family. The duke has to believe this is not a ruse…even if it is a ruse."

"All the more reason why we shouldn't do this." He held out his arms in supplication. "Let me talk to the duke. I'll even enter a monastery for a fortnight if this will help."

"Out of the question. I need you here to answer questions on our funding requests. And what of our research projects? You're the only one who understands the incomprehensible science behind the steam mechanism. This discussion is over, Brayden. Let me know who this girl is, and I will make certain Stoke and his daughter hear of it. In casual conversation, of course. I do not want this courtship to look staged."

Ronan clenched his jaw. "And you will talk to the duke about his daughter? Get her off my back? Maybe talk to the daughter as well and let her know the importance of what we are doing and how she must stop interfering. She isn't a bad sort, just used to getting her own way."

The Lord Admiral glowered at him. "You are dismissed, Brayden.

Report back to me first thing tomorrow morning, and you had better have a name."

"Yes, my lord." He strode out, mad as a bull.

Joshua and Robbie were in their offices, so he stopped in at each. "Conference in my office," he said, popping his head in and then striding back to his.

He was looking for something to pound on or toss across the room when the two of them hurried in. "What's wrong?" his brother asked, settling into his usual chair.

Robbie did the same. "Ye look as though ye've just been through a court-martial. Are ye going to tell us what happened, or must we guess?"

"Lady Melinda has been at it again, spreading rumors that she and I are an item."

Robbie shook his head. "So?"

"Her father's vote is crucial for the navy's funding. If he believes those lies, he might express his displeasure by voting against our budget."

Joshua groaned. "What does the Lord Admiral want you to do?"

"Squash the rumors by courting someone else. I'm useless to Lady Melinda if I'm no longer viewed as the carefree bachelor. For the next two weeks, I must be seen with the innocent and charming object of my affection…whoever she may be. Oh, and she has to be beautiful, clever, and from a good family. The duke has to believe I am wildly in love with this girl. I have until tomorrow morning to give him a name."

Robbie sat up in his chair. "Och, dare I guess who ye're going to choose?"

He ran a hand roughly through his hair. "It can only be Dahlia, of course. But I hesitate to ask her. She's already been destroyed by Wainscott's deceptions. How can I ask her to be complicit in this?"

"And yet," Joshua said, "if you choose someone else, how will

Dahlia ever believe you care for her? More important, how will she ever trust you when she sees you've dumped this supposed girl of your dreams after a fortnight? She'll fear you will do the same to her."

He nodded. "She may never trust me, no matter what I do."

"But ye think ye have to take the risk and ask her to help out?" Robbie asked.

"I can easily pretend that I'm falling in love with her since I am doing exactly that." He lolled his head back and groaned. "However, I'll scare her off if I just come out and admit I love her now. The Wainscott incident is still too raw. So for now, I will just tell her it is all a pretense. Once the vote occurs, I'll let her know how I truly feel."

Robbie rose and gave him a companionable pat on the shoulder. "I thought my cousin Thad made a mess of his courtship. I dinna think anyone could mess it up worse. But I think ye're about to do it, laddie. Good luck to ye. Ye're going to need it."

Joshua remained in his chair, saying nothing until Robbie left. "I think Stoke, Lady Melinda, and the Lord Admiral are the least of your problems."

Ronan regarded his brother. "What do you mean?"

"You haven't thought of Miranda. She has just learned that her baby boy is moving into his own house. Now suddenly, you'll be courting Dahlia. I love that woman, but there is no telling what she will do to you if she finds out what is really going on. All she will see is that you haven't been courting Dahlia so much as using her to advance your political goals."

"Bloody hell. Josh, just keep her contained. I had better let Finn and Tynan in on this, too. Maybe she'll listen if all four of her sons are on their knees, begging her not to get involved."

Joshua rose and patted him on the back. "We don't stand a chance against her. But good luck, Ronan. You'll have your hands full these next few weeks."

Chapter Seven

"DO YOU THINK Ronan will stop by today, Violet?" Dahlia peered out the entry hall window to stare at the front gate. "Where is he? What if he's detained and cannot make it?"

Violet laughingly dragged her away from the window. "He would have sent word if he had to cancel. Come into the parlor and sit down. You can give me decorating ideas while we wait for him."

Heather had already taken a seat in the parlor and was pouring herself a cup of hot cocoa. "Currant scones. My favorite. Thank you, Violet. This all looks delicious." She stared at the platter of cakes set out on a side table for them.

"There's tea in the other pot, if you prefer." Violet sat in a chair beside Heather's, the two of them purposely leaving an open seat beside Dahlia on the settee.

"Do you think he'll be irritated with me for reading ahead? I ought to have waited for him before jumping to the next chapters, but yesterday's meeting went well and left me in better spirits. I couldn't wait. I'll read them again with him, of course. Is this how you felt with Romulus?"

Violet blushed. "Well, our circumstances were a little different. We only had a week to figure out if we loved each other. But it was exciting to read the book with him and discover the sort of man he was. Obviously, I quickly realized he was splendid and wonderful, and I fell madly in love with him."

"It won't be the same for Ronan and me. He's reading the book so he can find himself a duke's daughter to marry. I'm reading it to learn more about men and know which ones will betray me."

Heather winced. "Oh, Dahlia. That is so harsh. You must think of it as a means to find love. And who is to say Ronan will not fall in love with you? Then you can marry him, and everyone will be happy."

"No, it won't happen. He doesn't think of me that way. He is only helping me because he is a Brayden, and this is what they do, protect the weak and vulnerable. This is what he thinks of me."

Although he had been very kind in his description of her yesterday. She did not know how much of what he'd said was true. Even if he was greatly embellishing her virtues, it still meant a lot to her that he was taking the time to read the book with her and seemed to enjoy their time spent together. "Oh, where is he? Do you think he's forgotten about me?"

"No," the two of them answered together, and at the same time, their gazes shot to the doorway.

"Dahlia, how can I possibly forget you?"

She gasped and looked up to find Ronan standing there, big and dominant, and grinning softly at her. His arms were crossed over his chest, and he appeared every bit the magnificent warrior. "Sorry I'm late. Got held up in a meeting at the House of Lords."

Dahlia groaned. "I hope you did not cut it short on my account."

He strode forward and settled on the settee beside her, taking up most of it because his shoulders were broad. "No, it ended of its own accord. Although I might have purposely nudged it along by boring them to tears toward the end. I began to explain the science of steam combustion. Their eyes glazed over, and they all suddenly remembered having prior engagements. You'd think the devil was on their tail, they fled the hall so fast."

"I think I would find it fascinating." She smiled at him. "Our cousin, Lily, would understand it all. None of us would be surprised if she had a hand in designing your steam invention."

Violet nodded. "She is brilliant. The Duke of Lotheil adores her. She married his grandson, Ewan. I think the duke was not quite so enamored of her at the start. She had a way of deflating his pomposity that he found quite irksome."

Heather giggled as she motioned to the teapot. "Would you care for a cup?"

"Perhaps later." He turned to face Dahlia. "What do you say we get started? We have a lot to get through this evening. Violet, do you mind?"

"Not at all. Heather and I have plenty to do to occupy ourselves."

He led Dahlia into Romulus's library and surprised her by shutting the door behind them. She cast him a puzzled glance. "Shouldn't we leave it open?"

"There's something sensitive that I must discuss with you and don't wish us to be overheard. I'll open the door in a minute."

She nodded. "You look so serious. Is something wrong?"

He raked a hand through his hair. "This is most awkward, and I hope you will not take offense by what I am about to ask you."

She clasped her hands together, suddenly worried she'd done something to irritate him. They were still standing together, he looking as magnificently rugged as ever. "Do you no longer wish to see me? Because I'll understand if you'd rather not. You've been kind to me, Ronan. The last thing I wish to do is cause you further embarrassment."

He stared at her in obvious surprise. "Dahlia, you are not an embarrassment to me. Why ever would you think that? What I am about to ask...well, it is about you and me, but not in the way you think." His hand raked through his hair again. "I'd like us to see each other on a far more regular basis. I'd like for us to be noticed as a couple."

"A couple?" Her heart fluttered. Was it possible he wanted to court her? Then why did he look so perplexed about it? "I'm not sure I understand."

He groaned. "Because I'm making a complete mess of this explanation. Let me start at the beginning. Do you recall the discussion we had about Lady Melinda and how the gossip rags are reporting that she and I are being seen around town together?"

She nodded.

Oh, she knew it! He was going to tell her the two of them were in love and had been going about in secret this whole time despite her father's disapproval. Ronan loved Lady Melinda, and she loved him and–

"Those gossip rags are still spewing those lies, and now the Lord Admiral is worried her father will convince the other members of the House of Lords to slash our navy budget in order to punish me on the mistaken belief I am courting his daughter against his wishes. Of course that petty action will hurt the entire Royal Navy. We cannot allow it to happen."

"Would he really do something so hurtful?"

Ronan shook his head. "I sincerely hope not, but it is quite possible. The Lord Admiral is very concerned. He is going to try to talk sense into father and daughter, but we doubt it will work. Lady Melinda won't stop planting those fake gossip items in the rags until her marquess offers for her hand."

"Surely her father knows this."

"Perhaps, but Lady Melinda and I have a history."

"You do?"

"Not much of one, I assure you. But the longer the gossip lingers, the more suspicious her father will become. It's already happening. He must have said something to the Lord Admiral to send him into a fit."

"What exactly is your history with Lady Melinda? I know you do not wish to discuss it, but if I am to consider helping you, then I must be aware of what is going on."

"Very well, I'll tell you." He motioned for her to take a seat, but she sensed their meeting might come to an abrupt halt over this discussion and preferred to remain standing. Ronan did not appear pleased but continued. "She was hoping to make more out of our friendship at one time. I escorted her to several parties. The duke noticed and quickly put an end to it."

"So, there was something between the two of you."

"No, not on my part. I quickly saw she was not right for me. However, the possibility that she wants me and not the marquess has to be stuck in the back of her father's mind. The longer her game goes on, the more suspicious he becomes."

"What if her desire for the marquess is a ruse, and you are really the one she wants?" Dahlia realized this book was already working its magic for Ronan. He was about to get the duke's daughter to marry him after all.

Of course, he'd have to hide the fact until after the vote.

But once the vote was behind them?

"I don't think so, Dahlia. Honestly, I don't know."

"Would it be so terrible if she did want you? This is your chance to marry into a higher circle. She is the duke's only child, isn't she? He will never disown her. And once you are married, he will do all in his power to support you because he loves his daughter and will want to keep her happy."

"She is pampered. Spoiled. Headstrong. Absorbed in her own comforts rather than of those less fortunate. She is not a terrible person, mind you. But as I said, she just isn't right for me."

"She is beautiful and wealthy."

"So? This might make her desirable to most men, I suppose. But not for me. Why are you pushing me toward her? I'm not interested, nor will I allow her to destroy all I've worked for to indulge her game. The Lord Admiral has asked me to find a young lady to court. Someone beautiful, intelligent, and of good upbringing, because it has to be convincing."

Dahlia nibbled her lip. "Oh, I see. And this is why you are here tonight. You want me to help you come up with a name?"

He laughed softly. "I have the name."

It was her turn to appear surprised. "You do? Then what do you need me for?"

"Lord, are you purposely being dense? You are the name."

"Me?" He had to be in jest. "Do be serious. Shall I call in Heather and Violet? If we all put our heads together, we might be able to find you someone suitable."

He took her hand to stop her when she turned toward the door. "Dahlia, I meant what I said. You are the one. I am choosing you."

Her heart shot into her throat. "Are you mad? Do you hear yourself? Of all the young ladies in London, I am the worst choice possible."

"Why?" He still had hold of her hand, his touch sending tingles shooting through her body.

"I am a laughingstock. Gerald humiliated me and dumped me. All of London must be aware of this by now. How will Lady Melinda's father ever believe you? I doubt even the local rat catcher will believe I am the object of your fascination."

"Why is it so improbable? You and I get on well, don't we? You are beautiful and clever. I always feel comfortable around you. I like your liveliness and wit."

She tried to ease her hand out of his grasp, but he would not let go. He'd been holding it gently, and she hadn't been tugging very hard. She supposed he would have released her if she'd persisted. She sighed and cast him a stern look. "Indeed, you are mad. I have been an insufferable watering pot for the last two days. I cry and grumble and mope."

"I've known you for several months now. You did not cry, grumble, or mope before that weasel Wainscott crushed your soul. I liked that happier Dahlia very much." He finally released her and stepped away to casually lean his hip against Romulus's desk. He folded his arms across his chest, another casual gesture, but it only brought attention to how muscled he was. Now, she was tingling again.

He continued, unaware of the effect he was having on her. "I even like the crying, moping version of you. Let me put this another way. I won't accept to do this with anyone but you."

She sank into one of the overstuffed chairs and emitted a long, ragged breath. "I repeat, you are mad. What will happen if I refuse you?"

"The House of Lords will likely decline most of our funding requests. In turn, the Lord Admiral will strip me of my rank and assign me to swabbing decks on a scow for the duration of my commission."

"He couldn't possibly…he wouldn't ever…"

"He most certainly would."

"But that's awful."

"I certainly think so." He shrugged. "My future is entirely in your hands. The choice is yours, Dahlia. If it's any consolation, we only have to keep up the pretense for the next two weeks. The vote comes right before Christmas. This will also give us more time to read that book together. No one will be surprised to see me come around daily if they believe we are courting."

"When you put it that way, it sounds most efficient."

He nodded. "But it has to be our secret. Everyone has to sincerely believe I am besotted and now courting you."

She struggled not to cry. This was awful. But if she refused to go along with his plan, the safety of every seaman could be put in jeopardy. Indeed, the safety of England. Not to mention the inexcusable waste of having him demoted. He was brilliant. The navy needed him. "Then, after the two weeks, you'll decide you don't love me after all, and you will end it?"

He moved to settle in a chair beside hers and took her hands in his again. "I would never do that to you. I don't know what will happen at the end of that time. Hopefully, we will be done reading the book and have a better idea of what love and marriage entail. But if this courtship is broken off, it will not be done by me. Only you can break it off."

"Well, it's the same thing, really. It will be broken off, but you'll allow me to save my reputation by being the one to do it." She shook her head again. "It won't work, you know. There is not a young lady in London who would ever walk away from you. Everyone will know you were only being polite to allow me to end the courtship. Having two men walk away from me in less than a month will ruin my chances of ever making a match."

Her heart felt as though it was being torn to pieces. She'd dreamed of her come-out season for years, silly, magical dreams where she would be the diamond of the ball, declared an Incomparable, and catch the eye of England's most eligible bachelor. He would be someone as handsome and splendid as Ronan, of course. "I don't care about this second humiliation for myself. But Heather's chances could also be hurt simply for being related to me."

"Dahlia, you are my Queen Pea. I will never let this happen."

She rolled her eyes. "That was just a game."

"Not to me. I give you my oath. Upon my honor, I will not break off the courtship. If it happens–"

"*When* it happens," she corrected.

He tossed her an impatient look. "*If* it happens, then it will be because you chose to end it."

She frowned. "And if I decide not to break it off with you?"

"Then I will marry you," he said with steady resolve.

She stopped breathing. "Marry me?"

"Yes. I believe that is what I just said." His expression turned achingly tender.

She stared into his eyes and tried her best not to burst into tears. How could he do this to her? "Am I supposed to be grateful for this?

The noble Captain Brayden comes to the rescue of the sad spinster and endures a lifetime of unhappiness for the sake of her honor and his precious navy budget?"

"What? Where do you come up with such nonsense?"

Her mind was in too much of a muddle to take in what he'd just told her. "I would never hold you to any such promise. How could you think I would force you to marry me if you did not love me?"

"You wouldn't be forcing me."

"Of course, I would. Do you not see? This is your protective instincts flaring up again."

She glanced at the book, resting quietly on the desk, waiting to be picked up and read. Her eyes widened in horror. "It's that thing. This is why you are speaking so oddly."

"What thing? What are you talking about?"

"*The Book of Love*. It is making you do this…spout ridiculous notions of marriage."

He growled as he rose and lifted her up along with him. "Are you too blind to see how lovely you are?"

"Are you so overcome by duty that you would sacrifice your happiness for the sake of a budget?"

"It isn't just a budget. Lives are at stake over this. Even so, you will never be a duty to me. You'll just have to trust me, Dahlia. Do you trust me?"

"Of course I do. But that is hardly the point."

"It is entirely the point." He drew her into the circle of his arms, holding her with a gentle intimacy she'd never experienced before. He touched her cheek with a delicacy she'd never felt before. "Close your eyes," he said with a gruff rasp to his voice.

"Why?"

"Are all Farthingales this obstinate? I want you to close your eyes because I am going to kiss you."

"But you–"

"Do you never stop talking?" He lowered his head and gently pressed his lips to hers, catching her with an open mouth just as he had done when she was his Queen Pea, and he was her King Bean. But this was not like their first kiss, for this was no light, sweet brush, and he did not draw away after a moment.

Instead, he deepened the kiss, slowly heightening the exquisite pressure until his lips were devouring hers, his mouth warm and provocative as it melded with hers and coaxed a muffled sigh out of her.

She felt his tongue dip into her mouth, teasing and softly exploring, sweetly invading and rousing sensations she never imagined possible. She could lose her heart to this man. Everything about him overwhelmed her. His exquisite touch. The taste of his kisses. His soft growl as he conquered her resistance.

His kiss held the promise of something deep and abiding.

Or was she mistaken? The humiliated spinster and the handsome-as-sin Royal Navy commanding officer? It could not be.

How could he feel this way about her?

They'd hardly started reading the book, and yet he was kissing her as though he loved her with all his heart.

He was kissing her as every girl dreamed to be kissed.

Tears began to stream down her face. Yet another reason why he could not love her. She was a watering pot.

"Queen Pea, why the tears?" he whispered against her lips.

Her response was to kiss him back with a breathless ardor to match his own. How could she not be swept away by this man? This was Ronan, her valiant gladiator, doing what he thought was right, convincing himself it was more important to protect her than to seek his own happiness.

Even if he enjoyed their kisses, it signified nothing. He would feel the same about a thousand other women. Wasn't this the point of a man's low brain? To seek out as many desirable women as possible and mate?

But she wanted true love, not merely the pretense of it.

She wanted the gift of it.

The treasure of knowing his kisses were for her and her alone. The pleasure of seeing his eyes turn to starlight and a smile cross his face whenever she entered a room. The heat of his body turned to flames because he wanted *her* so badly.

Was he offering all this with his kiss?

"Queen Pea," he said in an anguished whisper, drawing his mouth away from hers ever so slightly, "I'll never hurt you. I promise."

He cupped her cheek and ran his thumb lightly across it to wipe away her tears.

She rested her head against his chest, amazed that something so hard and solid could feel this divine. "Ronan, I'll help you out. I would never forgive myself if I put the lives of so many valiant seamen at risk. But it won't be easy for me. My heart is so bruised."

"I know. This is what worries me most of all."

"Let's not think beyond these next two weeks, and don't make me promises you won't keep." She remained in his arms, her head resting against his chest and his gloriously muscled arms around her. After a long moment, she reluctantly drew away.

She was surprised he hadn't been the one to move away first.

But this was Ronan. Now that he'd given her this promise, he was going to fulfill it to the utmost. If she wanted more kisses, he would indulge her. If she wanted to be in his arms, he would take her in his arms.

She would have two weeks of this.

More, if she desired.

She understood now why it had been important for him to choose her. Few women would ever let him out of the bargain they'd just made. Most would have used it as an opportunity to trap him into marriage.

Let me put this another way. I won't accept to do this with anyone but you. Those were his exact words of a few minutes earlier. It pleased her that he trusted her and considered her honorable. She felt the same about him.

With great difficulty, she drew away and returned to her chair. "What is our next step?"

He smiled at her and gave her cheek another sweet caress before crossing the room to open the door. "We get back to this book and its lessons in love."

She laughed shakily. "After that kiss, I'm not sure I'll be able to concentrate."

"It caught me off guard, too, Queen Pea." He grinned and returned to settle in a chair beside hers, the book now in his hand. "There's no rule to how fast we must read through it. We'll have plenty of time now, in any event. I'll make it a point to visit you every day."

She nodded. "I have a confession to make."

"You do?" He arched an eyebrow, looking quite amused.

"I read ahead to the next chapters. But I suppose it is a good thing because…" She sighed. "Your kiss is still affecting me."

"Me, too," he said quietly and opened the book to the second chapter. "Shall I skip it then?"

"No, it is important. Also, reading with you is different from my reading alone. Better, in truth. My head was hopelessly muddled, and I probably overlooked important bits. These next chapters are about the five senses. Sight. Touch. Taste. Hearing. Scent."

"What did you learn from reading them?"

"That our own expectations often get in the way of what our sense organs are showing us. These chapters teach us how to clear our minds and look at a thing without judging it in advance."

Since he seemed to be listening with interest, she continued. "Perhaps the biggest mistake we make when searching for love is our refusal to accept that we've selected the wrong partner. This is how I was with Gerald. After reading these chapters, it was as though a stone wall had toppled on my head. How could I have been so dense? Had I bothered to look at him with my eyes wide open, I would have recognized so many failings, not only in him but in us as a couple."

"You refused to acknowledge what he was."

"And you saw him so clearly." She nodded. "I wanted to fall in love now that I had become a woman. I was excited and thrilled to finally be making my debut. He was right there, a friend of long acquaintance. He was writing me love letters. So I was determined to fall in love with him. More important, I made myself believe he loved me. I ignored all the warning signs, refused to accept what my own eyes and ears were telling me."

He pursed his lips. "Men approach love quite differently, but we lie to ourselves as well. Women want to fall in love, and men want to avoid it desperately, at least early on when they are young bucks stepping out in society."

"It all goes back to the differences in our brains, doesn't it?" she said. "The man needs to sire and populate. The woman needs to find the best protector for herself and her children."

"But it is not quite as straightforward as all that." He stared at the pages a moment before returning his gaze to hers. "Our feelings also get corrupted by greed, ambition, revenge, envy."

"Gerald's certainly were. Yet, I saw none of his faults until now."

He took her hand. "Not all men are as selfish as Wainscott. We are also guided by feelings of respect, honor, duty, love of family."

She laughed. "Oh, you Braydens are a fine example of those nobler sentiments."

She listened while Ronan quickly read through the next chapters, loving the richness of his voice and the warmth of his body next to hers. But she shook out of the errant thoughts. She had just gotten herself out of one mess and was not ready to leap into another.

She would accept Ronan for the good friend he was and not allow her heart to push her toward a hopeless end.

"What do you see when you look at me, Dahlia?" he asked, setting the book aside once he'd finished reading through all five senses.

"Didn't we go through this yesterday? Naming twelve things we liked about each other."

He nodded. "But I want to try it again. This time with each of us really looking at the other. Choose the five things that you like best. One thing for each sense."

"In order of importance?"

"Not necessarily. In whatever order you prefer."

"Very well, but shouldn't we be making this a bit more general. We seem to be concentrating on each other instead of thinking outwardly."

"Is there something wrong with that? I think it helps us to better understand what the book is teaching us if we test it out on each other first."

If it made sense to him, she was not going to argue the point. All she had to do was remind herself that this was merely experimentation and pretense. "I'll start with the sense of sight first. The look of you." She cleared her throat.

Dark hair.

Emerald eyes.

Big muscles.

Exquisite in every way.

She tried not to sound deflated as she said, "You look like the man of my dreams."

He cast her a soft smile. "Would you care to elaborate? How do I look like the man of your dreams?"

"Just the way you are put together. It is very pleasing. There is a warmth to your smile and intelligence in your eyes. Your hair is dark and thick. Your body looks as though it could have been carved out of stone. You have a fine, firm jaw and a nicely shaped mouth. You look like a man, not an indulged, little boy."

She blushed under the force of his stare. "Now for the sense of hearing, I like the sound of your voice as well. It is deep and commanding." She laughed. "I suppose that is a requirement of being a captain. There is a strength to your voice, a quality that inspires confidence and trust. This is what makes you a natural leader."

He grinned at her. "I shall become quite full of myself if you keep this up. Is there something you don't like about my look or my voice?"

She reached up and rested her palm against his cheek. "The bristles of your beard. You may start out the day clean-shaven, but by the end of it, your cheeks are rough. I don't consider it a fault. I rather like it, if you must know. As for your voice, I think if you were ever angry with me, I might find it frightening. Well, that's about it. This is the best I can do. Shall I move on to the next sense?"

He nodded.

"I think I'll mention the sense of smell next." She eased closer and put her nose to his neck to inhale him. "Your scent is awfully nice. Is it sandalwood? My cousins, Honey and Belle, work in their family perfume shops. Belle designs the fragrances, as you must know, since your brother is married to her. She taught me a little about this. Sandalwood is an ancient fragrance. It feels timeless, doesn't it? It smells very nice on you."

He was still grinning at her affectionately.

"The sense of touch next." She took hold of his hand. "This feels awfully nice as well. There is strength in your touch, again, something that inspires trust and confidence. As for taste, I don't know how I am to test this."

"Our kiss."

She hadn't thought of that, but they did have their lips pressed together for a while. "I tasted ale on your lips. Your breath was pleasing, although that really belongs with the sense of smell. I'm not sure what else to say about this sense. Perhaps that I would feel very favorably inclined toward you if I tasted chocolate on your lips next time?"

He laughed. "I'll keep that in mind."

"Your turn now. I've done enough talking."

"All right, Queen Pea. I'll count them off in the same order as you did yours. How does that sound to you?"

"Perfect." She took a deep breath, eager to hear his comments.

But Violet knocked on the open door and ducked her head in. "I do apologize for the interruption. It is getting late, and Heather is yawning, and–"

"Of course." Dahlia jumped out of her seat. "How thoughtless of us."

"No, not at all." Violet smiled at her. "I'm glad you were having such a nice time together."

Ah, yes. Well-meaning cousin whose matchmaking instincts were on fire. Dahlia turned to Ronan. "Shall we expect you at the same time tomorrow evening?"

When he stood up beside her, his shoulder lightly grazed hers. Of course, his mere touch sent tingles shooting through her body…something that never happened with Gerald. Yes, she had been so foolish.

Ronan did not seem to be at all affected by their bodies in such close proximity. "No, I have something altogether different planned. Will you three be available tomorrow afternoon?"

Dahlia glanced at her cousin, and when Violet nodded, she turned back to Ronan. "Yes, we are. What is the plan?"

"I'd rather keep it a surprise."

Oh, she hated surprises. What did he have in mind?

Chapter Eight

DAHLIA WAS READY when Ronan drew up in a carriage in front of Uncle John's townhouse the following afternoon. Violet was feeling a little under the weather, so Ronan had picked up their sister, Holly, along the way. Since she was now married to Ronan's brother, she had agreed to serve as a chaperone for her and Heather.

This had originally been Holly's designated role when the three of them had come down to London from York. As a young widow, she'd had no plans to put herself on the marriage mart, but all that had changed upon meeting Ronan's brother, Joshua.

Dahlia was pleased to see her. "Do you know where he is taking us?"

Holly shrugged. "No, he wouldn't tell me anything."

She looked up at Ronan. "Why are you being so mysterious?"

He smiled at her as he helped her into the carriage. "You'll find out soon enough."

They were on their way a moment later. It did not take them long before they turned off Park Lane onto a beautiful, tree-lined street that was as lovely as Chipping Way.

Dahlia put her nose to the cold glass to peer out the window as they passed one well-maintained home after another.

She was still peering out of the window when they turned onto a small square. In its center was a gated garden with yew trees and boxwood shrubs that looked quite beautiful covered in snow. Their carriage slowed as they drew up in front of one of the elegant houses. "Are we to pay a call on someone?"

He nodded. "Yes, Lady Wellbrook. She's expecting us."

Dahlia exchanged confused glances with her sisters. After her humiliating encounter with Gerald, she really was not keen on surprises. But this house intrigued her. There was just something about it, a stately charm and an aura of faded elegance she found captivating. "Oh, I could do so much with this grand house," she muttered under her breath.

Ronan must have heard her, for he was smiling once again. "Are you eager to go exploring?"

She nodded. "But will Lady Wellbrook allow me?"

"Yes, I'm sure she will. Perhaps after tea." He took Dahlia's arm as they walked to the front door. Holly and Heather followed close by their side.

"You are being very secretive," she whispered to him. "What is this all about?"

The door opened before Ronan could reply. "Captain Brayden," the frail, elderly butler said with a nod and stepped aside to allow them in. "Lady Wellbrook will be down in a moment. She asked me to show you into the winter parlor."

Dahlia's eyes widened as she took in the beautiful detailing in the entry hall. The cornices, the niches, the high ceiling, and grand staircase. She was so busy looking everywhere, but where she was going, she bumped into a wall.

"Give me your hand, Queen Pea." Chuckling, Ronan tucked it securely under his arm and then placed his hand over hers so that he could draw her closer to him each time she was about to walk into something.

She turned to him, giddy with excitement. "I am in love with this house."

"Good. I hoped you would be. I bought it yesterday."

She inhaled sharply. "What?"

"Well, it isn't mine yet. But I put in my offer. Lady Wellbrook has accepted. Now our solicitors are handling the transfer."

Dahlia's heart beat faster. "Do you plan to make any changes to the house? The detail work is exquisite, but much of it is lost among the clash of colors. Will you paint the rooms? Oh, forgive me. It isn't even yours yet. I know it isn't polite to ask. But this place is quite splendid. How did you come across it? I had no idea you were even looking."

"I don't mind your questions. I'm glad you like the house. It's quite grand, isn't it?" He shook his head and laughed. "I can see you hold some strong opinions about it."

"I do," she blurted.

There was a glint in his eye as he laughed again. "Queen Pea, you look as though you're about to burst. Do you have any suggestions? I wouldn't mind hearing them."

"You wouldn't?" Her heart was now soaring. "I do, in fact. Would you…that is…could I…, you can tell me to mind my own business…"

He arched an eyebrow. "Are you asking if you can help me decorate this place once it is mine?"

"Would you consider it, Ronan?" She held her breath while awaiting his response. "It would be a dream come true for me."

"Well, who am I to dash your dreams? The answer to your question is yes. I would greatly appreciate your advice."

Had they not been in company, she would have thrown her arms around him and possibly kissed him. "Thank you," she said with a depth of feeling that surprised even herself. But this was exactly what she needed to move beyond Gerald and reclaim a part of herself.

Her hand was still tucked in his arm and covered with his own. "You'd think I had just given you diamonds," he said with amused affection.

She held him back a moment, feeling happier than she'd been in a long while. "You have."

"I'm glad then, Queen Pea."

"This is the best gift anyone's ever given me." To allow her to help. Indeed, to value her judgment enough to want her help was a tremendous honor worth far more than any diamonds.

"You are the one helping me out. If anyone has received a gift, it's me."

She shook her head in disagreement. "Oh, no. I'm the one who's been given the gift."

Heather giggled. "By the way, since you are both feeling quite generous at the moment, I would like to mention that I am quite partial to gifts. Feel free to bestow as many as you wish on me."

Ronan chuckled heartily. "Duly noted, Heather."

Lady Wellbrook was a lovely dowager who charmed them all. She was thin and frail, but quite sharp and up on all the gossip. When she mentioned Lady Melinda, Ronan stiffened. "No, I was with Lady Melinda's father at the House of Lords, not at the theater with her. The account is in error."

He glanced at Dahlia, as though to tell her, *see, this is why I need you.*

Then he turned back to Lady Wellbrook. "When not engaged with members of Parliament or attending meetings at the Admiralty, I have been spending my time with Miss Farthingale."

Dahlia blushed, knowing the others would believe it was her coy response to his statement. In truth, she was flustered. Their ruse was now officially underway, and she hoped no one would notice it was all a fraud.

Holly and Heather eyed them curiously.

Holly cleared her throat. "More tea, anyone?" She'd taken over responsibility for pouring since Lady Wellbrook's hands shook too badly to manage it.

After their tea and cakes, Lady Wellbrook took them on a tour of the main rooms of the house. Despite leaping out of her skin with excitement to see all of it, Dahlia understood that the upstairs bedchambers were private, and she would simply have to wait until the house was Ronan's before exploring it from attic to cellar.

She hung upon the dowager's every word as she led them through the parlor, the dining room, her late husband's study, his library, a music room that obviously served as a ballroom for their grander functions, a smaller dining room covered in a floral wallpaper that resembled a summer garden, a small sitting room, and large pantry.

She smiled inwardly, loving the size of the pantry but wondering if Ronan would ever fully stock it. Yes, he would. He was a wildebeest, big and strong. He ate like a lion, not like a little bird. The pantry and larder would be kept generously stocked.

But it was a shame he would be living alone. The house was quite large for merely one person. Most of these beautiful rooms would go to waste. No wonder Lady Wellbrook had found it too much for her to maintain. However, this had been a happy home, quite joyful when her children were younger, and her husband was alive.

She could feel the warmth of this house seeping through her bones.

Since ladies did not go into the kitchen, and Lady Wellbrook was quite the traditional lady, she did not show them that part of the house.

Still, Dahlia had seen enough for now and could not wait to offer her suggestions at the proper time.

The moment they climbed into Ronan's carriage for the return ride home, she let him know how much she liked the house. However, she stopped herself from throwing her arms around him and gushing about it.

After all, it was not yet his to do with as he wished.

She couldn't bear to think the purchase might not go through.

"Holly, did you like it?" Ronan asked.

Her sister nodded. "I did. Very much. And now I have a question for both of you. Would you mind explaining what is going on?"

Dahlia cast Ronan a nervous glance. "What do you mean?"

"Do not give me that innocent look. I am your sister. I know you too well. Is this true? Ronan, are you really courting my sister?"

Heather squealed. "I knew there was something going on between the two of you. Admit it, you weren't merely reading. You were caught up in the magic of *The Book of Love*. It has drawn you together in love, hasn't it?"

Dahlia glanced once more at Ronan, preferring he take the lead in this discussion since she was not comfortable with their arrangement and certainly did not like the prospect of lying to her sisters.

"Obviously, it is quite new to us," Ronan said. "We don't know what might develop, but as for me, my intentions are serious."

"Why did you not say anything before this?" Heather asked, her smile as bright as the beacon of a lighthouse.

"I am a gentleman, Heather. Your sister and Wainscott…well, now that he is out of the way, I wanted to make my feelings known to her before others came along."

Holly appeared a little harder to convince. "Then there is nothing to the rumors about you and Lady Melinda?"

"No, as I've told you all before. It is a ploy on her part to bring her marquess to heel and make an offer of marriage."

Holly was still wary. "Because if you hurt my sister," she said, glancing at Dahlia, "I will never forgive you."

"I give you my oath, it will not happen."

He'd spoken the last with a confidence that troubled Dahlia. They were not going to last as a couple, and she did not like that the lie had tripped so easily off his tongue. Also, Lady Melinda's name kept coming up…and Ronan had not denied there had been something between them not so very long ago.

Was it possible she was being duped again?

No.

If she could not trust Ronan, then there was not another man in the world she could. He had been honest with her in every detail, stating exactly what was to happen, and why it needed to be done. He'd promised not to embarrass her, even promised to marry her if she so wished it.

Holly was still staring at her. "You look ashen."

She nodded. "I won't deny that Gerald hurt me very badly. It isn't easy for me to jump straight into another courtship so soon. It scares me."

She turned to Ronan, saw the tension in his eyes, and realized she had to go along with the charade for now. "But I want this. At least, I want to try and see where it might lead. We'll take our time. But my feelings for Ronan are much as his feelings are for me."

There, she'd given the impression they were courting. But she hadn't actually confirmed anything. It was a deception...but not quite a lie.

Her sister's expression softened as she reached forward and patted Dahlia's hand. "I'm very happy for the two of you. Having found unimaginable happiness with Joshua, I can only wish the same for both of you."

She nodded, unable to actually utter a *thank you* since it still felt wrong.

Her heart remained troubled after they dropped Holly off at her home and returned to Chipping Way. Dahlia switched seats to sit beside Heather, who was squealing and bouncing beside her like an overexcited child. In truth, Heather had felt Gerald's betrayal as strongly as she had. Her relief at this new romance was boundless.

Ronan said nothing, merely gave a slight quirk of his eyebrow.

When they stopped in front of Violet's house, Dahlia turned to him. "It has been a wonderful afternoon. Thank you for showing us Lady Wellbrook's house. Perhaps we ought to part company now.

Violet is feeling a little under the weather, and I would not like to impose on her more than we already have."

Heather, obviously swept away by romantic fantasies, would not hear of it. "She merely complained of a mild queasiness. I'm sure she's fine now. She looked perfectly fit last night. Let's ask her before you send Ronan on his way."

Dahlia forced a smile. "Very well."

She tried not to appear reluctant because Ronan was already regarding her with some concern, no doubt afraid she was going to ruin their courtship before it had ever started. She took a deep breath and smiled up at him, allowing all the affection she felt for him to show.

"There's my Queen Pea," he murmured, placing her arm in his as they walked to Violet's door.

Heather once again beamed at their exchange.

Violet happened to be the one to fling open the door, likely shouldering aside her butler before the poor man had a chance to greet them. She caught the look they exchanged, and her eyes lit up. "I was hoping you'd stop in."

"How are you feeling?" Dahlia asked, glad that her cousin had gotten over her earlier stomach upset. In truth, she looked radiant.

"I'm in the pink. Do come in. I'd love the company." She began to rattle off questions. "Where did you go today?"

They quickly related all they had done.

She clapped her hands and gave Ronan a quick hug. "Congratulations! I had no idea you were searching for a home of your own."

"It was time, Violet. I'm the last of the wildebeests to remain a bachelor. With Romulus, Finn, and Joshua marrying within a few months of each other, I thought I had better start planning ahead."

Violet cleared her throat. "They all married Farthingales."

He laughed and glanced at Dahlia. "It has not escaped my notice."

Oh, goodness. She could actually *hear* the excited flutter of Violet's heart. Well, not quite hear it so much as feel it. But this is how they were as a family, each one wanting happiness for those they loved.

Violet tipped her head up. "I'm sure you have much to discuss with Dahlia. The library is all yours. Heather can tell me the rest of what happened while you get back to reading the book."

They were herded into the library, but thankfully the door was left open. Her cousin had retained some common sense while in her matchmaking fervor.

Once alone with Ronan, Dahlia sank onto the settee with an *oof.* "That was difficult."

He settled in a chair across from her. "I'm sorry you thought so. It doesn't have to be a pretense."

"How can it be anything else?"

"Why are you so closed off to the possibility that there could be something between us?" He shook his head and groaned. "No, that was not fair of me. Your wound is still too raw. I have no right to push you in a direction you are not yet ready to go."

She nodded. "But I'm happy for your new purchase. It's a beautiful house."

"Will you help me? I would love your input, no matter what happens over the course of these next two weeks."

"Yes," she said with a laugh, "I think you would have to wrestle me to the ground and pry the fabric swatches out of my hands before I'd ever give them up."

"Once the house is mine, I shall give you a key so that you may come and go as you please. You'll need one since I don't think I'll be hiring any staff until most of the work is done. But you mustn't ever go there alone. After what happened to Holly, not that either of us has a lunatic after us, but it's still best to be cautious."

"You needn't worry about me ever being alone there. I think there will be a daily party at the house. Between your mother, your sisters-in-law, my sisters and cousins, and additional assorted relatives who just happen to be passing by and decide to pop in, there ought to be a good twenty or thirty ladies in your parlor on any given day."

He eased back in his chair and smiled. "Good. I want you to feel safe whenever you are there. The Lord Admiral allowed me time off this afternoon because of the Lady Melinda situation, but with the budget vote drawing near, I dare not take much more time away from my work. However, I will make it a point to escort you to the next few *ton* affairs. We need to be seen together as much as possible."

"I know."

"There's a musicale at Lady Broadhurst's home tomorrow evening and a dinner party at Lord Fielding's home the evening after that. Lady Melinda will be at Lord Fielding's for certain. I don't know about the musicale. I hope she is. The sooner we address the damage she's causing, the better."

He reached over and took her hand. "We left off last night with me about to tell you what I like about you. Are you willing to hear it now?"

She pinched her lips, uncertain of what he intended to tell her. "I suppose you must since this is the point of our meeting like this."

"But you're still skittish about it." He had a way of looking at her that made her tingle. It was those green eyes of his, so deep and thoughtful. There was also something a little bit naughty about them, a slightly hooded look that hinted of pleasures one might read about in scandalous novels.

"I'll start with the sense of sight first since this is where you started with me." He paused a moment and laughed softly. "I'm not very good at romantic conversation. I'm used to speaking plainly, barking orders, and having them immediately obeyed. I don't think this will work with you, will it?"

"I'm afraid not." She smiled. "We Farthingales are terrible at obeying. We like to know the reason why before we do anything. But I like that you are straightforward. I don't think I'd have the patience to listen to a flowery speech."

"Good, because I'm really not good at this." He took a deep breath. "Here goes. You are like a rose amid a field of weeds."

She burst out laughing.

"Don't mock me, Queen Pea. I am trying my best."

"I know. It just feels odd. I'm sorry. Do go on. I really am enjoying this."

He shook his head and continued. "You simply stand out, even though you are little in size."

She grinned. "I am of average height. It's you, Braydens, who are big."

"Yes, perhaps. Stop interrupting me." He cast her a mock angry look, then ruined the effect by smiling. "I like that your hair is not one bland color. It's rich and silky to the touch. Well, I jumped a little ahead of myself. I'm still on the look of you, not touch. I like that your eyes are the vivid blues and greens of the ocean."

"They are?"

He nodded. "There is a depth to them, no mere surface shimmer. I like the way your face lights up when you smile. When I look at you, I see beauty and intelligence. I see a young woman with talents and strengths she has yet to discover."

He pressed on before she could comment. "This is how you appear to me, Queen Pea. And that is another thing. I like that you are the one who found the pea in the Twelfth Night cake."

She rolled her eyes. "That was days ago and quite by chance."

"It doesn't matter. You will always be my Queen Pea."

Would Gerald ever in his life have said this nice thing to her?

"Now for the sound of your voice. It is direct and firm, and at the same time, deliciously smooth and sultry." He tossed her a naughty grin. "May I be completely honest with you? Even if it embarrasses you?"

"Yes, of course. This is the entire point of the book, isn't it? To teach us to see things clearly and be honest in our feelings toward each other."

"Good, because if I ever had you in my bed…no, that's a little too honest for your innocent ears. Let's just say that I very much like the sound of your voice. Before I move on to the next sense, let me add that your laughter is also sweet and alluring. No girlish giggles or drunken cackles that would make a man cringe."

He moved over to settle beside her on the settee. "Next is the sense of smell."

She almost shot out of her seat when he leaned in close and nuzzled her neck. Her blood heated, and her heart began to race. His lips were so close! When she felt his mouth upon her skin, everything stirred to life inside of her.

The butterflies in her stomach were in a frenzy.

She eeped.

The fiend! He knew exactly the effect he was having on her. "Why are you kissing my neck?"

"Two birds with one stone, Queen Pea. Scent and touch." He did not stop nuzzling her or breathing her in.

And now he was also nibbling her ear.

Sweet heaven!

No one had ever done this to her before. How did any woman find the strength to resist this man?

"Three birds with one stone," he whispered. "Scent, touch, and taste." He kissed her along her neck and throat, then moved lower to place a feather-soft kiss on the swell of her breast before moving back upward and capturing her lips in a searing kiss that shattered any resistance she might have ever felt toward him.

Her traitorous lips sought his with torrid eagerness.

Even her body surrendered to his touch. Indeed, craved it.

They both seemed to realize something was happening that shouldn't be and broke off the kiss hurriedly. "Ronan?"

He smiled and glanced down at their positions. She had somehow found her way onto his lap. His arms were still around her, and his eyes were hooded and smoldering. "That was nice, Dahlia.

"Heavens," she whispered. "No, it was quite wicked. I think they would call this a compromising position. We behaved very badly just now."

He arched an eyebrow, obviously amused. "Would you care to do it again?"

She scrambled off his lap. "I don't think this is what the author of that book had in mind. Let's pretend this never happened and read on. You're supposed to find your duke's daughter and–"

"So long as it isn't Lady Melinda."

"Right. But after the vote, what's to stop you?"

"You, Queen Pea."

She shook her head, dismayed. "Me?"

"Do you think I am unaffected by what is obviously going on between us?"

She shook her head again. "Why is this happening? This isn't supposed to happen."

"Why not?"

"Because I'm..." She didn't know. But Gerald had ridiculed her and told her she'd been a fool. How could Ronan feel differently about her? She clasped her hands together and stared into her lap. "Ronan, is this real? Or are you manipulating me? I'm not wise to the ways of seduction. I don't know how to defend my heart against you."

"Blessed saints, how can you think I'd ever give you cause? You can always trust me."

"I want to, but it scares me."

"I know, Queen Pea. I've been telling myself not to push you so soon after Wainscott. Were it not for this blasted vote and the Lord Admiral's threats, I would have kept a solid distance between us for at least another month or two. But being in your company is proving difficult for me, as well. Perhaps it is a Brayden thing. Meet a girl and know within ten minutes she's the one for you."

"Not quite. We met months ago. It's only now that you are starting to notice me." Of course, this also assumed all of this was not a misguided error on his part.

"No, I meant what I said." He was giving her that direct, steady look again. The one that always set the butterflies in her stomach fluttering.

They were doing so, quite madly, just now.

And her head was spinning.

"Do you think it was mere coincidence that I sought *your* favor when Robbie and I were entertaining you, Violet, and Heather with those silly jousting games along the Parliament halls this past October?"

"Wasn't it?" She remembered those times vividly.

While Holly and Joshua were tucked away in Joshua's office reading *The Book of Love*, the rest of them had passed the hours playing frivolous medieval games. Ronan and his friend, Robbie MacLauren, were their valiant knights. Their clerks had served as their pages.

With both Houses in recess and all the lords up in Scotland shooting grouse, the entire wing of this Parliament building had been empty save for them. So they'd treated it as their jousting field.

"No, I sought your favor on purpose."

"Why did you not say anything to me back then?"

"I wish I had. Believe me, no one regrets the mistake more than I." He raked a hand through his hair.

"I gave you my handkerchief as the fair maiden's love token. And you were my valiant knight. Poor Robbie, you knocked him off his horse every time."

He grinned. "I was better at riding a broomstick than he was. In truth, he's in the Scots Greys. There is no finer cavalry regiment, and Robbie is among the very best of them. Had we been on horses rather than broomsticks, I would have been the one landing on my arse every time."

"I doubt it."

"Dahlia," he said softly, "I thought you were the loveliest thing ever to step foot in Parliament. I would have said something to you then, but Wainscott was courting you, or so I believed. Also, there was some reluctance on my part. Romulus had married your cousin, Violet. Finn had married your cousin, Belle. Joshua was about to marry Holly. It was obvious to all of us that he was wildly in love with her."

"We knew Holly felt the same. For years she'd avoided men, never once speaking of anyone but her late husband, and rarely even of him. Then suddenly, she was mentioning Joshua three times a day." She shook her head and smiled. "She may as well have worn a sign across her forehead that said in large letters, *I love Joshua.*"

"Same for him. But when I suddenly found myself having similarly strong feelings for you, I thought it had to be a mistake. The idea that some young woman I hardly knew could hold any power over me was inconceivable. And another Farthingale, no less. I expected to get over this odd malady that was ailing me."

"Ah, then I was little more to you than dyspepsia that you hoped would soon pass?"

"I think you are not someone I will ever get over. But let's speak no more about it yet. It's too soon for you, Queen Pea. Wainscott hurt you badly, and you need time to sort yourself out. When you're ready, I hope you will find that I am the right man for you."

Of course, he was going to be the right man for her. Who would not fall in love with him? Indeed, she strongly suspected Lady Melinda was being a thorn in his side because she did not want to give him up. Who could blame the young woman for her good taste?

More worrisome for her was Ronan's protective instinct. This was very important to her. She could not be certain what he was feeling until she stood on her own two feet, strong and capable. Only then would she believe his instinctive desire to protect her was not blinding him to his true feelings for her. What he felt right now could only be sympathy for her being jilted. How could he mistake it for love?

She glanced at the clock atop the mantel. "Oh, I think we ought to leave the rest for next time. Ronan, why don't you take the book and read the last few chapters on your own. We won't have time to meet like this until the end of the week."

He agreed, tucking it under his arm. But he held her back as she was about to walk out. "I'll look for you at Lady Broadhurst's musicale tomorrow night. You'll attend, won't you?"

She nodded. "Are you sure you can make it?"

"Where else would I be, but at your side, Queen Pea?"

Ordinarily, Dahlia would have been thrilled. But this was no ordinary time. Would Lady Melinda be there as well?

How would she respond when she saw Ronan paying court to her?

Chapter Nine

Dahlia adored her Aunt Sophie and Uncle John, and took comfort in the knowledge they would remain beside her throughout Lady Broadhurst's evening affair, allowing her to cling to them like a child if ever she felt the need. However, she hoped she would not turn coward and do so. She wanted to stand on her own and keep her chin up proudly, whether she was to face Gerald and his Lady Alexandra or the determined Lady Melinda.

Her gown for the occasion was cream silk overlaid with lace at the bosom, and her hair was styled in a loose chignon with a few curled wisps to frame her face. She strove for a muted elegance, having long ago understood that understatement was far more pleasing to the eye than ostentation.

This belief had been confirmed by the book she and Ronan had been reading, for a man's eyes were drawn to the female body, not the trappings surrounding it. Too many frills and bows and glittering gems only interfered with a man's ability to see what his low brain compelled him to seek. "Ronan is not here yet," she mentioned to Heather as they walked in and stood in line to greet Lady Broadhurst.

"He'll be here. I know he won't let you down."

Her Aunt Sophie locked her arm in hers. "You have nothing to prove to anyone, Dahlia. Just remember this. Besides, you look beautiful, and every young man here tonight will consider Lord Wainscott a great fool for ever letting you go."

Dahlia shook her head and laughed. "Oh, I think Lady Alexandra's dowry is too much temptation for any man to resist."

There were very few men such as Ronan, ones who would be led by their heart and not swayed by a large dowry. Of course, Ronan did not have a large estate falling into ruin that he had to protect for his ancestral line.

In truth, neither did Gerald. He just wanted the dowry and prestigious connection to Alexandra's father.

Since her aunt and uncle were quite popular, they were immediately surrounded by welcoming friends. Dahlia decided to venture away from them. She walked over to the bowl of ratafia with Heather, for her throat was already strained and dry.

To her dismay, Gerald and Lady Alexandra were standing near it.

She grabbed her sister's hand. "Heather, let's go the other way."

"Why? I thought you were thirsty."

She glanced toward Gerald just as he happened to catch sight of her. The coldness of his stare shook her. He looked away and drew Lady Alexandra further into the room, turning his back to her and Heather. Of course, she expected no less from the fortune-hunting bounder. But it saddened her tremendously that someone she'd known and trusted for so many years could turn on her and hurt her without remorse or hesitation.

It shook her faith in herself because she had never seen the warning signs.

"Oh, what a wretched man," Heather muttered.

"Look, there's William." Dahlia noticed their cousin chatting with Meggie Cameron. "Let's go talk to them. He's just back from his travels on the Silk Road. I'm sure he'll have plenty of exciting stories for us. I enjoyed Uncle Rupert's tales of adventure at the supper table the other night. Didn't you? I'm sure William will have more for us."

They spoke to him and Meggie for a little while, and even though Dahlia was facing them and paying no notice to Gerald, she could feel his malevolence toward her from across the room. What had she ever done to him? The evening had just started, and she was already desperate to escape. "Heather, I'll be back in a moment."

Her sister frowned. "Where are you going?"

She pointed to the doors leading to the balcony. "I know it's cold outside. But I already feel the walls closing in around me. I'll only be a minute."

Heather gave a reluctant nod. "Don't take too long, or I'll come after you."

"All right. I promise." She stepped outside and immediately felt the chill wind bite against her cheeks. The temperature had dropped further since their arrival. The silk gown she had on offered no protection whatsoever from the cold.

Oh, crumpets.

Coming out here had been a mistake. Her family would give her no end of grief if she fell ill.

She took a deep breath and turned to walk back in when she noticed Gerald had followed her out. She frowned at him. "I don't wish to talk to you."

She tried to walk around him, but he blocked her path. "What are you doing? Gerald, get out of my way."

Still, he said nothing.

His silence was far more unsettling than any angry words he might have spouted. She was already shivering from cold, but now a shiver ran through her for altogether different reasons. What did he mean to do to her? "My family is waiting for me. They'll notice my absence and come out here looking for me soon. They know exactly where I am."

His gaze was intense and unsettling.

"For pity's sake, say something. What do you want?"

He was about to grab her when she heard a low, menacing growl from the opposite end of the balcony. "Get away from her, Wainscott."

Ronan.

Relief washed over her.

He must have come out through the music room doors. She was never happier to see anyone in her life. Gerald, the snake, immediately slithered back to Lady Alexandra.

She cast Ronan an unsteady smile as he approached. "Thank you for that growl. You sounded like a magnificent lion about to pounce."

But he did not appear at all amused. "What were you thinking, Dahlia? Why are you standing out here on your own?"

She rubbed her hands against her arms to fend off the cold. "I would not have come out here if I thought he would follow me out. He'd already walked away from me earlier."

Ronan did not appear impressed. "Come with me, Queen Pea. You're shivering."

She felt it important to defend her actions even as he held out his arm to escort her back inside. He did not release her once they were in but led her along the periphery of the crowded room toward…she did not know where he meant to take her. "I did nothing wrong, Ronan. He was standing across the parlor in conversation with Lady Alexandra and her father when I last noticed him."

"You were outside on your own."

"Heather knew where I was. I did not sneak away. She and our cousin, William, would have come looking for me in another moment." She wanted to insist that she was never in any real danger, but something stopped her.

She had been scared, and Ronan would not have believed her if she had said she wasn't. "Don't be angry with me, please. I'm having a hard enough time getting through this evening, and it has only just started."

He raked a hand through his hair and emitted a long, ragged breath. "I'm not angry, Queen Pea. I was afraid for you. What if I had not been here to stop him?"

"Stop him from doing what? He was merely looking at me. No

doubt trying to intimidate me. He made my skin crawl."

"He should not have been anywhere near you."

"I know. As I said, I did not expect him to seek me out." She followed the direction of his gaze and saw his eyes were trained on Gerald. "Please don't make a scene here, Ronan. Let him be. The consequences will be far worse for me than for him."

She shivered again.

"You need warming up." He placed his hand over hers as it rested in the crook of his elbow. "Tonight was meant to be the first step toward declaring ourselves a couple."

She groaned. "Do you want to forget about this scheme entirely? We can come up with a better plan."

"No. It is a good plan. I meant it when I said I'm not angry with you. If you must know, it is me I was silently kicking. I've dragged you into the Admiralty's troubles, forcing a courtship on you while you are still struggling with a freshly broken heart." He looked her up and down. "Your lips are blue. They'll have pots of tea set up in the dining room. That ought to warm you up sufficiently."

She held him back a moment. "We need to let Heather and my cousins know I'm back inside and with you."

He nodded and led her toward them.

"Oh, thank goodness. We were about to go on the hunt for you and scold you for staying out too long. But I see now why you lingered." Heather grinned at Ronan.

In turn, he assured Heather he would not leave her side.

After exchanging more polite words with her family, he escorted her to the dining room. The pots of coffee and tea were set out along the back wall. The evening was still young, too early for the dinner bell to ring, so she and Ronan were among the very few guests in there. She took advantage of their relative privacy to continue their conversation. "Ronan, I will admit Gerald surprised me. But every time he reveals his mean and petty side to me, I find it harder to believe I could ever have loved him. I am merely relieved now that I escaped a terrible fate. My heart is bruised, but it is not broken."

He poured her a cup of tea and handed it to her. "Did he say anything to you?"

"No, that was the oddest thing about the incident. He just stood there staring at me. What do you think he meant by it?"

"I don't know."

"I suppose it doesn't matter now. I've learned my lesson and will remain close to others whenever he is present." She took a sip of her tea, closing her eyes a moment as a soothing warmth flowed through her.

Ronan was staring at her when she opened her eyes. "You look beautiful, Dahlia. I should have mentioned it sooner."

"And you always cut a fine figure in your uniform." Indeed, he always looked incredibly handsome. "I suppose you'll be wearing it to every function held over the next few weeks, a purposeful reminder that the navy is in need of support from the House of Lords? But I will admit, I very much look forward to seeing you out of uniform."

He chuckled.

It took her a moment to realize what she'd just said. "Not *out* of your uniform as in your having no clothes on. You know I did not mean that." But heaven help her, now that the thought was in her head, she could not get rid of it. Ronan without clothes? His muscled body on full display?

She felt her cheeks heat and knew she was blushing from her scalp to her toes.

"Queen Pea, try not to be so obvious in what you are thinking." His eyes were gleaming, and his mouth was turned upward in the hint of a smile.

"What?"

He caught her teacup and steadied it before she spilled tea on her gown. "Oh."

"Not that I mind your undressing me. Are you enjoying the fantasy?"

She eeped.

"Obviously, being male, this is the thought that crosses my mind every time I set eyes on you. This was my thought from the first moment I met you. Low brain fully in control. Heart in spasms. Lungs squeezed tight. Beautiful girl. The most beautiful I've ever beheld. How would she look without her clothes?"

"Ronan!" She ought to have slapped him and walked off. Fortunately, no one was close enough to have overheard their conversation. Since there was no harm done, she did not bother to feign outrage when she wasn't really offended. If anything, she was intrigued. "Do you mean it?"

"Yes, Queen Pea. You still have this effect on me."

"Most interesting. Well, lately, my heart has been fluttering whenever I see you. I feel suddenly breathless, too. I shouldn't be telling you this, I suppose. But since we are being honest with each other, you may as well know. You probably understand what's happening to me far better than I do."

"It's all set out in those chapters we read. The discussion about the five senses. This is the way our brain responds when in the company of someone pleasing to us. Remember the opening paragraph?"

She winced. "No. Remind me."

"Our brain controls our responses, sending signals to the other parts of our body. When I first saw you, my brain immediately recognized that I liked you. It sent commands to my organs. Heart, start beating faster. Lungs, stop filling with air. Eyes, open wider to take her all in."

She laughed. "I think I am far better off having you read the book and explaining it to me. I'm learning nothing on my own. I even peeked ahead a few chapters, for all the good it did me. I think my brain is still too numb to decipher what it is reading."

"Understandable. The other problem you have is that you do not have any romantic experience. Gerald was never a proper beau. That much is obvious."

"Yes, I agree. Gerald was very bad for me. This knowledge will not be wasted. It is a hard lesson learned and not soon forgotten. Hopefully, never repeated."

They spoke no longer as a bell rang to summon everyone to the music room for the concert that would soon begin. "Ready, Queen Pea?"

He held out his arm to her once more.

When she took hold of it, she felt a sudden awareness of his strength. Of course, she had always been aware of his size and brawn, but this time was different. She was responding with all the 'feels' described in *The Book of Love*. Heart flutters. Breathless feeling. Blood rushing. But there was another response that she was not quite prepared for.

It was as though her body was preparing itself for Ronan's intimate touch. Certain parts of her were awakened as they never had been before.

She began to squirm.

He glanced at her with concern. "What's wrong?"

"Nothing. Let's find seats. The place is filling up fast. Do you prefer to be up front or tucked away in the back?"

He shrugged. "Wherever you like."

She chose seats toward the middle, finding two that were at the end of the row. It would be easier for her and Ronan to leave if they needed to make a quick escape. Not that she expected to find the need, but if Gerald behaved oddly again, she wanted to keep her options open.

They had just taken their seats when she felt Ronan tense. "Lady Melinda is here," he muttered.

"What about her father? Do you see him?"

Ronan nodded. "Time to start gazing at me adoringly, Queen Pea. The game is afoot."

"I'll do my best. Let's hope Gerald doesn't ruin it."

He arched an eyebrow. "I hope he does. Fighting over you is not such a bad idea. Everyone would notice and be talking about it for the rest of the week, if not longer."

She inhaled sharply. "Ronan, you can't."

His expression turned stubborn. "I won't start anything, I promise. But if he tries something, I'm going after him."

"I hope he isn't that stupid."

He cast her a wry smile. "And I hope he is. It will make my life a lot easier if the Duke of Stoke believes I'm in love with you. Not to mention, it would add to your cachet to have two men fighting over you."

"That is an honor I will gladly pass up."

They spoke no more as the concert was now starting. A young man with flowing gold hair strode to the pianoforte in the front of the room and made an extravagant bow before settling on his stool and bringing his hands down on the keys to strike a vigorous chord. His mastery was excellent, and he cut quite the dashing figure.

Several young ladies were the first to jump up and applaud his performance. The other guests soon followed, for he was quite good and everyone had enjoyed his playing. Dahlia rose and clapped, then spared a glance at Ronan.

He was also on his feet, no doubt relieved the ordeal was over and eager to join the other men already running from the room to grab drinks and settle at the card tables the moment those were set up. "I see Heather seated with my cousins, Dillie and Daisy. They are the daughters of Aunt Sophie and Uncle John."

"I know their husbands," Ronan said. "Your cousins are legends among the military ranks. You do realize Daisy helped turn the tide against Napoleon. As for Dillie, she saved her husband's life twice."

Dahlia nodded. "I'd heard rumors to that effect. I think this is what I dislike most about what you and I are doing. There is nothing valiant in feigning a romance."

Ronan was giving her that bone-melting stare again. "Then don't let it be a pretense."

When she looked away to stare down at her toes, he sighed and tucked a finger under her chin to raise her gaze to meet his. "Sorry, Queen Pea. I spoke out of turn again. Come on, I'll escort you into the parlor."

"What will you do afterward?"

"Stay by your side. Dance with you if there is to be dancing. I'll introduce you to the Lord Admiral if he happens to put in an appearance. More important, I want the Duke of Stoke to see us together. Do you think you can give me an adoring look or two?"

She laughed. "It will be quite a hardship for me, but I shall endeavor to try."

By the time they walked back to the parlor, footmen were offering champagne. The glasses were carried on large trays poised on their shoulders. Ronan quickly took two. "Cheers," he said and raised his glass in toast to her.

She clinked hers with his. "Here's to successful new budgets and a beautiful home…and to decorating it."

Another bell sounded just then.

"Ah, the dinner bell. Are you hungry, Queen Pea?"

While they and the other of Lady Broadhurst's guests enjoyed a light repast, the music room was cleared of chairs to create a dance floor. When they returned to it, Dahlia saw that only a few rows of chairs remained, and those had been pushed back along the wall for guests who wished to sit and watch.

The parlor had now been set up for card games.

Dahlia knew Ronan would have preferred to play cards, but he was on a mission and determined to remain by her side. The Duke of

Stoke had seen them together; of this, she was certain. It was no hardship for her to play the role of adoring debutante. Ronan was the most handsome man in the room. But she did not allow herself to be distracted by her deepening feelings for him.

All that mattered at this moment was his budget vote. It was important to Ronan, and she did not want to fail him.

But their ruse also served another purpose. He was staying close to her because of Gerald.

The bounder would not stop staring at her.

His odd behavior was beginning to unsettle her.

Ronan had noticed it as well. "I'm going to teach him a lesson."

She missed a step and would have stumbled had she not been in Ronan's arms. They were dancing the waltz. She looked up at him in alarm. "Don't you dare. Can't you see? He's purposely goading you."

"It's working. I am goaded."

Dahlia began to nibble her lip, now fretting as the dance came to an end. "Please, just ignore him."

He was looking over her head and tossing Gerald a scathing scowl. "Let me go, Queen Pea."

"No. You shall make fools of us both if you take a step toward him because I won't let go. I'll be clinging to your arm like a limpet fish. You'll be dragging me along behind you."

He groaned. "Why are you protecting him?"

"Believe me, I'm not. I would love to walk up to him and punch him in his imperious nose. But I am trying to protect myself. Two men brawling over me as though I were a common doxy in a taproom? I'll be notorious. My reputation will be tarnished. So, ambush him in the park, if you must. But keep me out of it."

He regarded her as though she'd just slapped him in the face. "Ambush him?"

Oh, he looked so offended. "Bad choice of words on my part. I know you would never do anything so cowardly. Just don't fight over me. All right?"

His response was a frown.

"Oh, they're playing another waltz. Dance with me, Ronan. That will make two, and then you won't have to dance with me again."

He was still irritated. "Are you certain you wish to be in the arms of a coward?"

"I wish to be in the arms of the bravest, most intelligent man in the room…but unfortunately, I am stuck with you."

He chuckled in response. "Fine, I'll behave."

"You really are all those things. Handsome. Brave. Intelligent, usually. Just don't turn into a protective ape because of me. I think it is important that I stand up for myself. I know I made a fool of myself last time. But it is much like riding a horse, isn't it? If you get thrown off, just get back on and try again."

"It isn't as simple as that."

"I know, but look at what my cousins accomplished at my age?" She sought out Dillie and Daisy, spotting them across the room. "Why should I not push myself to do the same?"

They were so busy talking, they did not notice the Duke of Stoke come upon them. "Brayden," he said gruffly, "introduce me to your lovely companion."

Dahlia tried to keep her heart from pounding a hole through her chest. She had to remain calm. This was the opportunity Ronan and the Lord Admiral had hoped for.

"Your Grace, may I present Miss Dahlia Farthingale."

"A pleasure, Your Grace." She bobbed a quick curtsy and smiled at him with genuine warmth. If he was going to behave brutishly toward her, she was going to prove herself the better person and a lady.

But he did not appear to be a brute. Indeed, he looked quite elegant with his full head of white hair and tall, trim countenance. His eyes were a piercing gray, and there was a hawkish keenness to them. The man was obviously intelligent and missed little.

Graced with wealth, a title, and good looks, he must have been quite the rake in his day.

"So, you are the young lady who has captured Captain Brayden's heart. I did not credit it, at first. But now that I've had a good look at you, I can see why he is captivated."

She glanced at Ronan, then turned back to the duke. "I cannot speak for Captain Brayden. But as for me, I consider myself most fortunate to have made his acquaintance."

She did not look at Ronan but felt his approval.

So far, so good.

She did not wish to appear too eager.

"Have a turn on the dance floor with me, Miss Farthingale. It is not often an old man such as myself has the chance to waltz with a beautiful girl."

"Of course, Your Grace. It would be my pleasure. I don't believe I've ever danced with a duke before."

"We don't bite, I assure you."

She did not believe it for a moment. This man was going to question her and see if he could trap her into making a mistake. And then she would be in his jaws, and he would be drawing blood.

As expected, the questions began the moment they began to spin around the floor along with the other dancers. "How long have you known Captain Brayden?"

"I met him when I first arrived in London a few months ago."

"And you and he have been an item ever since?"

"No, Your Grace. I came to London believing another gentleman of my lifelong acquaintance was going to offer for my hand."

"That Wainscott fellow?"

She pursed her lips in a grim expression. "Then you've heard."

He spun her in a twirl. He was an accomplished dancer and as spry as any young buck strutting along the edges of the dance floor. "Seems the two of you parted ways only a few days ago. And now you are here with Captain Brayden?"

"You are polite in saying we parted ways. Lord Wainscott openly humiliated me and dumped me. In truth, I am still bruised over the public embarrassment. But I am not pining for him. I consider myself extremely fortunate to have seen his true nature before it was too late. As for Captain Brayden, again, I cannot speak for him. But he told me that he only held back from courting me because he thought I was about to be betrothed to another. He was there and witnessed the Humiliate Dahlia spectacle."

"What did Brayden do?"

"Jumped in and defended my honor. I don't think Lord Wainscott would be alive today if I hadn't begged Captain Brayden not to hurt him. I think he was more overset than I was about the sad affair. He has apologized to me a thousand times since for not pressing his suit."

"Do you love him, Miss Farthingale?"

"Captain Brayden? I expect I shall, Your Grace. But I am no fickle maiden. I'm still reeling from my first unhappy experience with love. I don't trust my feelings yet and will need a little time to regain my balance. However, I am not blind to Captain Brayden's merits. Is there any doubt he is magnificent?"

"My daughter seems to think so, too."

Dahlia instinctively flinched and then silently berated herself for giving away her reaction. "I see. Did she ask you to dance with me to pry information out of me?"

He frowned at her. "That is an impertinent question. I am no one's lap dog."

Did he expect an apology? He wasn't going to get one. "I've read the gossip rags. I know your daughter and Captain Brayden are supposedly an item. I know for a fact it is not true. What is it you wish to find out from me? Whether it is for your sake or your daughter's sake, just ask me, and I will answer it to the best of my ability. And if it is none of your business, I shall tell you so."

"You are quite direct for a young chit. You surprise me, Miss Farthingale."

"In a good way, I hope. But knowing the embarrassment I suffered, can you blame me for having very little patience for lies, evasions, or manipulations?"

The waltz would soon come to an end, but Dahlia dared not breathe a sigh of relief until the duke had returned her to Ronan. Only a few more spins around the room, and it would be over.

"Does your sudden infatuation with Captain Brayden have anything to do with my displeasure of him courting my daughter?"

"No, Your Grace. It has everything to do with my enjoyment of his kisses." She blushed. *Gad!* Why had she blurted this? She sighed. "Kindly do not report this to my aunt and uncle. They've been extremely kind and generous with me. In fact, to all their nieces. I would feel awful if I shamed them."

"Miss Farthingale, dukes are not in the habit of tattling."

She could not hold back her laughter. Perhaps it was her nerves getting the better of her. Or the shock so evident on his face when she so much as accused him of being a tattletale. It was both, most likely.

"One last question before the dance ends, and I return you to Captain Brayden. By the way, he has not taken his eyes off you the entire time."

"It is his protective nature. He knows I've been hurt once, and he has appointed himself as my guardian angel. As I said, I think that incident tore him up inside worse than it did me."

"I see." He emitted some harrumphs and grumbles, then asked another question. "What do you know of the Royal Navy's budget vote?"

"I know that Captain Brayden has poured his heart and soul into it. I know it means a lot to the navy that it passes."

"Enough that they would contrive this romance between you and Captain Brayden in the hope I'll believe he is not courting my daughter against my wishes? I know my vote is essential."

"What has one thing to do with the other?"

"It might. Will you answer my question?"

"Do you wish my honest answer?"

"Yes, Miss Farthingale. Surprisingly, I believe you will give me one."

"I will, Your Grace. I'm a terrible liar, and you would see through any falsehood at once. So here is the truth. Captain Brayden is in love with me. He is not in love with your daughter. If he were, he would not sneak around behind your back. It is cowardly, and Captain Brayden is no coward."

"I never said he was."

"You suspected him of going behind your back, and that is insulting enough. Now, about our courtship. It is not contrived. If it were up to Captain Brayden, we would be married tomorrow. But as I mentioned earlier, I do not trust myself yet. He knows better than to push me for an answer."

"And the funding vote?"

"Why should my answer matter? Aren't you going to vote on its merits? In which event you would have to approve it because I cannot imagine Captain Brayden putting anything extraneous or unnecessary in his budget."

"How little you know of the workings of government. Merit alone is never enough."

"Merit is all that should matter. Shame on all of you for even considering putting the lives of our noble seamen in danger over your petty suspicions and dislikes. Your Grace, those less clever than you would be guided by you on this vote. On any vote. You cannot hold back your approval out of spite."

"Who says I plan to vote against it?"

"Then why are you questioning me? Why have you asked me to dance with you?"

"Concern for my daughter, of course."

"And what has the Parliamentary vote on the navy's budget to do with her happiness? You have a moral duty to king and country to protect our fighting men and honor them to your utmost. How can you be so venal as to willingly destroy the Royal Navy because you are peeved at your daughter's choice in men? If anything, she has shown far better sense than you in this matter."

"My dear girl, I asked for an honest answer, not a public spanking." His eyes were gray embers, dark and stormy.

Crumpets.

She wouldn't blame Ronan if he throttled her.

If the duke were a dragon, he'd have flames snorting through his nose.

Had she just ruined Ronan's chances on this vote?

Chapter Ten

RONAN'S HEART SANK as he watched Dahlia being escorted back to his side by the Duke of Stoke. Dear heaven, what had she said to him? The man was grinding his teeth, and she looked to be in a panic.

He happened to be chatting with the Lord Admiral while Dahlia and the duke had been dancing. "Hellfire, Brayden. This looks bad."

"I know, my lord. I'll take full responsibility, of course. Miss Farthingale isn't to blame. I tossed an innocent lamb into the jaws of that wolf."

"No, son. It is my fault for forcing you into this bad idea. I hope your knees are in better shape than mine. I think we're going to be doing a lot of groveling before Stoke in the coming days."

The duke turned his angry gaze on Ronan. "I'll have a word with you, Brayden. Now." He spoke more politely to Dahlia, bowing over her hand. "Miss Farthingale, our time together has been…enlightening. Would you mind if I stole your captain away for a few minutes? I'm sure the Lord Admiral won't mind entertaining you until his return."

She nodded.

Ronan strode off with the duke. They stepped outdoors onto the balcony for privacy. Despite the cold, neither of them felt chilled. Ronan was certain they were both too hot and angry, and the temperature between them was about to rise even further.

He waited for the duke to speak first. "Miss Farthingale insulted me."

Ronan arched an eyebrow, trying to stifle his amusement, which would only take matters from bad to not-a-chance-in-hell-the-vote-will-pass. "She did?"

"I asked her to speak honestly, and she unloaded her full artillery. She's quite a girl."

"I think so. Your Grace, what did she say to you?"

Stoke leaned against the balustrade and stared out into the darkened garden. "She called me venal and manipulative."

"Lord, have mercy." Ronan knew he should not be laughing, but he was about to spend the rest of his days swabbing the deck of the ugliest, most sea-unworthy vessel in the navy. He no longer cared what the duke thought of him. The punishment could not be any worse.

He tossed his head back and laughed.

To his utter shock, the duke burst out laughing as well. "She is right, Brayden. I have been a monumental arse. I want you to know that you will have my vote. Not only that, I will actively support your appropriations and encourage others in the House of Lords to do the same."

Ronan was stunned. "Thank you, Your Grace."

"No, thank your young lady. Sometimes we are so caught up in ourselves that we lose sight of what's important. Are you in love with Miss Farthingale?"

"Yes, Your Grace. Utterly infatuated. From the moment I set eyes on her."

He grunted. "I'm not surprised. Do not let her slip away."

"I don't intend to." But neither would he push her before she was ready to commit her heart to him.

He thought the conversation would now end and expected the duke to walk back into the house, but he didn't. "Who is this fellow, Wainscott?"

Ronan's humor immediately fled. "A bounder."

"I saw him menacing Miss Farthingale earlier this evening. They were standing about where we are standing now. Then you came along, and he fled. What is his business with her?"

"He has none, as far as I'm concerned."

"Yes, yes. I know you wish to protect her. But I wish to know more about this man and what passed between them. Tell me all you know."

Ronan found the request odd but saw no harm in telling him. The news was already circulating in *ton* circles. He preferred the duke to learn the truth, not some distorted secondhand gossip encouraged by Wainscott to embarrass Dahlia. "He had made certain promises to her, led her to believe a betrothal was forthcoming. In the meanwhile, he was secretly courting the Earl of Balliwick's daughter, Lady Alexandra."

He nodded. "She's a nice girl. No brains, though. Her father's fairly dim, too."

Ronan figured they would have to be in order to align themselves with Wainscott. "He revealed the news of his betrothal to Balliwick's daughter in a most heinous manner, purposely designed to impose maximum hurt and humiliation on Miss Farthingale. She did nothing to deserve such ill-treatment."

"Yet, he does not take his eyes off Miss Farthingale. Why is that?"

"I don't know. I don't care. If he comes near her, I will kill him."

"Don't speak such utter nonsense, Brayden. You are far more clever than that."

Ronan raked a hand through his hair. "The man is lower than the slime beneath my boots. I am not at all clever when it comes to dealing with him. I just want to rip him apart with my bare hands. Dahlia…that is, Miss Farthingale, won't let me."

"She is right. You would only hurt yourself."

"Perhaps, but I still want to do it. I won't, of course. Unless he attempts to harm her. Then I will do it with a smile on my face."

"Let's hope it doesn't come to that." He sighed and shook his head. "Despite her forthright manner…a little too forthright for my taste…I like your Miss Farthingale. Do you think she would help my daughter?"

"Do you mean help with Lady Melinda's elusive marquess?"

He snorted. "If the man even exists, which I am beginning to doubt. She won't name him. No one knows who he is. I am sorry now that I gave her such a hard time over you. Miss Farthingale, while sternly berating me over my treatment of you, told me that my own daughter had better sense when it came to choosing a husband for herself."

Ronan winced. "Blessed saints, she said that?"

Lord, she'd taken Stoke to the woodshed and whipped him soundly.

"I don't suppose your courtship of Miss Farthingale is merely a ruse, and you'd be willing to court my daughter? I would not forbid it this time around."

Ronan shook his head. "I am in love with Miss Farthingale. No ruse, Your Grace. I'd marry her tomorrow if she'd let me."

"She said as much. I'd like to introduce her to my daughter. I'm truly worried about Melinda. Do you think she would agree to help me? Can I offer her anything in return?"

"She might agree to help you, but don't bribe her to do it. She'll take offense. These Farthingales do things from the kindness of their heart. Just ask her straight out."

"I will. Not tonight. I think she's boxed my ears enough for one evening." He turned to walk back inside. "Will she be at Lord Fielding's dinner party?"

"Yes, Your Grace."

"Good. She and I will chat then. I'll ask Lady Fielding to seat her beside me. It's a break with the rules of etiquette, but what's the use of being a duke if I can't be obnoxious and demanding?" He returned inside.

Ronan remained on the balcony, raking a hand through his hair and wondering what had just happened. He laughed as he sauntered in to rejoin Dahlia and the Lord Admiral. They were standing at the same spot where he'd left them, both still sporting worried expressions.

The Lord Admiral noted his smile. "Did you manage to repair the damage, Brayden?"

Dahlia was wringing her hands. "Oh, please say you did."

"There is no damage to repair. The duke apologized to me and assured me that we will have his vote. Not only that, but he'll throw his full support to us to be sure our budget request passes." He turned to Dahlia. "This is your doing. He was thoroughly charmed by you. In fact, he's going to ask Lady Fielding to seat you next to him at tomorrow's party."

The Lord Admiral emitted a sigh of relief. "Well done, Miss Farthingale."

She shook her head. "I'm not sure what I did. I thought I had angered him, and he was livid."

"You were honest with him, and he sorely needed it. Everyone panders to him. He recognized you as a person he could trust. It seems to be a precious commodity these days. However, tomorrow try to be a little more restrained in your opinions. I think you've sent him home with a blistered backside."

The Lord Admiral laughed. "Well, my thanks for saving the Royal Navy. I shall leave you to Captain Brayden now."

He bowed over her hand and then left them.

"So, I didn't sink your best-laid plans?" She smiled at him.

"No, Queen Pea. You were brilliant. Would you care to dance? Stoke stole the last waltz from me. They're about to play another, and I have a desperate need to hold you in my arms."

"I think that would be lovely. But isn't it unusual to play so many waltzes in an evening?"

"It is, but Lady Broadhurst has a daughter making her come-out. Three waltzes, three potential suitors. All rules are tossed out the window for this matchmaking mama."

"I won't complain. There is something quite heavenly about being in your arms."

"Feeling is mutual." There was a new awareness thrumming through him. Something had changed between them, and it took him halfway through their waltz to realize what it was. In helping him with the duke, they had just formed a very important connection. This had nothing to do with his response to her body or her beauty, which seemed to grow more spectacular with each passing moment.

This had to do with her becoming a part of his life. His assignment as navy liaison to Parliament defined him as a man. It was a prestigious position, even though it was not one he would have preferred for himself.

He would have been happiest in command of a battleship.

But liaison was the job he had been tasked to do. This evening, Dahlia had come through for him, saving his arse. More important, she'd saved him while remaining true to herself. For the first time, he realized how much richer every aspect of his life would be with her in it.

Until this moment, he had been thinking of her primarily as a pleasing bed mate. He had also been thinking of her as a wife and the perfect mother for their children, should they be blessed with them.

Those were important, of course. But he had not considered her as a confidante and partner in every aspect of his life. When it came to matters beyond their domestic life, he had only been thinking about what he could offer her.

Offer her marriage.

Offer his protection.

Provide a home for her.

Protect their children, should they have any.

He'd never once given thought to all she would add to his life. But he understood now what the author of *The Book of Love* had been describing. It wasn't merely about the senses. It was about the connections one built over the course of a marriage. It was about the strengths in each that enhanced the other.

He did not know if the Lord Admiral would ask for more from Dahlia. But knowing she could handle whatever they tossed her way was a source of pride for him. Also, she offered a fresh perspective. As helpful as Joshua and Robbie always were, the three of them were often of one mind.

Dahlia would bring not only a fresh opinion but a woman's opinion. Other men might dismiss it, but he'd been raised by a fierce, intelligent, and independent mother. He understood the value of her thoughts. Of course, he was not going to divulge military secrets to Dahlia. But his everyday worries?

"You are looking at me so oddly, Ronan."

They were spinning around the room along with the other couples, flowing to the music in a smoothly moving current. "Am I?"

"Yes. You are looking at me as though you are seeing me clearly for the first time."

"I am, Queen Pea. I thought I understood what the book described. But it is only now that I realize the full impact of the advice. We look at a person, but what do we really see? What we want to see. What we expect to see. But if we clear away our preconceptions and open ourselves to all possibilities, we suddenly notice an entirely new world set out before us."

He wanted to tell her that he loved her, but to do so amid a crowd was out of the question. Once he did tell her, he intended to seal the declaration with a kiss. Perhaps a string of kisses.

Perhaps more.

Definitely more.

He wanted to devour this girl.

"I've never felt like this before," he said, his voice husky as he struggled to hold back the words she was not yet ready to hear. But he wanted her to know that he was not going away. "You and me. I want you in my life forever."

"Don't say anything more, Ronan." He felt her tremble in his arms. "Let's wait until your vote is over. I may have done you a good turn this evening, but I could be the goat tomorrow."

When the dance ended, the Lord Admiral called Ronan over. "Something's come up. We have to go. Nothing to do with the vote. Forgive us, Miss Farthingale. And thank you again for all you did for us this evening."

Ronan took a moment to escort her to a group of her cousins who were clustered in a circle beside the balcony doors and merrily chatting away. He led her to them, knowing they would keep her safe from Wainscott. But he frowned at her to emphasize his concern. "Do not leave them."

She smiled at him. "I won't. If they migrate to the food, I shall migrate right along with them and keep to the middle of the herd."

"Brayden, let's go," the Lord Admiral said impatiently.

"Until tomorrow, Queen Pea." He raised her gloved hand to his lips and kissed it.

He dared not look back once he strode off.

Dahlia was not a child. She would know better than to give Wainscott the chance to find her alone again.

"What has happened, my lord? Who has summoned us?" They grabbed their cloaks and hurried out the door to the Lord Admiral's waiting carriage.

"Lord Liverpool. He's assembled his cabinet ministers at Westminster Hall and wants us there immediately."

Damn. This had to be something serious. Lord Liverpool led Parliament. He was the most powerful man in England, save for the royal family. Arguably, he was even more powerful than the royals. Ronan's eyebrows arched upward in surprise. "Any indication of why he needs us so urgently?"

"No." He rubbed a hand across his furrowed brow. "We'll find out soon enough. Merciful heavens, I am too old for this. My appointment as First Naval Lord was meant merely as a political favor."

"The sea is in your blood, my lord. They knew what they were doing when they put you in charge. If not for you, the civilians on the Admiralty board would have made a political mess of the Royal Navy."

The Parliament buildings were shuttered for the night, only the usual guards standing at the various entrances. Ronan was familiar to these soldiers since he often worked late into the evening. They were allowed in without question.

Each hallway had guards stationed at the ends. There were more guards posted in front of the banqueting hall. Once again, they were immediately allowed in. Ronan's gaze took in Lord Liverpool and ten of his cabinet ministers assembled, all of them looking quite grim.

More than grim, for there was so much tension in the room, it was like a powder keg. One had only to strike a match to set off an explosion.

Ronan's first thought was an attempt had been made upon the life of the king, for King George IV had only been crowned a few months ago. He had served as Prince Regent during his father's reign but had been officially invested and crowned only earlier this year.

Since Ronan was the lowest ranking individual in the room, he said nothing, merely listened while the ministers began to explain what had happened. "This is disastrous," Lord Liverpool said. "First the Peterloo massacre, then the Cato Street conspiracy. Now a mob in Tilbury has seized The Invictus and is threatening to blow it up."

"What!" The Lord Admiral was livid.

"In Tilbury?" Ronan was furious, but not yet convinced they were being given an accurate account. The Invictus was one of the newer ships of the line and also one of their largest. It was perhaps the finest vessel in their entire fleet. Of course, this is why it had been targeted. But it had been designed for combat on the open seas and was too massive to sail up the Thames, which it would have had to do in order to reach Tilbury.

Had it been on its way to London?

What idiot had ordered this?

And why did its admiral in command not ignore the order?

"How did The Invictus get to Tilbury?" he asked. "Why would this vessel be anywhere near there? Portsmouth or Harwich are the closest deepwater ports able to accommodate these large-hulled ships."

Apparently, he had asked a sensitive question.

These politicians were glowering at him instead of providing information.

He inhaled sharply. "Oh, hell. Did it run aground?" He bit his cheek to stop himself from saying more. Obviously, one or more of the men seated here, perhaps Liverpool himself, had demanded the ship to call in at the port of London.

No doubt, the intention was to show it off to the local citizenry and the well-heeled members of the *ton*. It would not surprise him to learn that a young lady or two had been promised a tour of The Invictus by one of these lords hoping to impress said young ladies.

"Watch yourself, Captain Brayden." One of Liverpool's cabinet members, a debauched peer he recognized as Lord Peckham, was glaring at him. The man sat on the Admiralty board, a civilian, as most of these board members were, and likely was the one who'd gotten them into this mess. "We are not schoolboys to have our ears boxed by a young upstart such as yourself."

"Of course, my lord. I meant no disrespect." *Bloody fool.* He ground his teeth in frustration. Dahlia had just saved the navy budget, and now Lord Peckham's idiocy was about to sink it. "Do we know who is leading this mob?"

He doubted there was any leader or organized assault. The mob in question was likely fishermen angered by the presence of this behemoth blocking their vessels from sailing to London to sell their fish or venturing out to the North Sea to catch more.

He did not see how they would have the means to capture such a prize, much less get their hands on explosives to blow it up.

"No," Lord Peckham said. "Fortunately, this rebellious uprising has been contained to Tilbury thus far."

Yes, definitely angry fishermen. Ronan doubted they had captured this battleship at all. But they might have surrounded it with a flotilla of fishing boats.

And by rebellious, did Lord Peckham mean they'd been throwing eggs and rotted vegetables at the ship?

Lord Liverpool turned to the Lord Admiral. "Sir William, I do not know that you are well enough to ride to Tilbury. Would you have any objection to my placing Captain Brayden in charge?"

"No, my lord. Indeed, I have every faith he can bring a peaceful end to this unfortunate conflagration."

Lord Liverpool turned to Ronan. "Then the task is yours, Captain Brayden. Take one of our regiments with you on the chance matters get out of hand."

He nodded. "I'd also like two barges and all the rope I can commandeer. The ship has run aground, has it not?" He'd asked the question moments earlier but had not received a straightforward answer.

"Yes," said Liverpool with a sigh. "You have my authority to take whatever materials you need. Get started at once."

He strode out with the Lord Admiral, slowing his step to accommodate the older man. "My brother, Joshua, still commands a regiment of dragoon guards. They were the soldiers who cleared out the criminal element in Oxford a few months ago. These are disciplined men, not likely to do anything foolhardy and make matters worse."

"Yes, take them with you. Bah! That Peckham, what an arse."

"Who is the idiot in command of The Invictus?" Ronan asked. "He ought to have known better than to risk one of our finest ships."

"Have you not figured it out yet? It is Peckham's brother, Viscount Hawley. I'll have him under court-martial if there is so much as a blemish found."

Ronan's expression turned grim. "She'll have scratches along the length of her hull for certain. Let's hope it is nothing worse. I don't want to be the one standing in front of Liverpool and his cabinet ministers informing them the costliest ship we've built in this century just sank at the mouth of the North Sea."

While the Lord Admiral returned to the Admiralty building, Ronan called on Joshua. "I need your help, Josh."

Fortunately, his brother and Holly were still awake. They settled in Joshua's study, and he quickly explained what had happened. "This is why I need you to muster your regiment as fast as possible."

Holly turned ashen. "How dangerous is this mission?"

The two brothers exchanged glances. Ronan spoke up since he was the one most familiar with the situation. "I think Oxford was far more dangerous. Lord Liverpool would have heard from the Tilbury magistrates had this uprising been more than a group of angry fishermen pelting cabbage at a stranded battleship to vent their frustration."

She clasped a hand to her throat. "I pray this is all it is."

Ronan nodded. "I'll watch over my big brother."

He knew Holly had lost her first husband toward the end of the Napoleonic Wars when the ship carrying his regiment had been attacked and destroyed. Now newly wed to Joshua, she was not keen on losing him just yet. "Holly, will you do me the favor of letting

Dahlia know what is happening. I was supposed to join her at Lord Fielding's supper party, but there is no way we will be back in time. I expect we'll be gone for three or four days at a minimum."

She nodded. "I'll tell her. Do you know if Wainscott has been invited?"

"I don't, but it is likely he has been since the Fieldings are friendly with Lady Alexandra's father. Will you alert Finn and Tynan? Let my brothers know the situation. I need them to protect Dahlia from that weasel if he decides to cause trouble."

Holly nodded, but Ronan was not sure how much she was taking in. That Joshua was about to ride off to help him quell a local confrontation had her trembling and ashen.

"Holly, please. I'll be mad with worry if Dahlia is left unguarded while he is anywhere close by."

She nodded. "I will. Of course. I love my sister. I won't let any harm come to her."

Joshua rode off to his regimental headquarters while Ronan left to arrange for the barges and round up as much rope as he could gather. His hope was to tow the battleship out of the shallows and into deeper waters. This could be done if the river bed was soft enough. The vessel could be harmlessly pushed through silt and reeds.

Finding the rope proved to be a fairly simple task. One of their biggest suppliers of rigging for their battleships had a warehouse at the London docks.

It took Ronan another hour to summon the owner, one Lord Stonehurst. In turn, Lord Stonehurst sent word to his foreman for his workers to start loading the ropes onto the barges immediately. Once this was underway, Ronan rode to the Admiralty to gather whatever maps he could find that charted the Thames seabed around Tilbury.

Shortly before dawn, he watched the barges pull out of their slips at the London docks. He then rode in the graying light to Joshua's headquarters to travel overland with his brother's regiment while the supply-laden barges sailed to Tilbury.

He was exhausted.

But now was not the time to rest. He would catch a few winks while in the saddle. He glanced up at the sky, hoping for good weather. Getting that leviathan back into the North Sea would be a Herculean task. He had no wish to do it with snow and ice pelting down on them.

Having to work in icy waters was bad enough.

He couldn't send divers down to assess the damage, for they wouldn't survive more than five minutes in those frigid depths. Also, the Thames was murky. Very little light would filter down to the lower depths of the hull. The divers would be exploring in the dark.

No, he would simply have to rely on the maps and pray hard they were accurate.

"Ronan," his brother said, grabbing his arm as he was about to slip off his mount. "Are you all right?"

"Fine, Josh." But he wasn't really, and his brother knew it. The political storm the navy would have to face over The Invictus stranding itself on the Thames was going to be bad. He was now in charge of this thorny operation. Being a mere captain, it was more than likely his name would be put forth as the one to blame if it failed.

More damning was his role as naval liaison to Parliament. He was the face these politicians saw every day.

Yes, they would have a merry old time kicking his arse.

Perhaps the true incompetents would be disciplined eventually, but he doubted they would ever be seriously touched. Viscount Hawley, the obvious culprit, had powerful connections to see him through this incident more or less unscathed.

Ronan thought no more of the headaches he was facing.

He would deal with each problem as it arose.

His greatest concern was for Dahlia. Would she make it through Lord Fielding's dinner party on her own? Lord Stoke was going to have her seated beside him. She had handled the duke brilliantly at Lady Broadhurst's party. Would she be as successful tonight?

And what of that weasel, Wainscott?

Did he have more humiliation in mind for Dahlia?

Or was he plotting something more sinister?

Chapter Eleven

"HOLLY, DO YOU think I can send my regrets to Lord Fielding?" Dahlia was dismayed to learn Ronan had left for Tilbury. The hour was early still, but Holly had wasted no time in stopping by to fill her in on all that had happened after Ronan and the Lord Admiral departed Lady Broadhurst's musicale.

The two of them were now seated in Aunt Sophie's parlor, chatting alone. Neither Aunt Sophie nor Heather had come down yet. Hortensia was awake and somewhere in the house, but she never liked to engage in conversation before having had her morning coffee.

Her sister frowned. "No, you cannot send your regrets to Lord Fielding. His party is tonight. He will be terribly offended if you back out."

She sighed. "I suppose you're right. Then Ronan will think I am a coward. I need to show him that I can stand on my own."

Holly reached over to give her hand a squeeze. "You have more spirit and independence than I ever had at your age."

Dahlia laughed. "You are only three years older, but the way you talk sometimes, one would think you were thirty years older."

"Well, I never had your effortless charm. Until Joshua came along, I was on my way to turning into a younger version of Aunt Hortensia." She made a wrinkled prune face, then glanced around. "Oh, dear. I hope she didn't catch that. But I've gotten off the point. Ronan is very proud of you. He knows you are no simpering debutante prone to the vapors. However, he cannot help but feel protective of you. This is who he is. But enough about him. Now for the next important issue…"

"What is that?"

Holly grinned as she came to her feet. "What are you going to wear tonight? Come on, let's go upstairs and wake Heather. Did Violet sleep over?"

"No, she's in her own home." Which was only next door, so she did not have very far to walk if she was inclined to join them. "Romulus is due back any day now, and she did not want him returning to an empty house."

Holly smiled. "She must be eager to see him. As for you, show me your gowns. Not that I will be any help whatsoever in choosing what you or Heather should wear this evening. You were always the one who helped me with my wardrobe."

They ultimately chose a rose silk gown for her and a silvery blue one for Heather. The silk fabrics were from the Farthingale mills. As Dahlia cast a final critical eye over their choices, Dahlia recalled her Uncle Rupert's stories about his travels east, the mulberry trees and silkworms. The gowns were beautiful, but also of special significance now that she knew the tales behind the origins of this fabric.

Holly's eyes were sparkling as she gave them a final inspection. "You will both look stunning."

They had rustled Heather out of bed to choose their gowns. She stifled a yawn, not yet fully awake. "I hope so. I need to make a good impression on the Marquess of Tilbury."

"Tilbury?" Dahlia's thoughts immediately shot back to Ronan and his miserable assignment. She was not yet wise to the workings of politics but knew someone would have to take the blame for this glaring mistake.

She curled her hands into fists, determined to start garnering favors that could be called in to protect Ronan, if necessary. She'd start with the Duke of Stoke. If he wanted her to befriend his daughter, then she would ask him to help Ronan. But only if there was no other recourse. She knew Ronan would not appreciate her interference otherwise.

"Has Lord Tilbury given you any indication he is interested in you, Heather?" Holly had asked the question, bringing Dahlia's thoughts back to her sisters.

"I think so. Nothing obvious yet. But he sought a dance with me last night and asked if I played whist and would partner him once they set up the card tables at Lord Fielding's party."

Dahlia smiled at her sister. "Oh, Heather. That is exciting. I shall discreetly inspect him and give you my opinion…that is, if you'd like my opinion. I'm hardly a good judge of character."

Heather frowned. "Of course I do. Stop kicking yourself for Gerald's deceit. He had all of us fooled."

The rest of the day passed swiftly for Dahlia.

Before long, she and Heather were climbing into the carriage with her aunt and uncle. Shortly afterward, they were on the receiving line, waiting to meet Lord Fielding and his wife as they stood by the grand staircase of their elegant home. The light of a thousand tapers guided their way, casting a magical glow about their home. "It feels as though we are entering a fairy kingdom," Heather whispered.

Dahlia nodded, wishing Ronan could be by her side.

Lady Fielding was a formidable woman who wielded quite a bit of power among the *ton*. Dahlia was surprised by the warmth of the greeting she received from her and Lord Fielding. "It is a pleasure to be here. Your house is exceptionally lovely."

"Why, thank you, Miss Farthingale. That's quite a compliment coming from you. The Duke of Stoke tells me you are very talented in matters of design."

She shook her head and laughed. "He exaggerates. But I am delighted to have won him over."

"He was raving about your talent," her husband said. "I hear you are going to help his daughter redecorate their home."

She was?

"It's just an idea tossed around at the moment." She wasn't certain how much to say about it. Dear heaven, she and Lady Melinda had never even spoken.

Lady Fielding's eyes were gleaming. "Well, I have been bothering Lord Fielding for years now about his study. It is old and ugly, but he claims it is comfortable."

"It *is* comfortable," he insisted in good nature.

"It is old, just as we are," said his wife, gently berating him.

"You, my dear? Why you are as youthful and lovely as the day I met you."

Dahlia sighed. "Beautifully said, my lord. Well, I shall be happy to offer my suggestions whenever you are ready."

She and Heather moved on to the parlor since they'd noticed one of their Chipping Way neighbors, the kindly dowager countess, Lady Eloise Dayne, seated there. She was in a corner with one of her elderly friends, Lady Withnall, the two of them settled in the most comfortable chairs in the room.

While Aunt Sophie and Uncle John were once again accosted by friends to slow their progress and distract their attention, she and Heather skittered over to the dowagers. "Good evening, Lady Dayne. Lady Withnall."

Lady Dayne smiled at them. "Dahlia. Heather. How lovely you girls look." She motioned to a footman to bring over chairs for them. "Do join us. How are you, Dahlia?"

She blushed. "Much better than a few days ago."

"I should think so," her diminutive companion intoned. "That toad, Wainscott, is never to be trusted. Lady Alexandra's father is just catching on to this fact. Their betrothal will not hold, mark my words."

"It won't?" She leaned closer, eager to learn more. Dahlia had heard Lady Withnall was a gossip feared by all. But she and Heather had nothing to hide, and therefore, nothing to fear from her. "Truly? What has happened?"

"Wainscott has already been caught with another young lady, a duke's daughter this time. I shall not name her, of course. Discretion forbids it."

Dahlia refrained from rolling her eyes. This woman was dishing out the juiciest gossip most indiscreetly, and now she was worried about naming names? Someone would soon figure out who his new victim was, and she would become the object of whispers. Dahlia actually felt sorry for Lady Alexandra.

But a duke's daughter? She worried that Lady Melinda, the Duke of Stoke's daughter, was his latest victim.

No, Stoke would not be here tonight if that were the case. She'd noticed him standing near the entry doors as they'd walked in. He had been engaged in conversation with others and not looked up when she and Heather had been announced.

"Poor Alexandra," Dahlia said, more to herself. Even though the girl had not shown much remorse or compassion to her, she did not find any satisfaction in her being hurt by that scoundrel.

Who was this as yet unnamed duke's daughter?

"Of course, we won't hear anything yet from Balliwick or Alexandra, not until she has started her monthly courses. Let's hope they arrive on schedule. Once he is assured she is not with child, that betrothal contract will be burned to ashes."

Dahlia gasped.

Lady Withnall was not at all remorseful for her crudeness. "Do not look so shocked, gel. This is how things work in this world. Wainscott's ambitions will leave him with nothing in the end. If it is any consolation, I think in his weaker moments, he cared for you."

Dahlia was surprised. "He was merely pretending all along. It is obvious he cares for himself most of all. No young woman will ever capture his heart since he's claimed it for himself already."

Lady Dayne nodded. "I'm glad you see him now for what he is."

"Oh, I do. I will be happiest if our paths never cross again. But I fear he will be in attendance this evening. I shall avoid him as best as I can."

"Oh, no. He will not dare show his face here tonight," Lady Withnall said with a comforting certainly. "Nor will Balliwick and his daughter."

"That's a relief. But Lady Withnall, why would you think he ever cared for me?"

"My dear, I would have thought it obvious. Because he did not touch you. He treated you as the lady you are."

Dahlia emitted a mirthless laugh. "Until the moment he humiliated me."

Perhaps there was a kernel of truth in the comment. Twice now, Gerald had been caught with his pants down about his ankles. Yet, he had never taken a step out of turn with her. It really was not any consolation. Even caring for him as she did, she would never have allowed him to seduce her.

Because there had been no spark between them.

It would not have torn her apart to deny him. She had never ached for his touch, and it never bothered her that they did not kiss on the lips.

But Ronan?

He set her in flames.

"A word of advice, Miss Farthingale." Lady Withnall was now eyeing her as avidly as a bird of prey eyed a field mouse it wanted to eat. "Do not remain so caught up in what Wainscott did to you that you push away the right man when he comes along."

Was she speaking of Ronan?

He had come straight out and told her that he wanted her in his life, and she had put him off exactly as Lady Withnall had just intimated. Heat ran up her cheeks. "Thank you. I will take your advice to heart."

Heather's eyes were as wide as full moons. "Lady Withnall, do you have any advice for me?"

She *thucked* her cane up and down on the polished wood floor. "Gel, what do you think I am? A fortuneteller?"

Heather looked as though she was about to cry.

Dahlia grabbed her hand to comfort her.

Lady Dayne was scowling at her companion. "Honestly, Phoebe. Behave yourself."

The little woman grumbled and then turned her piercing gaze on Heather. "Very well, here's my advice to you. You have already met the man who loves you. He is not obviously suitable for you, but that is on him. He tries very hard to hide his true nature."

"Lady Withnall, if you know his name, can you not just tell us?" Dahlia asked.

"No. Heather must learn to see through all these elegant trappings and seek the true treasure that is his heart." She waved her hand to take in their surroundings. The glimmering crystal and shining silver. The elegant ladies in their shimmering silks and the brilliant gemstones dangling from their ears and necks. "This is all I will say on the matter."

"Why does courtship have to be so hard?" Heather muttered when they sauntered to Aunt Sophie's side a short while later. "I don't understand any of what Lady Withnall meant just now. I can see beyond the glitter. The Marquess of Tilbury is no prancing peacock. Do you think he will be here? I don't see him yet."

"It is possible he was called home, seeing as how The Invictus has run aground in his back garden."

"Oh, do you think so? What a disappointment. Now that I wore this gown tonight, I'll have to wait at least a fortnight before wearing it again. And it's so pretty."

"It's just a gown, Heather. What matters is who you are inside and out. You are a beautiful girl with a beautiful heart. This is what counts to any man of substance. Smile, Heather. No one is prettier than you when you smile."

"How's this?" She put on an exaggerated grin, crossed her eyes, and lolled her tongue to the side.

"Och, pixie. That face will haunt my dreams tonight. What in blazes are ye doing?"

They both turned in surprise to find Robbie MacLauren striding toward them. "None of the Braydens were able to attend tonight, so I was sent here to watch over Dahlia." He glanced at Heather. "Seems ye need watching, too."

"Any news yet from Tilbury?" Dahlia asked. "I suppose it is too soon."

"Aye, too soon. I'll come around to Chipping Way to let ye know if I hear word. Likely the first reports will begin to arrive tomorrow afternoon. I'll do the same for Holly. I know how worried she is about Joshua."

Dahlia nodded. "We were thinking to stay with her for the next few days."

"Aye, that is a splendid idea. It canno' be easy for her. Let me know if ye do. I'd rather no' be traipsing about town delivering the same news to all of ye."

The dinner bell sounded, leaving no more chance for conversation. Robbie was about to escort her in when the Duke of Stoke approached. "I'll do the honors, Captain MacLauren, since Miss Farthingale and I are to be dinner partners." He turned to Dahlia. "My daughter will be seated across the table from us. I'm eager to have you meet her."

Robbie offered his arm to Heather. "Come along, pixie. Seems it will be just us."

Dahlia was curious where her sister had been placed, for the far end of the table is where she ought to have been seated, too. She was relieved to see her settled beside Robbie. On her other side was a minor nobleman, a baron whose name she could not recall. Not that it mattered. The man had no interest whatsoever in speaking to Heather and had barely sat down before he began to fawn over the woman to his right.

"MacLauren's a good man," the duke said, obviously noting the direction of her gaze. "He'll look after your sister. Baron Brookings is a bore and an idiot. She's better off being ignored by him."

She took her seat beside the duke and found herself staring across the table at a very pretty young lady who could only be his daughter. She and the duke had the same eyes and a similar curve of the lips. Curiously, she also resembled Dahlia's own younger sister. There was something in Lady Melinda's aspect that reminded her of Heather.

She turned to the duke. "I understand your daughter and I are about to undertake the decorating of your home together. Apparently, we have become fast friends."

"Fielding told you that already, did he?" He chuckled. "Yes, I thought it was a good subterfuge."

"Your daughter does not look like a simpering idiot. She'll understand your game immediately. What will you do if she does not like me?"

"Miss Farthingale, simply talk to her any way you feel is right. I do not want to deceive my daughter. I only wish to make her happy. I don't suppose there are any more Braydens left to marry off?"

"I don't think so. Ronan is the last, as far as I know. But I will inquire. They are very good men. Do you no longer care about a title?"

"You are rubbing salt in the wound," he said with a wince. "I will admit my mistake only this once and never again. A title is preferable, of course. But no longer required. Having strong family connections will do. But nothing less. No shopkeepers, farmers, or blacksmiths. No stable hands, horse breeders, or estate managers. I will shoot any who dare come around."

Society being as elitist as it was, she supposed the duke did not have it in him to simply accept whomever his daughter chose to love. However, he'd taken a step forward in not ruling out military men. "But soldiers are acceptable?"

He sighed. "Yes. Indeed, I regret my mistake. I suppose not every Brayden can be an earl, although three of them are."

"I am sorry, Your Grace. I did not mean to insult you. I simply wished to be clear on the matter. I will help your daughter if I can. I think it is commendable that you care for her happiness. But surely you must be aware that if she is in love with Captain Brayden, then my presence will make matters worse, not better for her."

"I know. But I am terribly concerned. She has shut me out completely, and I am not used to this. We have always been very close."

The table was long but not very wide, so the duke managed to introduce them without having to shout. They were able to engage in occasional conversation across the table. Dahlia was surprised to find Lady Melinda witty and intelligent.

She liked her. Perhaps it was because of how much she really did resemble Heather. They were similar in height and build, had the same dark hair, and even had similar gestures and laughs.

So what was going on with her?

Why was she giving her father fits by behaving so secretively?

When their feast was over, Dahlia made a point of approaching her to continue their dinner conversation, even if it was considered forward of her. She knew that she risked being given the cut direct. To her surprise, Lady Melinda was actually quite friendly. "My father rarely likes anyone," she explained. "Nor is Captain Brayden an easy one to please. If they both like you, then perhaps there is something to you, Miss Farthingale."

"They both have only good things to say about you, Lady Melinda.

Of course, it is to be expected in a doting father."

"What is this nonsense my father has been spouting about redecorating our home? It is much the way it was when my mother was alive. I am not keen to change anything."

Dahlia's heart gave a little tug. How awful it must be for an only child to lose her mother. "I am so sorry for your loss. You must have loved her dearly."

"I did. So did my father." Sadness reflected in her eyes. "But it was a very long time ago. Almost ten years past."

"I expect you are missing her, particularly now." She smiled sympathetically. "Fortunately, my mother has remained in York with my father. She is wonderful, and I love her, of course. But her advice is usually terrible. If she suggests a thing, we immediately know to do the exact opposite."

Lady Melinda laughed. "Did she advise you to run from Lord Wainscott? She would have been right about that."

"Alas, she gave me no guidance on him. The mistake was all my own, and I got quite the comeuppance for it. But I have a large and loving family in London to help me get over the embarrassment. By the way, all Farthingales love to meddle. If you ever need help, please do not hesitate to ask. Offering our opinions, whether wanted or not, is something we excel at."

"Miss Farthingale, I can see why my father and Captain Brayden like you. Even though I ought to consider you competition for his affections, I find I cannot gather even a smidgeon of resentment. I like him, mind you. But I do not love him."

"Is there someone you do love? Someone other than the fake marquess you've been spreading the word about?"

She arched an eyebrow in surprise. "How do you know he is fake?"

"Because you are a beautiful woman, Lady Melinda." Indeed, she had her father's gray eyes, but hers were warmer, almost slate blue in color. Her hair was dark and was done up in a style that perfectly framed her pretty face. "You are also smart and witty. If he exists and you've set your cap for him, I don't think he'd have the will to resist you."

"Your Captain Brayden did not fall in love with me."

Thank goodness. But she was not going to repeat this to Lady Melinda. "Toss in your dowry and your father's title, and I think your marquess would have at least made his presence known. Yet he remains unseen by anyone except you."

"Fine." She shrugged. "If you believe there is no man, then you may report this to my father and ease his mind."

"No, it is not my place to tell him what you are thinking or feeling. I wish you would. Just don't lie to him. He raised you and loved you and cared for you, would give his life to protect you. Does he not deserve something better?"

She emitted a wistful sigh. "I'll think about it."

Dahlia did not press Lady Melinda any further on this topic. Perhaps there was no marquess, but Dahlia suspected there was someone else. What if this someone else was married? *Oh, dear heaven.* That would be a disaster in the making.

"Has my father invited you to our home yet? On the pretext of viewing it for our redecorating scheme? If not, I shall do so now. We are at home to visitors tomorrow. Our calling hours start at two o'clock. But do come around at one so we may have some time alone to chat." She glanced over at Heather. "Bring your sister along, if you'd like. Who is that big Scot standing beside her? He keeps looking over at you."

"Captain Robert MacLauren. He is best friends with Ronan and Joshua Brayden. I'm sure he'd rather be anywhere else but here watching over me."

Lady Melinda nodded. "I see. These men look out for each other, don't they?"

"Yes. I think this was ingrained in them during the war, to protect each other in the heat of battle. It is something that will never leave them."

"My father's estate manager also served in the war. He was shot and now limps because of it. I'm sure it must be painful, especially on stormy days. But he never complains about it."

So this is the man.

"Will he be at your house tomorrow?"

She nodded. "He is always around. My father relies on him heavily. Why do you ask?"

"My Uncle George is one of the finest doctors in London. He was an army surgeon for a while, during the earlier years of the war. I'm certain he would not mind having a look at his leg. Perhaps there is something he can do."

Her widened with excitement. "Do you think he would?"

Dahlia nodded. "Yes, most certainly."

Lady Melinda gave her a hug, a gesture noticed by everyone in the room, including the Duke of Stoke. Well, he'd been telling everyone that she and Lady Melinda were close friends. Perhaps they would become that now. "Thank you, Miss Farthingale. I've been suggesting to the stubborn man this is something he ought to do. I will be forever indebted to you if you can make this come about."

She laughed. "I have done nothing. It is my uncle who would be working this miracle, assuming anything can be done. Since this estate manager has now become the object of our meddling, what is his name?"

"James Dawson."

Yes, this was her secret love. Dahlia could tell by the breathy way Lady Melinda said his name. Did the man know of her feelings? More important, were they reciprocated?

Heaven help them both.

What would the Duke of Stoke do when he found out?

CHAPTER TWELVE

RONAN STUDIED THE Invictus listing ever so slightly in the icy waters at the mouth of Tilbury's harbor. She was surrounded by a circle of boats. However, only the smaller vessels had been able to circumvent the massive obstruction and sail out of the harbor. The larger fishing boats were either trapped inside, unable to get out or trapped outside, unable to get in.

"Bloody, blasted mess," Joshua muttered.

Ronan merely grunted, unwilling to say anything while they stood beside the harbormaster and the Marquess of Tilbury who had raced home like the wind to personally inspect the dung heap left at his doorstep.

Well, The Invictus was no pile of dung.

But the situation certainly could be described as that. Ronan, having been assigned to save the day, had stepped into it up to his neck.

"What's your plan, Brayden?" the marquess asked, barely containing his rage as he stared across the harbor.

The barges had arrived. Since they were too big to maneuver around the battleship and pull up to the docks, they were now floating idly in the river. "The plan is to tow her out to sea. I'll need to be brought to the barges first, then to The Invictus. May I commandeer one of the smaller fishing boats for this purpose? The navy will pay the man, of course."

The marquess was still frowning. "And what of the cavalry regiment?"

"Since there is no uprising to quell, I–"

"Uprising? In my town?" The marquess was livid. "What arse ever told you that?"

"An entire cabinet ministry of arses," Joshua retorted.

Ronan shot his brother a quelling glance. He did not need this conversation to make its way back to London and gain more enemies. "We dismissed the possibility at once, of course. But I wanted the regiment to use as muscle. We'll have to get the ropes secured to The Invictus, among other things."

"What other things?"

"Lord Tilbury, I do not know yet. Perhaps constructing a temporary bridge. Perhaps assisting the injured on the ship. Whatever arises." He turned to the harbormaster. "I'll need that small boat as soon as possible. We need to accomplish as much as we can in daylight."

Once the harbormaster ran off to wave back one of the fishing vessels, Ronan returned his attention to the marquess. "How well do you know these waters?"

"This is my home. My family has ruled here for centuries. What do you wish to know?"

Ronan gestured to the maps in his hand. "I cannot tell how accurate these are. Where are the hidden dangers? Boulders. Sunken ships. Shoals. Other obstructions. Is the seabed soft? Once The Invictus is moved out of the shallows, she will need to keep a steady course within the deepest waters until safely out to the North Sea. Can I trust these maps? If so, which one is the most accurate?"

Ronan took a breath and let it out slowly, watching the frosty vapor trail blow out and disappear in the chill wind. "Then we need to test her seaworthiness. I would not like for her to sink before she returns to Harwich. We have the facilities there to check the damage to her hull."

The marquess laughed. "Lord Liverpool is praying hardest she doesn't find a watery grave. The press will roast him alive. But they'll roast you, too. It is a pity, Brayden. You are well-liked."

He shrugged. "I am no politician. I'd much rather be put back in command of a ship."

"Speaking of command, who is the idiot in charge of The Invictus? It is a flagship, is it not? It must have an admiral of the fleet in command."

Ronan winced. "It is Lord Peckham's brother, Viscount Hawley."

"Blessed saints! He was a schoolmate of my father's. My father, may he rest in peace, often referred to him as the vainest man alive. How can Liverpool have allowed it?" The marquess shook his head. "Never mind. It is done. Hopefully this incident will allow us to put in some reforms, start promoting men on the basis of merit instead of connections. The House of Commons is already screaming for this."

When the fishing vessel arrived, Ronan strode onto it and was surprised when the marquess hopped aboard as well.

Joshua had no intention of being left behind, either. "My men are settled in and awaiting my orders. It is best if I have first-hand knowledge of what they'll be required to do."

The Marquess of Tilbury knew this fisherman. "Don't sink us, Ralph. At least, not before we get that giant tub of lard out of our way." They were hardly under sail before the marquess turned to Joshua. "I hear you recently married one of the Farthingale girls. Holly, is it?"

Joshua gave a reluctant nod. "Yes."

"Tell me about her sister."

Ronan immediately tensed. "Dahlia?"

He shook his head. "No, the other one. Heather."

Ronan exchanged glances with his brother. Joshua, being the married one, answered for them. "Why are you asking?"

"Isn't it obvious? I like her." He grinned at him and Joshua. "Although I may have to rethink the family connection if this ship sinks."

SINCE LADY ELOISE Dayne had planned to call upon Lady Melinda and her father today, Dahlia asked her to serve as her chaperone and ride over earlier. She preferred not to bring Heather or involve anyone else in the family since the duke and his daughter were new acquaintances, and there was no telling what might happen if the duke found out about the estate manager.

Also, her aunt and uncle were busy planning their traditional family holiday parties. As their daughters and nieces were growing up and marrying, not to mention raising children of their own, these intimate family affairs were growing unwieldy. She did not wish to add to their burden. "His Grace has invited us for one o'clock, Eloise. He and his daughter would like some time to show me around before their other callers arrive."

Eloise was quick to accommodate, as Dahlia knew the kindly dowager would. Besides being related by marriage to the Farthingales – her grandsons were married to Laurel and Daisy, two of Sophie and John's daughters – she was also intelligent, pleasant company, and capable of discretion.

The Duke of Stoke's Belgravia house was a magnificent work of architecture. Large, stately. Imposing. Dahlia could not imagine actually decorating the place. But what a prize it would be to have the assignment.

They were shown in by the Stoke butler, who led them to the receiving parlor, a grand room in muted shades of yellow and green with an Aubusson carpet of similar colors to pull it all together. She'd also noticed two Aubusson tapestries on the entryway walls and several statues of white alabaster. "The things I could do with this place."

Eloise laughed. "I can see how eager you are."

The butler rolled in a tea cart, and shortly thereafter, the duke and his daughter hurried in. The duke had a genuinely warm smile for Eloise. "Lady Dayne, a pleasure to see you."

"I hope you don't mind my accompanying Miss Farthingale. Of course, she could not ride over on her own."

"Not at all, I'm delighted you are here. Would you care to join us in a tour of the house? We've promised to show Miss Farthingale around, and I'd rather it were done before our other guests arrive."

"Dear me, no. My knees are quite creaky today. I shall sit here and enjoy my cup of tea. Do not mind me. I am perfectly fine waiting right here."

The duke frowned. "No, that won't do at all." He turned to his butler. "Reems, summon Mr. Dawson. He shall keep you company in our absence."

Dahlia tried not to show her curiosity. *Dawson.* This was the man Lady Melinda loved. He hurried in soon after and greeted them politely. "Lady Dayne. Miss Farthingale."

She had no time to engage him in conversation. They were given only a brief introduction before the duke and his daughter led her away.

Still, it was enough for Dahlia to form a first impression. He was not at all what she'd expected. He was tall and slender, had a swarthy complexion, and wore spectacles. He walked with a pronounced limp. He had dark hair, light green eyes that were jarring against his otherwise dark complexion, and a serious air. A nice-looking man, but he did not have a commanding presence. If anything, he was shy and retiring, not at all the sort who would have a bevy of young ladies fluttering around him or ever feel comfortable having a bevy flutter around him.

"Dawson," the duke said in a commanding but respectful tone as they walked out, "keep Lady Eloise company. We won't be long."

"Of course, Your Grace." He did not look at Lady Melinda.

Nor did she look at him.

They were good at hiding their feelings.

Dahlia thought it very sad. Indeed, truly a shame. She did not believe the duke would ever permit his daughter to marry his estate manager. But she kept her opinions to herself. There was always hope where love was involved. Perhaps Mr. Dawson was somehow distantly related to a nobleman. She would do a little digging and see what she could turn up.

Unfortunately, it was more than likely he was the by-blow of a nobleman and a young beauty from one of the islands. Perhaps Jamaica, or somewhere else exotic on the other side of the world.

"The house is stunning," Dahlia said when the tour came to an end.

The duke nodded. "It is in desperate need of rejuvenation."

His daughter did not look at all pleased. "What would you have Miss Farthingale change, Father?"

He studied his daughter for a long moment. "I'll leave the decision to you, my dear. You and Miss Farthingale can decide what to do."

Lady Melinda looked so stiff it was a wonder her back had not cracked in two. "And if I wish to leave everything as it is?"

"I think it will be a mistake, Melinda." Her father spoke kindly, but Dahlia sensed the determination behind his words. His daughter would not win this standoff.

"Lady Melinda, might I suggest we take one room to start. Any room you'd like. Your mother's touch is everywhere in this house. I think what your father is saying is that he'd also like to have a little of *you* here as well. Even if you decide to do nothing more than the one room, it is still something that he can look upon as a thing of pride as he thinks of you."

Lady Melinda cast her a wry smile. "Very well, Miss Farthingale. You have convinced me. One room." She put a finger to her lips as though seriously contemplating her options. "If I am to choose, then it must be my father's study."

The duke arched an eyebrow, not at all pleased. "Melinda, this is where Dawson and I conduct our work. Can you not choose another? It will be very disruptive."

"No, Father. This is where you spend most of your time. I want you to think of me whenever you look up from your ledgers. You were the one who pushed for this. Will you not honor it now?"

He clenched his jaw in obvious displeasure. "No. My study it is. When do you plan to start? Dawson and I will have to move to another room while you are tearing this one apart."

"Not at all," Dahlia said. "In the first stages, we will only be sketching out a plan. Then it is a matter of choosing colors and patterns. There will be perhaps a week of upheaval as we paint and have the floors refreshed. But it does not have to be done immediately. We can take care of it whenever you are out of town."

"Since Mr. Dawson practically lives in here, I shall ask for his opinion as well," Melinda added. "We'll show both of you the design and take your comments. However, the decision will ultimately be mine. Is that agreeable to you, Father?"

She was smiling at him, and Dahlia sensed that Lady Melinda had not smiled in a long time. Her father, as fierce and powerful a duke as he was, melted. "Yes, my dear. It is agreeable. Come, give your father a hug."

Dahlia looked away a moment in order to lend them privacy. This was a special moment between father and daughter, and she did not wish to appear to be gawking at them. In truth, she was unsettled. Would these two remember their love for each other when the truth came out about Lady Melinda's feelings for Mr. Dawson?

Not likely.

All hell would break loose.

And if the duke found out she had guessed the identity of Lady

Melinda's love and hadn't told him?

The punishment would not fall on her so much as on Ronan.

Indeed, the duke would be a one-man destruction force in the House of Lords, ranting, shouting, condemning, as he pounded on his lectern. He would not stop until there was nothing left of the Royal Navy budget. And then he'd make it his life's ambition to destroy Ronan.

She would not allow this to happen. There was only one thing to do, and that was to stall.

Yes, she had to come up with an excuse to delay the start of their project until after the vote. This way, if the duke went on a rampage, they'd have a year before the next budget came up to calm him down.

She was not married to Ronan. He had not asked her, merely hinted at it. And yet, they were already embroiled in problems that could tear them apart as a couple.

A sinking ship.

A secret love affair carried on under the duke's nose that could very well turn into a current day tragedy to put the likes of Romeo and Juliet to shame.

Not to mention, Wainscott was still in London, creating problems.

What a jolly Yuletide season this was turning out to be.

The duke and his daughter had ended their sentimental moment. "Miss Farthingale, you seem to be contemplative. Is something amiss?"

"No, Your Grace. All is perfect. What could possibly be amiss?"

Chapter Thirteen

Dahlia had put off commencing work on the duke's study for the week, stalling him by making up excuses about having to remain with Holly. It was not far from the truth. Although Holly was putting on a brave face to the world, she was dying inside. Joshua was still with Ronan in Tilbury, and all sorts of wild accounts were circulating in the newspapers, mostly gossip rags.

"Put down that paper," Dahlia said, stealing it out of her hands and tossing it over to Heather. "Throw it into the fire."

"No!" Holly shot out of her chair and tried to grab it back from their younger sister. But she was too late and could only watch in despair as the paper caught flame and quickly burned. "Why did you do that? You are being very cruel, Dahlia."

"You shouldn't be reading that rag. How can you believe their ridiculous rumors of sea monsters smashing up the ship and eating sailors?"

Holly sank back in her chair. "Because it is preferable to reading true accounts. All the legitimate newspapers are reporting there is an angry mob growing more restless and frustrated the longer The Invinctus remains run aground. It has been five days now, and I've received not a word from Joshua."

"You know he and Ronan are busy," Heather said, coming to her side. "Robbie's come by every day to give us a report. He wouldn't lie to us."

Dahlia poured her sister a cup of hot cocoa. "Indeed, he's done his best to keep us apprised. He's probably revealed information that he wasn't authorized to give out. No military secrets, of course. Just news that could be politically damaging to Lord Liverpool and his cabinet, especially Lord Peckham and his idiot brother, Viscount Hawley."

She handed Holly the cup. "Heather, would you like some?"

"Oh, yes. Please."

She poured two more, deciding to have one as well. "A four-year-old child would have known better than to sail that ship up the Thames. Surely, Hawley's officers must have been pleading with him not to do it."

"I will personally eviscerate Peckham and Hawley if any harm befalls Joshua." Having said that, Holly then whipped out her handkerchief and began to cry into it.

Dahlia exchanged an exasperated glance with Heather. But they had no chance to distract their sister, for they suddenly heard a heavy pounding at the front door. Although Holly's butler was there to answer, Heather immediately started for the door. "Let me see what this is about."

Her young sister, too curious to contain herself, hurried out before Dahlia could stop her.

Dahlia considered following her, but Holly now appeared about to faint, and she dared not leave her. Dahlia grabbed her hand, trying not to show her own exasperation. "It is not a dangerous mission. There is no uprising. Just a group of jeering onlookers. Ronan is–"

Heather burst into the room with Robbie right behind her. "They're back," he said, looking remarkably glum for bearing such good news. Unless…

Dahlia rose, now clutching a hand over her heart. "What is it?"

Holly had turned ashen. "Joshua?"

"Och, no. Yer husband's fine, Holly. He's no more than a few minutes behind me." He turned to stare at Dahlia.

The blood drained from her face. "What's happened to Ronan?"

"He's been hurt. Joshua is bringing him here to recover. I stopped by yer uncle's infirmary and asked him to meet us here."

"Uncle George?" Dahlia's head was spinning. Ronan hurt and in need of her uncle's medical care? "How badly?"

Robbie came to her side and guided her back into her chair before she fainted. She was no meek flower, but it was shocking how quickly one's body could fall apart when dealt bad news. "He was caught in the tow ropes when the ship suddenly lurched forward. Ye know he was no' going to let anyone but himself take on the most dangerous assignment. I dinna know just how badly he was injured. But I saw him, Dahlia. He's breathing and conscious. He insisted on riding back to London."

"He was able to ride?" Her eyes rounded in surprise. "Oh, the fool! Why would he do this? He ought to have stayed in Tilbury to recover."

Robbie now glanced at Heather, who had been standing beside him all the while, absently gripping his arm as he relayed the news to the three of them. She'd stuck to him like a barnacle to a ship even as he'd helped Dahlia to her chair. "Och, men do foolish things when they're in love."

Holly was now on her feet and ready to jump into action. "Heather, ask Cook to prepare a hearty soup and send one of her scullery maids out for fresh bread. I know it is early yet, but they'll be hungry after their long ride. Yet, I dare not give Ronan anything too difficult to digest. Oh, where shall I put him?"

Dahlia realized she and Heather were taking up the only furnished guest chambers. "Put him in my room. I'll move in with Heather." It would take her less than five minutes to carry her belongings out with the help of her assigned maid. She had only packed enough to stay with her sister for a few days.

Dahlia had just hurried out of the dining room when the front door opened again, and Joshua and his soldiers began to fill the entry hall. Robbie rushed past her. "I'll help carry him up, Josh. Holly's sisters have been staying here while ye were away. But he's to have Dahlia's room. She'll lead us up. Yer wife's in the dining room. Go give her a kiss to let her know ye're all right."

Joshua laughed. "Since when have you become so considerate of a woman's feelings?"

"Shut up, ye arse. Another smart word, and I'll give ye a set of broken ribs to match yer brother's."

Broken ribs?

Dahlia was determined to have a better look at Ronan once they got him into bed. Right now, he was surrounded by soldiers, and she could not see past them. "Right up this way." Too late to move her things out now. She'd manage it later, once everything had quieted down.

She scampered up the stairs and heard the thunderous clomp of boots behind her. Or was it her heart beating that hard and fast? "Over here." She led them down the hall to her bedchamber and opened the door to allow them in.

Her maid had already been in here to tidy up, but that was earlier, and before they'd realized Joshua and Ronan were coming home. These were the sheets she'd been sleeping on. They were still on the bed that was now neatly made up.

Well, it wouldn't matter for now. There was no time to change them. In any event, he was dusty from the road and possibly bleeding because he'd been too stubborn to remain in Tilbury. How badly had he damaged himself on the ride back?

She remained in the room but stepped back to allow Robbie and the soldiers to settle him atop the bed. Although she wanted to help make him comfortable, she knew it was inappropriate for her to even be in here. The less she did to make herself noticed, the better.

Robbie handed her Ronan's cloak.

She held onto it a moment, wanting to breathe in his scent and not caring that it would likely smell of his sweat and possibly of dried blood. Worse, what if his blood was still fresh? She inhaled, the scent not quite as bad as she expected. Mixed in with the dust and travel grime was the subtly fragrant sandalwood soap Ronan liked to use and the rugged, male heat of him.

She set the cloak aside with care and then hurried to gather his boots as they hit the floor with a thud. Ronan had emitted a wrenching groan as Robbie pulled off each one. Tears formed in Dahlia's eyes. But she held them back.

Robbie knew what he was doing, and Joshua's soldiers obeyed him without hesitation as he quietly issued orders. Only when the soldiers had cleared out did Dahlia dare approach Ronan. He was stretched out on the counterpane, his clothes stripped off save for his breeches.

Dahlia shuddered upon catching sight of his body. There was an ugly red welt resembling a vicious burn running along the entire width of his chest. The skin had been scraped off in spots, leaving caked-on blood and remnants of raw skin. "Ronan…"

Her heart was aching so badly, she could barely speak.

He opened his eyes and smiled at her. "Queen Pea, you're a sight for sore eyes."

She reached out and took light hold of his hand. "Oh, even your hands are badly scraped." She meant to draw hers away, but he would not let her go.

"Your touch doesn't hurt me."

Robbie cleared his throat. "Let me stoke the fire in the hearth. I'll add a log or two and then go down to check on the others. Dahlia, will ye stay with the lunkhead and see that he does no' do anything foolish?"

She gave a laugh, one of relief that was badly needed to break her tension. "Yes, Robbie. I will."

She returned her gaze to Ronan. A mistake, she realized at once.

Her body immediately responded to the sight of him. There was something magnificently raw and masculine about his unkempt appearance.

He wasn't unkempt so much as wounded and in obvious pain, looking very much like a magnificent medieval warrior returned from battle. Big and muscled and not a whit of softness to be found on him.

She did not know what to do to ease his agony. If only Uncle George would arrive. He would make him better.

All she seemed capable of doing was gawking. She had seen statues in museums, of course. But she hadn't realized men were actually built like this. Ronan's arms seemed sculpted out of granite. His shoulders were broad, and his body exquisitely hard and lean. She noted the dusting of dark curls across his chest and itched to touch it.

She was also fascinated by the way his muscles rippled whenever he moved, and she wanted to run her fingers along those ripples. But she was too much of a coward to touch him boldly, so she merely placed a hand on his shoulder.

His skin was hot. He tried to shift his position but winced in pain.

"I think you may be running a fever."

"No, I'm just hot for you."

"Oh, for pity's sake. Lie still. I'm sure you're feverish. Don't you dare move. I'll get you whatever you need. Is there anything in particular you want?"

"A kiss from you. Why else do you think I rode back to London, risking a punctured lung? I may have also cracked three ribs between Tilbury and here."

She gasped. "Are you jesting? You are a lunkhead! How can you be so reckless? What good will you be to me dead?"

"I'm not going to die. Although I feel like death right now. Bollocks. Everything hurts. But I had to see you."

Yes, he was definitely feverish.

"Will you kiss me, Queen Pea?"

She stopped him when he tried to roll his body toward her. "You fool. Yes, I'll kiss you. Lie still and don't move your head. I'll come to you." She cast him a gentle smile. "But I need to get the correct angle. It may seem a simple matter, but it is actually a rather complex set of mathematical calculations," she said, teasing him just as he had teased her before they had shared their very first kiss.

He laughingly groaned. "Enough. I want that kiss."

She eased onto the bed and carefully leaned over, trying not to touch any part of him for fear she would hurt him. But he wrapped his arms around her and drew her down atop him. Her breasts pressed against his chest. "Let me go, Ronan. I must be hurting you."

His entire chest had to be a raw wound.

"Best ache I've ever felt," he whispered, easing one hand around her waist and raising his other to the back of her head to draw her lips to his.

Before she could utter another word of protest, he captured her mouth in a searing embrace, pouring so much heat into their kiss, she was certain the bed would catch fire. Yes, this is what she'd always dreamed the right kiss would feel like. Hot. Burning. Exquisite.

Her body was already thrumming in unladylike ways.

She wanted to crawl into bed with him and–

He ended it quickly and fell back, gasping for air. "Ronan! You idiot. Did I hurt you?"

"No. Kiss me again, Queen Pea."

She moved away. "You are a low-brained idiot. What if you do have a punctured lung? And aren't three cracked ribs enough? You cannot support my weight atop you."

He grinned wickedly. "I'll position you under me."

"Ronan! This is serious."

"My ribs are merely bruised. So's my arse after bouncing around in the saddle on the ride back here. This is why I prefer sailing ships. No sea captain ever complained of a shredded arse."

She rolled her eyes. "I am going to hit you if you don't behave."

"You can't hit me. I'm going to marry you."

Her breath caught in her throat. She stared at him for the longest time before uttering a word. "Is that a command?"

He was smiling at her with a warmth that stole her breath away, and his eyes were seductively gleaming. "It's a promise and a sincere wish."

She settled beside him again and took his hand because she loved him. How foolish she'd been not to notice what had been right in front of her all along. She'd been so caught up in lying to herself about Gerald that she'd refused to believe what her heart was telling her. But realizing she almost lost Ronan brought on clarity of thought. She wanted to be with this man forever. That diminutive little gossip, Lady Withnall, had been so right in her advice.

But was he speaking merely due to his delirium? He was in agonizing pain, and anyone in his condition could say something he would regret having said once he'd healed.

He raised her hand to his lips and kissed it. "I love you, Queen Pea. I should have told you before I left, but it was never my intention to force words on you that you were not ready to hear. Near-death has a way of sorting out what's important and what is not. You are the most important thing to me. I had to come back here and let you know."

Tears once clouded her eyes, but she hastily wiped them away. "You could have written me a letter. I would have come to you."

He cast her a melting smile. "I couldn't wait that long. And what if your family did not allow it? Besides, I am better off here to defend myself when the members of the House of Lords begin their inquisition."

"You saved the day," she said with a gasp, her indignation rising. "Why should they question you at all? You were in London and nowhere near the vessel when it went aground. How can they possibly blame you?"

He tried to shrug his shoulders but had barely moved them before he winced. "Someone has to take the fall."

"Those fiends! There is no way I will let this happen. Nor will your family. If I have to descend upon the House of Lords with sword drawn like a vengeful Valkyrie, I shall do it. I will take exquisite pleasure in gutting Lord Peckham and his foolish brother, Viscount Hawley."

"Sweet mercy, you'd make a glorious shieldmaiden. But stop talking like that or I'll pull you under me and probably puncture both lungs making mindless, low-brain love to you. Lord, you're beautiful when you're fiery."

She couldn't help but laugh. "Tell me the rest of what happened to The Invictus."

"Not much to tell. It ran aground. We managed to tow it back to deep waters. It is safely on its way back to Harwich, although who knows what else might happen between Tilbury and there since Viscount Hawley is still in command of the vessel. But he will be called back to London. I expect there will be a summons from Lord Liverpool waiting for him when he docks the ship at Harwich. Fortunately, there appears to be only minor damage to the hull. The seabed is mostly soft silt. We don't believe she struck any boulders. But we'll know more once she's properly inspected."

"So, your budget is safe?"

He cast her a pained look. "For the most part. But the navy will have to absorb the cost of this incident within that budget. The barges, the ropes, the local fishermen who had to be paid off to assist in the operation, and those who could not get out to sell their catch of the day."

"Too bad Peckham and his brother cannot be made to pay for it," she muttered. But this was the way of things, noblemen promoted to positions for which they were grossly unqualified merely because they were titled or closely connected to titles. Their rise to important ranks had nothing to do with merit. No wonder the members of the House of Commons were screaming for reforms.

"Indeed, too bad. Joshua wouldn't let me near Viscount Hawley. He feared what might happen if I got close enough to put my hands on him. Specifically around his neck. Well, it's done. Whatever is going to happen, will happen." He closed his eyes, and they sat in silence for several minutes. But he hadn't fallen asleep. Each time she tried to slip her hand out of his, he grasped it tighter and whispered, "Don't leave me, Queen Pea."

As if she ever would.

But she thought he might want a cool cloth against his head, for he did appear a little too hot. She wouldn't touch his wounded chest, afraid to do more harm than good. In any event, her Uncle George would be here shortly to take care of the ugly gash, his bruised and perhaps broken ribs, and whatever else he had done to damage his body.

Would her uncle be able to tell if Ronan had suffered a punctured lung as well?

She dearly wanted to climb in bed with him and wrap her arms around him. Perhaps later, when they had more time to spend alone. Perhaps he'd raise the topic of marriage again, and they'd discuss it once he was more lucid. Although, in truth, he did seem lucid now. "I'd like to put a cold compress on your head. Will you let me fetch it?"

He nodded. "Queen Pea, you didn't say it back to me."

She knew what he meant. *Don't be a fool. Listen to Lady Withnall.* "Ronan, I–"

Robbie came back in the room, followed by her uncle. She moved away from the bed to give her uncle the space to examine him. "So, I understand you got tangled in the tow ropes," Uncle George said, opening up his medical bag.

"Just a little." He opened his eyes and glanced at Dahlia.

Robbie snorted. "A little? That is no' the way Joshua tells it. He says Ronan would have been crushed had Joshua not grabbed a hatchet and cut the ropes. But in cutting them, Ronan could no' hold on and plunged into the icy waters. Joshua had to dive in after him and pull him out."

Dahlia gasped.

"Robbie, you talk too much." Ronan frowned at his friend. "It wasn't quite that bad."

Her uncle shook his head. "Dahlia, go downstairs for a few minutes. I have to check his ribs and lungs. He is going to howl when I do."

"I want to stay, Uncle George. I can hold his hand."

"I also need to remove his trousers to see if he suffered more bruising that he hasn't told anyone about. Captain Brayden, how high up were you when you fell into the water?"

"About two stories."

"Dinna believe him Dr. Farthingale. Joshua says he was at least twice that high up when he fell."

"I'm going to check you for a possible concussion as well," her uncle calmly remarked. "How does your spine feel? I'll have to check it, too."

"Oh, dear heaven." Dahlia was now trembling noticeably. "Ronan, if you ever do anything so foolish again, I will put my hands around *your* neck and throttle you. Do you hear me?"

He grinned. "Loud and clear, Queen Pea."

She desperately wanted to kiss him, but how could she with an audience? "I'll come back when your examination is over."

She hurried out before any of them saw how overset she was. If the ropes hadn't crushed him, then falling from that height might have killed him. How could he be so calm about it? She walked back into the dining room where Joshua, Holly, and Heather were now seated. "Where are your men?"

"On their way back to the barracks. I'll join up with them later." Joshua's expression remained grim. "I'll have to let Miranda and our brothers know about Ronan's condition. I suppose my cousins will insist on hearing the details as well. But I'd like to hear your uncle's assessment of his injuries first. I want to give my family an accurate account."

"Uncle George will be thorough. I left because he's going to check Ronan from head to toe."

Joshua turned to Holly. "Love, do you mind if I go up and watch?"

Holly kissed his cheek. "Do whatever you must. I'll have Cook prepare some simple but hearty meals as I'm sure we'll have more company today. Tynan and Finn will rush over and bring Abby and Belle with them. James and Marcus will want to stop by as well. That means Sophie and Lara will insist on coming, too. They might arrive before their husbands."

Dahlia listened quietly as the pair conversed.

These Brayden men were eight in all and close in age. They were lovingly referred to as the wildebeests by their parents because these gorgeous, big men had been wild as beasts when they were younger. Much tamer now, of course. But still very much a beastly herd that would gather protectively around any one of them who happened to be injured.

"I'll send word to Romulus and Caleb once we have all the information," Joshua said as he and Holly began to review what needed to be done while she followed him to the door. "They will be very upset their duties kept them out of London. But Romulus may be back within a day or two. It won't be so easy for Caleb to leave his post in York. However, I don't think Lord Liverpool will dare stop him from riding down here once news reaches him."

Holly nodded. "Do you think your mother might want to stay over?"

"Miranda? Good heavens, no." Joshua shook his head. "She's a handful. Besides, there's no room. I'm not going to kick your sisters out. Ronan won't let me, in any case. The only person he really wants to see is Dahlia." He turned to her with a wincing smile. "He hardly spoke the entire ride back because he was in so much pain. But the few words he did manage were all about you."

She nodded. "I didn't want to leave his side. I'll stay with him once Uncle George is through."

"He'll feel better having you near. But I don't know what he's going to do about the budget matter. Fortunately, he's already met with most of the committees. We've both lost this week, and now he might lose next week, which is when the House of Lords will vote. He'll ignore your uncle's directive to stay in bed. I know my brother will be stubborn about it. He'll get to Parliament even if he has to crawl."

Dahlia pursed her lips, knowing everything Joshua said was accurate. "What about the Lord Admiral? Can he not take over for these next few days?"

Joshua nodded. "I know he'll do whatever he can. But Sir William is not in very good health himself. Robbie and I will do what we can, of course. But we aren't Royal Navy, and our own superiors will frown on our lending too much help. We have our own budgets to worry about. I'll probably receive a blistering set down for riding off with my regiment to Tilbury. But I could not assign the matter to anyone else. Who would protect my little brother better than me?"

Dahlia managed a chuckle. "Little? He's big as an ox. Even bigger than you, Joshua."

"Big pain in my arse, too. Stubborn oaf."

Holly rolled her eyes and gave an impudent cough. "And you're not?"

"No, love. I'm perfect. You tell me so often enough. Especially at night, when in my arms, right after I–"

"Joshua! My sisters!" But now that Joshua was home safe, Holly seemed much more composed. She shot him a warning scowl, and then faced them all with an expression of determination that commanded everyone's attention. "Let's get down to important business. There's also been rumblings in the gossip rags about who is going to be blamed for this blunder. Ronan's name was mentioned."

She pointedly eyed her sisters. "You tossed the paper into the fire, but burning that trash will not erase the fact that someone is already working to pin the blame on Ronan."

Joshua appeared stunned. "You must be jesting. He almost lost his life saving that vessel."

Holly pursed her lips. "I wish I were. We cannot ignore this news item, even if it is obvious nonsense. The Braydens are a powerful family, and several hold important titles. But we Farthingales also have our connections."

"Indeed, we do. And I won't hesitate to call on them to help Ronan." Dahlia's thoughts were already on the same path as her sister's. "He is not going to take the fall for this blunder."

Heather chimed in, too. "Knowing our cousins, they are going to insist on helping whether asked to or not. And Robbie is the grandson of an earl. Scottish," she said with a shrug, "but an earl nonetheless. Not to mention that Poppy is married to the Earl of Welles, and Honey is married to the Earl of Wycke."

Joshua groaned. "Enough with the Farthingale marriage connections. I am vastly impressed. But we don't need the Earl of Caithness or you meddlesome Farthingales stepping in and starting an insurrection."

Holly curled her hands into fists. "We will fight for your brother if we have to. Don't ask us to sit idly by and watch him get battered any worse than he already is because all those lords who are to blame for putting Hawley – that incompetent – in command in the first place are looking to save their hides and offer up your brother as the scapegoat."

Joshua held up a hand. "Sweetheart, I think you are getting a little ahead of yourself. Yes, we will flex some Brayden muscle to make sure the right men are called to account. And yes, it is good to have the Farthingales on alert if more is needed. But Ronan is well respected. He'll also be mad as hell if we interfere before he's had a chance to deal with the matter on his own."

Dahlia was still worried. "How can he help himself when he is hardly able to move out of bed?"

Joshua sighed. "We are Miranda's sons. I did not even bring her into the equation, but rest assured, that woman will personally light a torch under any of those pompous arses who dare falsely accuse her baby boy. Indeed, I think we can all sit back and watch the spectacle unfold while safely perched in the House of Lords spectator's gallery."

Despite their concerns, Dahlia and her sisters could not help but laugh. "Hooray for Miranda," Dahlia said, and her sisters cheered.

"Indeed," Joshua said with a roll of his eyes. "And now I really need to go upstairs and see what is going on with my brother."

But their lively moment came to an abrupt halt as their Uncle George suddenly walked in, almost bumping into Joshua on his way up. He looked as though someone had just died.

"No," Dahlia said in an agonized whisper, putting a hand to her heart that was now beating with unrestrained frenzy. "Uncle George?"

Her uncle said nothing for a long moment.

Dahlia was sure her heart was about to burst. "What's wrong? How badly is Ronan hurt?"

Chapter Fourteen

Dahlia's uncle cleared his throat. "I haven't completed my examination yet. But he is insisting his *Queen Pea* stay by his side. I cannot claim to approve of his behavior, Dahlia. But he is going to do serious damage to himself if he attempts to get out of bed."

He sighed and ran a hand through his hair. "So come back up with me, at least until I've finished looking him over. The good news is that he has no punctured lungs. Nor any broken bones along his spine, which was my greatest worry the moment I heard the height from which he'd plunged into the water. Incredibly, I don't believe he's sustained so much as a hairline fracture."

Dahlia let out a breath. "Thank goodness."

"But he may have suffered a mild concussion along with those three damaged ribs. They're badly bruised, not broken. But they're still fragile and might break if he doesn't take care of himself. For now, there is not much to do other than keep him resting so that his rib cage can heal on its own. This means he cannot run around. He has to stay in bed and let his body recover. His brain must also heal. This is probably most important. These concussions are insidious things if not properly tended. He may think he's all right, but years later, he will begin to feel the effects. Headaches. Dizziness. Loss of memory."

Dahlia's hand was once more at her heart. "I'll do my best to keep him at rest."

She hurried upstairs, leaving her uncle while he took another moment to speak to her sisters.

In truth, she did not wish to be anywhere but by Ronan's side.

Robbie breathed a sigh of relief when she walked in. "Och, he's a pain in the arse. He even riled yer uncle, and I dinna think the great George Farthingale could ever be ruffled. But ye'd better keep yer eyes closed. And do no' think to lift the sheet to look at his injuries. He is no' dressed. Not a stitch on him."

She gasped, and her gaze shot straight to Ronan.

Ronan returned her bemused gaze with a steamy one of his own. "Leave us a moment, Robbie. Please."

"I want yer promise, ye'll keep that sheet covering you."

"Of course, I will." Ronan rolled his eyes. "I'm wounded, not insane. You have my word on it."

"Well, I suppose there's no harm then, not in yer condition. Ye have two minutes alone with her. That's all I dare give ye. Dahlia, just shout if he does something stupid. He is no' to be trusted around ye. I blame it on that book the two of ye have been reading. He'll be spouting love sonnets in another moment. I'll hit him if he does."

Once Robbie left, she sat on the bed, her hip grazing Ronan's hip as she sank onto the mattress. "Why are you behaving like an ill-tempered brat?"

His eyes were filled with pain, although she did not think the pain was from his physical injuries. "You didn't say it back to me, Queen Pea."

She took his hand and drew it to her lips. "Is this what has you so worked up you'd risk a brain hemorrhage?"

He arched an eyebrow. "Did your uncle tell you to say this?"

"No. I actually know a few big words. Some even with ancient Greek or Latin roots. *Hemo* means blood, and *ragia* means to burst or break."

"Gad! Enough. You are arousing my sense receptacles. I think I'll ask you to read Latin to me once I have you in my bed."

"I am already in your bed. Have you not noticed?"

"*On* my bed is altogether different than *in* my bed. *In* means me doing all sorts of wicked things to your delectable, bluestocking body while you surrender to my irresistible prowess. *On* means you're primly perched atop my bed with your lips pinched and about to berate me, as you are doing now. It does not count."

"You are quite irascible, you know."

"Kiss me, Queen Pea."

"All right. Stop talking long enough for me to place my mouth on yours." She bent forward and planted a soft but heartfelt kiss on his lips. "I love you, Ronan Brayden," she said in a broken whisper once she'd pulled away. "There. You've had your kiss and my admission of love. Will you behave now?"

"Not a chance in hell. Do you mean it? Do you love me?"

She nodded. "Hopelessly, you wickedly handsome clot."

"I love you, too." He caressed her cheek. "Now tell me how you are doing. What have you been up to while I've been gone?"

She nibbled her lip, not wanting to add to his concerns. "The Duke of Stoke introduced me to his daughter. She and I are going to redecorate his study."

Ronan groaned. "There's a big *but* hidden in there somewhere. I can feel the sudden tension in your hand."

"The duke wants me to help him with his daughter. He knows you are not the man she has her heart set on. And she has finally admitted there is no marquess."

"That is good, isn't it?" He studied her features. "Bollocks, what's the problem?"

"The *but* is…I think I know who it is she loves." She sighed. "And here's the bigger *but*…the duke will never approve of the man. How can I tell the duke his name? It would be betraying Lady Melinda. I know that using you to further her deception wasn't right, but I truly believe she never meant to hurt you. And yet, if I don't tell her father…and he finds out I knew all along, he will take it out on you."

He caressed her cheek again. "Queen Pea, don't worry about me. I can take care of myself."

"Says the man who is lying helpless in bed right now after almost getting himself killed in Tilbury." She sighed. "Forgive me if I don't believe you."

They spoke no more as Robbie marched back in with her uncle close on his heels. "Let's get back to it, shall we?" Uncle George said, shooting both of them a warning frown. "Dahlia, why don't you take a seat over there?" He pointed toward one of the comfortable chairs by the hearth.

"No." Ronan was not at all in agreement with the arrangement.

"Seems my presence has done nothing to cure his stubbornness." But Dahlia was not really put off by Ronan's highhandedness. An enveloping warmth flowed through her as she realized her importance to this magnificent man. She still did not understand why he wanted her, but it seemed he did, and she was not going to toss his gift of love away. "I'll draw up a chair on the other side of the bed. This way, I'll still be close enough to take his hand…if he intends to continue being a big baby about this important medical examination."

Ronan chuckled, but even that small laugh brought him pain. "Indulged and insulted at the same time. You are a marvel, Queen Pea. Will you take my hand now? You know you already have my heart."

"Uncle George, is he drugged?"

Her uncle was smirking. "If you consider love a drug, then yes. Otherwise, no. I've given him nothing yet."

"Should I do as he asks?" She awaited his instruction, reluctant to interfere with whatever he needed to do.

Examining Ronan thoroughly was most important. Once her uncle was done, she would take his hand and hold it for as long as he wished. But Uncle George was in charge now.

"Go ahead, Dahlia. I'll let you know when you are in the way."

She took Ronan's blistered hand in both of hers and ran her thumbs in slow circles over it. His attention remained on her as he was poked and prodded, on occasion painfully. However, her uncle was doing his best not to purposely hurt him.

The oddest feeling came over her as Ronan continued to look at her. She could only describe this feeling as one of permanence. Perhaps forever was a better word for it. That he would love her forever. That he would desire her forever.

That she was in his heart forever.

She squeezed his hand lightly and smiled at him, hoping he understood the feeling was reciprocated. He was still staring at her as he spoke to her uncle. "Patch me up as best as you can. There is something important I must do tomorrow."

Her uncle groaned. "You are to stay in bed tomorrow. What is it about my instructions you do not understand?"

"I understand them perfectly. But I need to marry your niece as soon as possible and must obtain the special license first."

"*Need* to? Dahlia, what in blazes–"

"Uncle George! No!"

"*Want* to," Ronan said, correcting himself. "The need is my own. I cannot bear to be apart from her a moment longer. Since I am forced to lie abed anyway, why can I not make the most of it?"

Dahlia wanted to smack him over the head with a pillow. But she dared not do him any more harm. She released his hand and rose to stand over him. "You have declared it as fact. You have made plans and decisions on your own. You have assumed my answer. But you haven't actually asked me yet. What game are you playing? Why won't you simply ask me straight out?"

She was taken aback by the pain evident in his eyes, and immediately wished she could take back her words.

"How can you think I would ever trifle with your affections? It isn't a game for me." He emitted a ragged breath. "I haven't asked you straight out because…I'm afraid you'll refuse me."

"Oh, Ronan."

"I know it's too soon for you, Queen Pea. You've hardly had the chance to get over Wainscott."

"Get over him?" She shook her head and emitted an exasperated laugh. "I have been giving thanks every day since he did me the favor of dumping me. I may have felt heartbroken in those first few days afterward. But even in my lowest state, my deepest misery, I knew I was well rid of him."

His gaze turned hopeful. "Is that true?"

"More important, I have been giving thanks every day that you are in my life. I held back telling you because I didn't want you to think I was a fickle, frivolous girl. But if ever you were to walk out of my life, that is a heartbreak I would never get over."

"Are you certain, sweetheart?"

"It is rushed, I will agree. Under normal circumstances, I would insist upon waiting." Her eyes began to tear, and her voice became shaky because she was too overwhelmed to remain composed. "You almost died in Tilbury. I could have lost you. My heart would never have recovered from this."

Robbie groaned, reminding them others were also in the room. "Bloody hell, just ask her already. That bloody book has ye both babbling like *idjits*."

Ronan glared back at him. "How about a little privacy here?"

Her uncle was shaking his head and rolling his eyes. He was used to this by now. Falling in love with a Farthingale was a dangerous proposition in many ways, the most obvious being the physical danger. How many times had her uncle come to the rescue of these injured swains?

Robbie was more obvious in his impatience. "Ye had yer chance in the two minutes I gave ye earlier. Ye wasted it." He crossed his arms over his chest. "What are ye waiting for? Stop dawdling and ask her."

Ronan turned to her apologetically. "This is not at all how I wished it to be."

She took his hand in hers again. "Just say it already, or I'll think you don't really mean it."

"Blessed saints! I've never meant anything more in my life." He tried to roll to a sitting position and sank back in agony. "Ow, that hurt. Oh, bollocks. That still hurts. Dr. Farthingale..." The last came out in an alarming wheeze. "I think my lungs are about to rupture."

Suddenly, no one was grinning. "Robbie, get Dahlia out of here. Now!"

"Uncle George, what's happening?" She felt as though her legs were about to collapse from under her. But she held herself together with sheer force of will. Ronan was the one in dire straits and in need of her uncle's full attention.

"Those tow ropes did damage to his rib cage. One of his ribs may have just cracked and punctured a lung."

Dahlia fainted.

When she awoke, she found herself in Holly's parlor, sprawled atop the settee. Her sisters were staring at her, their brows furrowed in worry. "Ronan? How is he?"

Holly brushed a hand lightly over her forehead. "Joshua and Robbie are back up with him now. I don't know how much help they will be to Uncle George, but they needed to be upstairs with him."

"I need to be with him, too."

Heather was in tears. "You will, but not now. Ronan forgets how badly he's injured when he is with you. You make him feel invincible. He's fortunate he only has a punctured lung. Uncle George is still optimistic that he'll recover. He says it is not life-threatening when properly treated."

Dahlia shut her eyes tightly as a shudder ran through her. "Thank goodness. Holly, is love always this difficult? He was attempting to propose to me when it happened. Perhaps this is an omen. I'm bad for him, and we shouldn't be married."

Holly cupped Dahlia's face in her hands. "Don't you dare think like that. Viscount Hawley's idiocy caused this, not you. If anything, you are giving him strength and hope through his ordeal. He loves you so much that despite his injuries, he had to come home to be near you. This is the most precious gift anyone can bestow on you. Don't you dare spurn it."

Her sister was now squeezing her cheeks so that her lips were bunched like those of an openmouthed trout. "You can let go of me," she said. "I wasn't going to spurn him. I love him. Will you stop squeezing my face?"

"Move over." Holly nudged her legs aside to settle on the settee beside her. "You must understand you are doing him no favor by deciding what is best for him. I never understood what love meant until I met Joshua. The two of you simply cannot *be* without each other. This is why he's behaving like a child, throwing a tantrum. He needs you by his side. He will move heaven and earth to make it happen. So, do not make it difficult for him. If you love him…"

"I do."

"Then marry him and stay by his side."

Heather was weeping again.

Holly went over to their younger sister. "Not you, too? Why are you crying?"

"I want to find a love like the two of you have found."

"You will," Holly said, giving her a hug. "Don't be impatient for it, or you will make the same mistakes Dahlia and I made. Wanting to be in love is not at all the same as truly falling in love with the right man. I jumped into a hasty marriage and was not happy. Dahlia convinced herself that Wainscott was the man for her even though he'd done little to prove it."

Heather shook her head. "But he wrote her all those adoring letters."

"Anyone can do that. Was he ever there when Dahlia really needed him? Was he ready to put her desires ahead of his own? Would he ever risk his life to protect her? Ronan would."

Heather dabbed a handkerchief to her cheeks. "How am I to find a man like that? You two got the last of the Brayden men. Who's going to love and protect me like this?"

"Och, Heather. Why are ye still crying, lass?" Robbie was standing in the doorway, filling it with his size and brawn. He crossed his arms over his chest as he stared at the three of them.

Dahlia sat up. "How is Ronan?"

"Better. Yer uncle's done all he needs to do for now. He's given Ronan some laudanum, but he isn't permitted to take too much. Will ye go upstairs to him before he does something stupid again?"

She nodded. "I'll go right now."

"What can we do to help?" Heather asked.

Robbie stared at her. "Stop crying, for one thing. Help Holly with whatever she needs to do. Joshua's about to ride off to tell his brothers and Miranda. I'll be riding out to report to the Lord Admiral and Lord Liverpool. Parliament will not convene until Monday, but those two need to be kept current on all that's happened. The Marquess of Tilbury has assured Josh and Ronan he'll be giving a favorable report, but who knows with these noblemen? Some of them will say and do whatever is to their advantage. Although, Tilbury is one of the better ones. He's always been fair in his dealings with me."

Heather patted away the last of her tears. "Will you come back here afterward, Robbie?"

"Aye, pixie. Ronan is one of my best friends. I will no' abandon him."

Dahlia hurried upstairs while her sisters remained talking to Robbie. She encountered Joshua on the stairs, but he paused only long enough to mutter that he was riding off to tell the family and would be back shortly.

Her uncle had closed his medical bag and had just finished washing his hands when she walked in. He dried them on one of the washcloths. "I should tell you it is most improper for you to be in here alone with Captain Brayden. But since my words of warning have held no sway whatsoever over any of my nieces throughout the years, I'll spare you the lecture."

"Thank you, Uncle George. Not about sparing me the lecture, but saving Ronan's life. I don't know how I can ever repay you for this."

He picked up his medical bag, then walked over and kissed her on the cheek. "It is what I do. Nothing is required in return. Just be happy. And follow my instructions as I've written them." He pointed to the note he'd left on the night table beside Ronan's bed. "Tonight will be rough for him. Send for me immediately if he begins to struggle for breath. I'll be at home with Evie."

She hugged him. "Give her my love."

"I will." He strode out, leaving her alone with Ronan.

The first thing she did was read the note her uncle had left for them. It seemed simple enough, so after perusing it, she set it back down and turned her attention to this man she loved.

The handsome brute was stretched out in the middle of the bed, his eyes closed, and his arms at his sides. His back was propped up by several pillows. The covers were drawn up only far enough to cover his body to his waist. His chest was exposed, and she could see that her uncle had placed an unguent across the length of the rope burn, no doubt applying the foul-smelling substance to his flesh to prevent infection.

She sat beside Ronan on the bed and took his hand onto her lap.

His eyes flickered open, and he cast her a gentle smile. "Queen Pea, I missed you."

She laughed. "I was only gone a few minutes." Perhaps it was longer. She could not tell for certain how long she'd been unconscious. Her sisters would have been frantic if she had been out for more than a minute or two, so she doubted it was any longer than that.

"I still owe you a marriage proposal. Let me get this right before something else happens." His voice was little more than a raw whisper. "Will you marry me?"

"Yes, my love. I will marry you."

His smile broadened. "I'll try to obtain the special license as soon as possible. My brothers will help me since I'm not allowed out of bed for another three days on pain of death…my death, or so your uncle warned if I don't lie still."

"I'm sure Tynan and Finn will be able to accomplish this on your behalf. They have connections to everyone important in London." She cast him an impish smirk. "Just remind them my name is Dahlia, not Queen Pea."

"I think they'll figure it out for themselves. I love you, sweetheart. Will you marry me tomorrow if I obtain it?"

She inhaled lightly. How was this possible? He couldn't get out of bed. "You don't waste time once your mind is made up, do you?"

"Is that a yes?"

"Uncle John is my guardian while I am here in London. My parents have given him authority over all decisions, so I assume it includes giving his consent and signing the betrothal contract."

"Bollocks, I'll sign a blank piece of paper. He can fill in any terms he likes."

"You will put Finn's heart in spasms if he ever hears you speaking so foolishly. It doesn't have to be a formal agreement. But you have to think this through, Ronan. You can agree on the general terms and seal it with a handshake."

"I want you. That is my only term. I still don't have your answer. Will you marry me tomorrow?"

If she agreed, then she would deprive herself of the elegant wedding she'd always dreamed of having. Nor would there be time to put together an informal affair hosted by her aunt and uncle at their home on Chipping Way. The ceremony would have to be quick, held right here, with Ronan lying in bed while she stood beside him.

She glanced around, taking in the proportions of the bedchamber.

Oh, dear. They wouldn't be able to squeeze more than fifteen people in here. Her sisters. His brothers. Maybe their wives. Miranda and Robbie had to be here, too. Aunt Sophie and Uncle John if they could spare the time between their own family obligations.

It would have to be a bare-bones service since Ronan could not kneel in prayer. She doubted he would be allowed out of bed. Would he even be able to toss on clothes for the occasion? She did not think so.

He sighed. "I'll understand if you don't wish to give up your wedding dreams. I had just hoped…"

Her mind began to spin. "Yes, Ronan. I will agree to it."

Because what really mattered was sharing the rest of her life with him. When the less essential concerns were stripped away, it really was a simple choice. She did not want to spend any more nights without him.

Once their house was decorated, they could hold their own belated wedding breakfast. "I'm going to kiss you now, you brainless but incredibly handsome clot. Don't you dare move."

He emitted a pained laugh. "You'll get no complaint from me. Why am I brainless? For riding back here to be with you? Don't berate me for that, Queen Pea. But I'm truly sorry for depriving you of your wedding dreams. I wish I could make the day special for you. I realize how much you are giving up for my sake."

"I am giving up nothing important." She kissed him on the lips, teetering over him so that she did not touch his unguent-riddled body. Not that she cared for herself, but he was in a bad way, and the slightest pressure to his chest could be dangerous.

His lips were warm and inviting.

His expression was rueful as she drew away. "I was intent on seducing you before we were married. But it seems I'll be taking you completely innocent to my bed. Perhaps it is for the best. My intentions were always honorable. I would never have touched you unless I meant to marry you...and I always wanted to marry you."

"How could you want me when I was exactly what I just accused you of being, brainless?"

"No, Queen Pea. You were never that. Naive. Misguided. Duped. Nothing worse. Wainscott is the villain here. He took advantage of your inexperience."

Her heart ached whenever he spoke to her in this gentle and encouraging manner. "You are being too generous with me. I have to bear some of the fault for refusing to see the sort of man he truly was. One of lowest character. I allowed myself to be blinded by his fine trappings. His fancy clothes and carriages. His family's prominence and aristocratic connections."

She shook her head and groaned. "I wish I had read *The Book of Love* last year. Although who knows if I would have understood its meaning? Had I really *looked* at Gerald, what would I have seen?"

"Stop kicking yourself, my love. I think this is a trait you and Holly have in common, this insistence on being too hard on yourself."

She smiled at him. "That sounded nice, especially the soft way you said it."

"Said what?"

"You called me your love."

He arched an eyebrow. "Because this is what you are. Oh, bollocks. Are you going to cry now? Don't you dare. Not while I'm trying to seduce you."

She gazed at him in surprise. "You're trying to seduce me?"

"And obviously doing a terrible job of it if you have no idea this is what I'm doing."

"Are you saying this to make me feel better?"

"No. I'm saying it because I want to hold you in my arms and kiss my way down your exquisite body. I want to breathe you in. Taste your quivering flesh."

She snorted. "You are teasing me. Stop it. My flesh does not quiver. I'm not sure I even know what that means."

"You will once I get my hands on you. Don't mock an injured man, Queen Pea."

"Sorry. I can't help it. You are helpless in bed and forbidden to move. You must own that the situation is ridiculous."

"Desiring you can never be ridiculous. I want to run my fingers through your hair. There are other things I would do to you with my fingers, but you'll slap me if I tell you. However, as soon as I am able, I will prove to you just how enjoyable the experience will be."

"Without hurting yourself in the process? I have read those naughty books the elders are always forbidding us to read. They do use words like quivering flesh and crashing waves of splendor." She grinned. "And you are going to show me this?"

"Yes, Queen Pea. I promise. You will quiver, and waves will crash splendidly. You will enjoy it."

"I have an admission to make," she said quietly, blushing as she stared at her toes.

"What is it, love?"

She cleared her throat. "The men in these stories are always handsome and nicely muscled. However, I cannot believe they are as nicely formed as you. Will you think I am wanton if I admit to being eager to explore your body?"

"Thank The Graces! Here I thought I was the only one straining at the tether. My agony has nothing to do with my plunge off the ship into the icy river. I've been in frenzied, low-brain lust over you from the moment we first met."

"I still don't understand why you've singled me out for these feelings."

"All that matters is that I have. It's explained in that book. You are the one who is perfect for me, just as I am the one for you. I like that you are in hot, panting lust for me."

"Aren't you getting a little ahead of yourself? I merely admitted to curiosity. Worrying about you is not the same as–"

"You are terrible at hiding your feelings. You've been licking your lips and eyeing me as though I were a plump Christmas goose roasted to perfection." He grinned wickedly. "I'm not bashful, Queen Pea. Touch me wherever you wish. But be gentle. My chest is on fire just now."

Even though inwardly he was in sad shape, outwardly, he was magnificent. Dahlia could not get enough of staring at his chiseled body. Was there ever a Greek god who looked finer?

Nor could she resist touching him. Very carefully, of course. She reached out tentatively to wrap her fingers around the bulging muscle of his upper arm.

Sweet mercy.

It was hard as a rock.

The butterflies in her stomach began to flutter.

Was it possible his glorious body would be all hers to play with?

His face was a thing of beauty, too.

She put her hand to his cheek and felt the rough, stubble of his beard.

Then she ran her fingers through his hair, lightly brushing back a few stray curls. She liked the way the ends hugged the corded muscles of his neck.

His eyes held amusement. "You are not very adventurous, are you? You will put me to sleep if this is all you dare to do."

He slid his arm around her waist to nudge her closer. "Ronan! The unguent!"

"We'll work around it. I'll show you how it's done. You shall be *my* test frog. Close your eyes, Queen Pea."

"Why? What are you going to do to me?"

Chapter Fifteen

Ronan knew he was behaving like an idiot, but he didn't care. He could blame his clouded thinking on his injuries? Why not? Life was fragile and easily stolen in a moment. He wasn't going to waste time being polite. "I'm going to make wild, low-brain love to you, Queen Pea."

Dahlia gasped and opened her eyes. "How can you do such a thing in your condition? Do you think I would ever allow it? The effort might kill you."

"I'm not going to hurt myself. Nor will I hurt you. Keep your eyes closed. I want you to clear your mind of everything but the sensation of my touch." Ronan's chest was tight, and every movement caused him pain, but Dahlia soothed his heart as no one and nothing else could.

Perhaps he was being a monumental idiot, but he'd ridden from Tilbury in excruciating pain just to be with her. All worth it, for she had now promised to be his wife.

More than that, she had given up her dream wedding because of him.

She was a beautiful, sacrificing angel.

He wasn't going to do anything obscene with her.

But he wanted her to know his touch, which would be loving and reverential. The quivering flesh part would come later, once they were married, and his chest was no longer coated in this foul poultice that was necessary to keep him alive and free of infection.

"What should I do with my hands?"

"Keep them primly folded on your lap, if you wish. You needn't do anything yet." He was fighting against the laudanum because he wanted to stay alert and focused. Having her all to himself would not last long. His brothers and cousins would be tromping up the stairs shortly. Lord help him, so would Miranda.

He had little time to show Dahlia how pleasurable his touch could be.

Oh, bollocks.

The damn poultice would interfere with this lesson.

But she looked so delectable. "I need to kiss you, Queen Pea."

At some point, he expected she would club him over the head and tell him to stop calling her that. But he couldn't help it. The kiss they'd shared after she'd found the pea in the holiday cake had sealed matters for him.

She was the woman he would love to the end of time.

"Again? We just kissed." She nibbled her plump lower lip, now fretting. But her eyes were still closed.

She looked lovely and trusting and achingly innocent.

She had the most beautifully shaped mouth. He could explore it for hours. Full bottom lip and sweetly curved upper lip. Her mouth was perfectly designed to be crushed against his.

Indeed, he would enjoy delving his tongue into its velvet warmth. "Will my every request be a negotiation?"

"No. But I dare not hurt you."

"You will never hurt me, sweetheart." He caressed her cheek, the mere movement causing him agony. But if it was a choice of touch or not touch, then touch would win every time.

She smelled of cinnamon and roses.

Well, his nose was off, so he couldn't tell exactly what he was inhaling over the fumes of that foul unguent. Something nice, to be sure.

He slid his hand down her neck, brushing his thumb along the gentle line of her jaw. Then he traced his fingers down her throat and further down to cup her breast. Her eyes opened wide, but she did not scamper away. "Ronan?"

"You are beautiful, Queen Pea." Her breasts were lush but not too weighty. They filled his hands. "Close your eyes. I want you to *feel* the way I touch you." He drew her forward and placed his mouth against her breast. It did not matter that there were layers of fabric between his lips and her skin. When she gasped again and arched toward him, he knew she'd felt the intimacy and the promise of passion it held.

But he soon released her with a groan. Even the slightest exertion was causing him pain. "Let's try this again tomorrow."

She opened her eyes and kissed his damp forehead. "Then we can close the door and truly explore this magical sensation. Did you know I would respond this way to you?"

"I had hoped."

"We ought to proceed with all due caution. I would not like you to puncture your other lung on our wedding night."

He grinned. "It would be worth it to touch and taste you. Your uncle said a punctured lung is not life-threatening."

"If properly treated. And don't forget your concussion." She cast him a prim frown and puckered her lips in worry.

Which brought him right back to wanting to drag her down atop him and kiss those perfect lips quite thoroughly.

Unfortunately, he smelled like a goat at the moment.

Their time alone, which had been pretty much wasted since he couldn't touch her the way he wished, was now coming to an end. He heard footsteps on the stairs and knew the first family members were arriving and would be anxious to see him.

Miranda and Finn were the first to rush in.

By this time, Dahlia was seated in a chair beside his bed, trying to pull her hand out of his. But he refused to let go of her. "You're to be my wife," he whispered, merely intending to convey they were doing nothing wrong.

"Wife?" Miranda came to an abrupt halt, this new thought completely distracting her from whatever she was about to say.

Finn smiled broadly. "Well, I'll be damned. You took the leap, tadpole. Congratulations to you both. Dahlia, you do realize my brother is getting the better part of the bargain."

She shook her head. "I am satisfied. No complaints yet."

"She's an angel," Ronan said, realizing how easily she was letting him off. "We'd like to be married tomorrow."

Finn stared at him. "Sure, I see no problem with that." He was obviously being sarcastic. "Have you sought her uncle's permission? Do you have the special license?"

"No to both. John Farthingale won't deny us. But I'll need your help to obtain the license. Tynan may be able to pull some strings and get it done for me if you don't think you can–"

"Who said I couldn't do it? My connections are better than Tynan's. He's just an earl." He shook his head and groaned. "You arse. Stop manipulating me. Fine. I'll help you. I suppose the ceremony will have to be held here."

"Literally here," Dahlia said. "In this bedchamber. He is not permitted out of bed for the next three days."

Miranda had been quiet this entire time. "Merciful heavens, three days in bed? Are you dying?"

"No, Miranda. At least, not if I can help it."

Her expression alternated between wanting to hug her baby boy and wanting to smack him across the head for getting himself tangled in the tow ropes and falling into the icy water. "But you could have died while out there trying to move that blasted ship. It is the lead story in the newspapers today. Viscount Hawley had better approach me on bended knee, or I shall tear him a new ar–"

"Mother!" he and Finn cried at once.

"What? Is this any different from what Dahlia wishes to do to him?" She sat on the chair Finn had drawn next to Dahlia's beside the bed.

Ronan arched an eyebrow as he glanced at his beautiful bride to be. "Perhaps not, but she would never express it in quite those terms. She's a lady."

Miranda was getting that dangerous gleam in her eyes. "Are you suggesting I am not?"

"Mother, you are a harpy. And I mean it as a compliment. I look forward to your cutting a swath of destruction within the House of Lords. My only concern is that I'll be laughing so hard after you are through with those hapless lords, I might rupture another vital organ."

She gave a harrumph. "I would do anything to protect my sons."

"I know." He was starting to sweat, and his pain was getting worse. But he wasn't going to confide this to any of them.

As though sensing his discomfort, Dahlia rose and went around to the other side of the bed to read the note her uncle had left for them. "Finn, what time is it?"

He removed his watch fob from his breast pocket. "Five o'clock."

She pinched her lips. "He's to get more laudanum in an hour. But I need to put a damp cloth on his forehead now."

Ronan knew the note did not say anything about a compress since Dahlia's uncle had discussed the instructions with him as he wrote them down. But he was sweating, and Dahlia was going to do her best not to alarm anyone. In all likelihood, this discomfort would pass.

He had closed his eyes but opened them now that Dahlia was seated on the bed, easing closer to place the cloth on his brow. She felt along his neck.

By her expression, he knew his skin was burning.

Damn it.

He wanted to marry her.

He wanted to spend a lifetime with her, and by lifetime he meant more than one bloody day.

By eight o'clock, George Farthingale was back. "Joshua, he needs to be put in an ice bath now."

Miranda, Joshua, Finn, and Tynan were in the room with him, but his gaze sought Dahlia. "Where is she?"

If she was still in here, she was hidden by his family of giants.

"Dahlia's downstairs grabbing something to eat," Miranda said. "She hasn't touched a bite since breakfast early this morning. I doubt she has the appetite, but she must get something in her, or Dr. Farthingale will have another patient to add to his list. Holly is looking after her. She'll be back in a few minutes."

Miranda's eyes were red. Had she been crying?

Hell, was he dying?

He had no intention of going without the fight of his life. He did not care about this for himself. He'd chosen a life in the military, and it was a hazard of the job. But he could not leave Dahlia. How was he to protect her if he was gone?

Once the ice bath was prepared, Miranda left the room while his brothers and Robbie carefully carried him to the tub and ever so gently set him in it. He was so hot, he could feel the ice melt as it touched his skin. But the cold water felt good on his body.

He hadn't washed up since reaching London. His hair could use a good scrubbing. "I need a washcloth and some sandalwood soap."

Joshua growled. "Damn it, Ronan. What do you think this is? A Roman bath? There are no handmaidens to do your bidding. You are in here to get your fever down and keep you from convulsing."

"Dahlia isn't getting anywhere near you for a while," Tynan said. "That unguent Dr. Farthingale will apply again once you dry off will have you smelling like moldy cheese."

"Och, I'll do it. The lad's in love. If he wants clean hair, that's what he'll get." Robbie surprised them all by kneeling beside him and carefully pouring water over his head. He then grabbed two soaps he found beside the ewer and held them out to him. "Ye have a choice. Do ye wish to smell like a rosebud or a stick of cinnamon? These must be Dahlia's soaps."

Finn laughed. "From the famous Oxfordshire Farthingale soap company. Yes, this one is definitely roses. And this other one is a cinnamon and apple blend."

Tynan arched an eyebrow. "I'm impressed. You've become quite the fragrance expert."

Finn shrugged. "It's a hazard of being married to Belle. Now, I can't help but think of scents. It's the first thing that hits my brain. Which one will it be, Ronan?"

Ronan had a lot more to worry about than smelling like a woman. Besides, they always smelled delectable. Especially Dahlia. He could breathe her in for hours. "The cinnamon and apples."

This was Dahlia's scent.

Robbie patiently lathered his hair and then rinsed it out. Of all his friends, Robbie was perhaps one of the rowdiest of all. He was a hard-drinking, womanizing Scot who would not back down from a brawl. He often gave the impression of being shallow and careless. And yet, he was quite the opposite.

Ronan trusted Robbie with his life. He could think of no one finer to guard his back in battle. And now, the big Scot was proving to be a true friend in every sense of the word. Odd, how this simple gesture of washing his hair showed the character of the man.

Ronan did not remember being carried back to bed. Laudanum had a way of addling one's senses. Perhaps he had passed out in the tub. But when he awoke, Dahlia was once again by his side, holding his hand in one of hers while stroking his brow with the other. "Queen Pea..."

She inhaled lightly. "You're awake. Thank goodness."

"What time is it?" He wanted to know how long he'd been asleep. Or had he been unconscious? Probably just asleep. Dahlia did not appear too alarmed.

"It's midnight. Finn and Belle took Miranda back home. Tynan and Abby also left. They'll all return tomorrow. I wrote a note to Uncle John asking for permission to marry you. Uncle George is going to deliver it and speak to him about it as well."

Ronan nodded, however, he was not pleased about this. "It is something I should have done. Out of respect for you."

"I know you respect me. He'll understand the circumstances. Robbie is here. He's going to sleep in the guest bedchamber where Heather was sleeping. This way, he can be nearby if he and Joshua need to lift you again. Heather will sleep on the sofa in Joshua's library."

"And you?"

"I'm not leaving your side. I know it is improper, but I am beyond caring what anyone thinks. My sisters will never tell. I doubt Robbie or Joshua will either." She ran her fingers lightly through his hair. It had dried hours ago. But at least it was clean. "You smell like a cinnamon bun. Your hair does, anyway. I love the scent."

"I know. It was your soap. This is your fragrance."

She inhaled his scent again. "Uncle George put that unguent on your chest. That part of you smells like moldy cheese. But he says you only need to apply it for the next few days."

He frowned when she resumed her seat in the chair beside his bed. "You'll topple if you think to sit there all night. Stretch out beside me, Queen Pea. I promise not to have my wicked way with you. Not that I can do anything. Every bone in my body aches. My chest is still on fire."

He was surprised when she made no protest. She removed her shoes and set the chair aside, then climbed onto the bed. She settled beside him atop the covers and rested one hand lightly on his shoulder. "I think this officially classifies me as a wanton and a ruined lady."

"I'm marrying you tomorrow, so I wouldn't fret too much about it. You'll be respectable by tomorrow evening."

"Are you serious? Do you still mean to go through with a wedding ceremony?"

He nodded. "More than ever. I need to give you the protection of my name. Whatever I possess will be yours. My family doesn't need my wealth. I want you to have it. I want my brothers to take care of you. You'll be a Brayden, and we always look after our own."

"Ronan, you are being ridiculous."

Since her hand was still resting on his shoulder, he covered it with his own. "It's important to me. Don't fight me on this, Queen Pea. I will not go to my grave abandoning you."

"You will not go to your grave at all. I'll never forgive you if you do. Don't speak of such things. You're a big ox. You are invincible. We are meant to be together. *The Book of Love* wouldn't part us like this."

"It's just a book."

She shook her head. "No, it's magical. Don't say it isn't. How else would I have found you? It's magical, and it will work miracles. It will make you better, and we'll live happily ever after into our dotage."

He took her small, soft hand and put it to his lips, irritated with himself for upsetting her. He was in pain, but so was she. Having to watch helplessly while a loved one suffered was almost worse than being the one injured.

She had to be taut as a bowstring and ready to break at the slightest provocation. "You're right, sweetheart. Close your eyes and get some rest. One of us ought to look decent for our wedding ceremony. Since I'm going to look like fungus and smell like rotted cheese, I think the least you can do is look spectacular."

She laughed at his remark, her voice gentle and melodic.

However, she was also exhausted, physically drained after this harrowing day. He hadn't been an easy patient. She skittered closer to his body, resting her cheek against his shoulder. "I love you so much, Ronan."

"I love you, too, Queen Pea."

He fell asleep, holding her hand.

Chapter Sixteen

RONAN AWOKE THE next morning feeling much better. His fever had subsided considerably, but he was still in no shape to get out of bed. Of course, Dahlia's uncle had warned him to stay put for another two days. He supposed he had no choice. Parliament would not be in session until Monday anyway. He would accomplish nothing other than hurting himself if he chose to disobey this simple instruction.

When he tried to move his arm, he felt it weighed down. "What the…?"

He looked over and grinned.

Dahlia had wrapped herself around his upper arm, clinging to him as she slept. Her face was buried between his shoulder and the pillows at his back, so all he saw was a mass of beautiful hair. She must have taken the pins out last night and left the silky mane long and loose.

She had spent the night atop his covers and refused to climb under them because he was naked. He realized she must have become cold at some point, and rather than leave his side to grab a blanket, she had sought the heat of his body for warmth.

"Ronan?" She stirred when he reached out to run his hand lightly over her hair. "How are you feeling? How's the fever?"

"Gone, I think. I'm much better, Queen Pea."

She did not appear to believe him and stared at him with her big eyes. "And your breathing?"

"No crackling or wheezing in my lungs."

"You sound good," she admitted, tipping her head toward his chest to listen for any railing sounds. "Do you feel a burning in your lungs?"

"Much less than before."

She sat up and put a hand to his brow. Then she touched his neck. "Your fever has gone down considerably. But you're not quite done with it yet." When she smiled at him, he thought his temperature might spike again. All to do with the heat of desire and nothing to do with the physical mangle his body was in just now.

With her hair unbound and the sleepy look in her eyes, she looked like a sultry wood nymph. Everyone knew wood nymphs had beautiful bodies, and Dahlia's was exquisite.

He could do nothing about it yet because of the damn unguent. It was meant to save his life, and he was not so foolish as to refuse to have it applied. He could wait two days to get himself healthy and spend a lifetime with this beauty who was to be his wife.

After spending last night with Dahlia beside him, he had no intention of waiting to get married. He would accomplish this today, assuming Finn had been able to obtain the special license on his behalf.

"Are you hungry?" she asked, taking him out of his musings.

"What am I allowed to have?" He could eat an entire wild boar, but he doubted he'd be permitted anything that hearty. No, he'd be placed on a diet similar to that of a toothless ninety-year-old.

"Porridge. Broth. You are also allowed fish and cheese, but Uncle George recommends plenty of liquids first. He also recommends keeping ice on your ribs to reduce the inflammation. I'll fetch some and wrap it in a cloth for you. Good thing there's plenty of it at this time of the year. I'll go downstairs and see if anyone is stirring."

Ronan watched her as she took a moment to pin her hair up and then smooth out the wrinkles in her gown. It amazed him how pretty she looked in the early morning light.

Waking up to a female in his bed was not something he was used to, for it was never his practice to stay with a woman after he'd satisfied himself. Of course, these were not the sort of women one wanted to look at too closely, especially in the light of day. Even the finer ladies – and some of them were quite elegant and beautiful – had a jaded, used look about them.

But Dahlia was a breathtaking vision. "I'll be right back," she said, casting him an impudent smile. "Don't you dare climb out of bed."

She hurried out.

The door had been kept open overnight, a nod to maintaining a shred of propriety. Holly and Joshua were not going to force Dahlia to leave his bedside, but neither were they going to allow that door to close before they were husband and wife.

It was an unnecessary restriction.

He'd been in too much pain last night to accomplish anything.

No sooner had Dahlia gone downstairs than Robbie walked in. He had yet to wash up, and he looked half asleep. His shirt was untucked, as though he'd tossed it and his breeches on merely as an afterthought. "I just saw Dahlia in the hall. She said ye were much better this morning. Is this true?"

Ronan nodded. "Yes. By the way, I wanted to thank you for what you did for me yesterday."

Robbie arched an eyebrow. "Ye're welcome, although I dinna know what I did to earn yer gratitude. Dumping water over yer head was not much of a chore."

"You looked out for me and proved yourself to be a true friend. I always thought you were, of course. But the truest friends are those who stick with you during hard times, as you did. Thank you."

He nodded. "Ye gave us quite a scare."

"I know. I'll be on my best behavior from now on. I meant what I said about marrying Dahlia today. I may need help getting dressed for the occasion."

Robbie laughed and shook his head. "Ye're not putting on clothes today, laddie. Do ye have a robe? Perhaps Miranda will think to bring one over for ye. Or Josh may have something he can lend ye. Well, it will be a ceremony to remember. It'll make a fine story to tell yer bairns. Yer da got married with his bare arse flapping in the icy wind."

He groaned. "Ouch, stop jesting. It hurts when I laugh. Are those eggs and coffee I smell?"

"I'm surprised ye can smell anything over whatever it is Dr. Farthingale slathered on yer chest. Aye, they're setting out breakfast on the buffet. Can ye have anything?"

"Dahlia's bringing up something for me. Her uncle left a list of what I should eat. In truth, I'm ready to chew the furniture, I'm that famished."

"That's a good sign. Yer color looks good, too." He sighed. "If ye're comfortable, I'll go downstairs to see Heather. I feel bad that I kicked her out of her own bedchamber. She gave it up for me last night, but all her things are still in there."

"Dahlia never moved her clothes out of here, either. I suppose it doesn't matter. She'll be my wife in a matter of hours."

"Assuming Finn gets ye the special license." Robbie frowned. "Are ye sure about this? Not questioning yer wanting to marry the lass. Just the timing of it. All jesting aside, it won't be much of a wedding for her."

"I know. I felt as though I was at death's door yesterday, and all the while, all I could think about was giving her the protection of my name. I know the Farthingales will always take care of her. It isn't the same. And it isn't merely a matter of protecting her. We belong together. She has my heart. I needed her to have all that goes with it."

"It's that damn book. I think I have to read it." He shook his head as he walked out.

Within minutes, everyone began popping in to see how he was faring. Heather came first since Robbie must have awakened her and told her she could have her bedchamber back. "Robbie said you were doing well this morning."

Ronan nodded. "I am. How did you sleep? Robbie still feels guilty about you giving up your bed for him. How was the sofa?"

"Very comfortable. I was fine. Robbie is too big to fit on it. His legs would have been dangling over the edge, and his shoulders are too broad for the seat. He would have rolled off at least a dozen times during the night."

Then Joshua and Holly walked in, and they had the same conversation. "Yes, I'm much better this morning. Slept well. No fever to speak of."

He felt as though he was the host standing in a veritable reception line, for the rest of the morning was taken up greeting family members who came by to ask after him. But he looked up eagerly when Finn strode in. "Did you get the license?"

Tynan and Joshua happened to be in the room with him at the time.

Finn shot him a look. "Of course, I did. Was there ever a doubt?"

"Were you able to find a minister willing to conduct the service?" Tynan asked.

Finn pursed his lips. "Working on it. Don't you think we ought to hear from Dahlia's uncle first?"

"I'm sure he'll give his consent. Why wouldn't he? Besides, you, Josh, and Romulus gave him enough practice negotiating betrothal contracts. As far as I'm concerned, I'll sign whatever he hands me."

"He and Rupert will be along later this morning," Joshua said. "Let's wait until then before you make your plans."

Ronan was not going to allow his brothers to delay him. "I'm marrying her today."

Tynan frowned. "What you are doing is barging ahead like a bull on a rampage. But there is someone important you're trampling over. Did you think to discuss the wedding details with Dahlia?"

Ronan sighed. "She is agreeable to marrying me today."

"Because you pushed her into it," Joshua said. "What was she going to tell you while you were on the verge of convulsions?"

No, his Queen Pea loved him.

But he knew they had a point. He was rushing her, forcing her to give up her special day. "I'll talk to her when she comes upstairs. What's she doing now?"

"Having coffee with Belle and the others in the dining room. Miranda should be here shortly. This week has been bittersweet for her. She's about to lose the last of her sons."

Ronan pursed his lips. "It will be an adjustment for her to be alone in that big house. But we'll all live close enough. Your wives have been good to her. I think she likes them better than she likes us."

Tynan nodded. "She and Abby have grown very close. We'll make it a point to stop by often to visit her. At least until she's used to being on her own."

"Holly and I will do the same," Joshua said. "But I wonder if we ought to hire a companion for Miranda. There are lots of genteel women who would be suitable for the position."

Finn chuckled. "Let's get through Ronan's wedding ceremony first, shall we? Don't you dare raise the possibility to Miranda until afterward. She'll eat you alive at the mere suggestion."

At one o'clock, the Lord Admiral stopped by to see how he was doing. Joshua led him into Ronan's bedchamber. Dahlia had been seated beside his bed, reading a collection of poems to him. She was in the middle of reading *Ozymandias* by the poet, Percy Shelley, but set her book aside and skittered out after hastily greeting the man.

The Lord Admiral watched her as she left. "I hear you are getting married."

"That's right. I want it to happen today, but there is a concerted campaign afoot to have my wishes overruled. The family believes I should at least be able to stand on my feet, not naked, and not smelling like fungus growing in a cave."

"Well, knowing you are to be married should square things with Stoke, although your lovely betrothed set him straight already and saved our hides." He settled in the chair Dahlia had vacated. "I won't stay long. I just wanted you to know that if there is to be any political chicanery over this navy scandal, I will make certain I'm the one to take the fall."

Ronan frowned. "Dahlia read me this morning's newspaper account. The Examiner is skewering Viscount Hawley, Lord Liverpool, and you. It isn't fair what they are saying about you. What choice did you have in giving him this commission? The blame falls on all the lords who pressured you into appointing him, and this includes Lord Liverpool. I like the man, but this was an enormous blunder on his part."

"Hopefully, some good will come of it. The incident would have been disastrous had we been at war. Having just ended a long and brutal engagement against the French, and having lost so many good men of our own, the country has no patience for this continued privilege nonsense. I only hope Liverpool isn't brought down along with Hawley. As for me," he said, shaking his head and chuckling, "I am eager to be booted out. I'm a tired, old man. I would enjoy being able to live out the rest of my life in peace and quiet."

"And leave men like Lord Peckham and Viscount Hawley in power in the navy? I would rather take the blame for this incident than ever see you gone. But is there anything to be done about Hawley?"

"Other than promoting him to some inconsequential position? Doubtful. Well, it's done now. Peckham, the arse, was hoping to place blame on you to misdirect everyone's anger, but it didn't work. The newspapers are touting you as the hero in all of this. Indeed, you are. I think the members of the House of Lords would have to be delusional to try to pin the blame on you. Mind you, many of them are."

"Too many of them are locked in the past and refuse to see the old ways disappearing."

"Then they will be smacked in the face by this changing world." The Lord Admiral patted his arm as he rose. "I'll leave you now. We'll see what political storm hits us on Monday. Congratulations, Brayden. Rest up. I'll need you in fighting shape as soon as possible."

Dahlia came back upstairs once the Lord Admiral left. "What did he have to say?"

He grimaced. "The lords are in turmoil, trying to figure out how to save their hides. Lord Liverpool's party might lose control over Parliament because of this. It was on his insistence that Hawley was promoted to a fleet admiral and given command of The Invictus. Liverpool is an able leader. I don't know who will fill his shoes if he tumbles. Hopefully, someone less keen on rewarding rank instead of merit."

"These lords have been holding power ever since the days of Magna Carta. None of them wishes to be in the generation that gives it up."

He reached out and took her hand. "Enough about politics. How do you feel, Queen Pea? My brothers think I'm an idiot for wanting to marry you today. How do you feel about it? Am I forcing you into it?"

"No."

He arched an eyebrow. "You sound hesitant. Are you having doubts?"

"About becoming your wife? None. I am marrying a hero. Or haven't you heard?" She grinned as she nodded toward the newspapers. "They are all claiming you are, so it must be true."

"I only wish to be your hero. I don't care what anyone else thinks." He kissed her hand.

"You are, Ronan. I don't need a newspaper to tell me about your virtues. But do you think your brothers are right? You must admit, it will be a lame affair. You can't even stand on your own beside me because your wounds are too fresh."

"I rode from Tilbury to London just to be with you. I can stand by your side for the few minutes it will take us to get through the ceremony."

She smiled at him. "Clothed?"

He chuckled. "Oh, hell. Don't make me laugh."

"Sorry. But we have overlooked these practical considerations."

"Are you saying you want to wait? As for me, although I've made jests about my low brain need for you, my desire for urgency isn't about that at all. It is about my heart needing you. It's a soul-wrenching ache, Queen Pea. But you have only to say the word. I will do whatever you wish."

"Then let us be married today. I feel the same way, Ronan."

"Thank you."

She gave him a kiss on the forehead. "I only came back in here for a moment. We've reclaimed Heather's bedchamber, and my sisters are now determined to fuss over me. So I must spend the next three hours in a dither, wondering how I shall ever be ready in time for my wedding, which hasn't even been scheduled yet."

He smiled. "Finn will have the minister for us today. He'll grumble and moan, but he'll get it done."

"And I'll be ready. Violet brought over more of my gowns. We will spend at least an hour pondering which one I am to wear. And another hour deciding how to style my hair because it has to be just right. And another hour simply fretting because everyone frets over wedding preparations."

"I suppose it is a much simpler thing for men. I just have to worry about getting my trousers on. But I'm truly sorry, Queen Pea. You deserve far better."

"We Farthingales are notorious for marrying in haste. We have raised these patched together weddings to a fine art. It has become a source of pride to see who can outdo all the others. I never thought I would be the one to claim the honor. But a naked bridegroom? Marrying in a bedchamber? On a few hours' notice? Our story will be a legend among the family."

He laughed again, the effort causing pain to course through his body. But he overlooked it because he was in too good humor. "Put that way, then I'm glad to be of service."

She leaned forward and gave him another light kiss, this time on the mouth. "I hear Uncle John and Aunt Sophie downstairs. What do you think? Will he withhold his approval or say *thank goodness* and kick me out the door?" She grinned impishly. "Let me go down to speak to them. And then I shall be locked away in Heather's bedchamber. Uncle John is not going to refuse your proposal."

Indeed, there was little to be discussed when John and Rupert called on him. Finn had come up with them. "I'll sign whatever you want," he said, impatient to have the minister scheduled.

Finn rolled his eyes.

John and Rupert laughed.

"What is it with you Braydens?" Rupert jested. "You take all the fun out of contract negotiations. Even Finn was ready to sign over the Crown jewels to marry Belle."

"I wouldn't be surprised if my brother actually owned those jewels. But my assets are not quite as impressive. They're similar to Joshua's. Just copy whatever terms he agreed to when marrying Holly, and let's be done."

When they left, despite fighting to remain awake, Ronan fell into a deep sleep for the next two hours. He awoke to the sound of his family and the Farthingales still gathered downstairs. However, Dahlia was across the hall from him. He couldn't tell who else was in the room with her, but there were definitely more than just the three sisters. Multiple giggles emanated from behind the closed door.

In truth, it made him feel better that Dahlia was being fussed over as his bride-to-be. He wanted her to have at least one frivolous memory because he was depriving her of every shred of her dream wedding.

Robbie and Finn sauntered into his bedchamber. "Thought ye might need help taking care of the necessaries now that ye're awake," Robbie said.

"I'm good. Took care of almost everything myself before I fell asleep."

Finn frowned. "You stood up all by yourself?"

"Sort of. I held on to the bedpost. Did you find a minister? I hope this is why the family is still downstairs. They had better not be holding vigil over me. I have no intention of dying anytime soon."

"Minister will be here within the hour."

"Thank you, Finn," he said with all sincerity.

"You're still an arse, but I know you love Dahlia. I was as much of an idiot about Belle."

Robbie scratched his head. "Ye took care of the necessaries with yer door wide open?"

"What? Yes." Ronan shrugged. "Couldn't be helped. I kept the sheet wrapped around me as best as I could."

"When did ye do this?" Robbie was horrified. "The pixie might have seen ye. At least the others are married and ken what a man looks like."

"Heather was busy with her sister. They haven't come out of that room in hours. Why are you scowling at me, Robbie? No one saw anything."

"I would have come up here and shut yer damn door." He sighed and shook his head. "Joshua gave ye a bell to ring if ye needed us."

"You aren't my servants. And I didn't want anyone's hands on me. I managed fine on my own…almost. Someone must have come in here while I slept and tidied up the mess I made. I see there's fresh water in the ewer, and the chamber pot has been emptied. When did you say the minister was coming?"

Finn groaned. "You really are an idiot."

"A royal pain in the arse," Robbie said. "Is this what love does to a man? Then I hope I never fall in love. I dinna think I've ever met a more lovesick fool."

"Hah! You'll see. When you fall, it will be so hard, all of London will quake."

Robbie rolled his eyes. "Not a chance."

Robbie and his brother were still giving him a hard time when Dahlia popped her head in. "May I come in?"

"Blessed saints," he said in an awed whisper. "You look beautiful, Queen Pea."

She had changed out of the gown she had put on this morning. This new gown was a soft rose color, which brought out the gentle blush in her cheeks and pink of her lips. Her hair was drawn off her face, curled and left to tumble in a glorious cascade down her back. The few pink and purple flowers in her hair enhanced the effect. She looked like an exquisite wood nymph. "What do you think of this gown and my hairstyle? Suitable for a wedding?"

He groaned. "Hell, yes. Finn, please. Drag the damn minister here already."

"Fine. Robbie and I will bring him over now." They complimented Dahlia on their way out.

Ronan was glad for a moment alone with her. "How do you feel, Queen Pea?"

She grinned. "Happy. Amazed. Is this really going to happen? Will I truly be married to you?"

"Yes, but there's still the matter of my husbandly duties to fulfill. We'll figure that part out later. You look so beautiful. I'm glad I was an arse about rushing the wedding day. I don't regret it."

"Nor do I." She sighed and reached for the unguent. "I had better coat you again."

"I'll do it. Why don't you go downstairs and join the others?"

She looked disappointed. "Are you eager to be rid of me already?"

"No. But I'll understand if you'd rather be downstairs than up here holding your nose while I smear this odious glop on me."

"I'd rather be with you, if you don't mind. Won't it be in our vows? In sickness and in health. For better or for worse. In odious glop and gagging scents."

"I think the good Lord would give you a pass on that one. But it feels nice, doesn't it? You and me? I think I shall write Wainscott a note. Thank you for being the biggest dumb-arse in existence. Thank you for being too shortsighted and narrow-minded to appreciate the gem you had within your grasp."

"Oh, don't ever mention his horrid name again. He was a beast to me. And now he's done the same to Lady Alexandra. Everyone is gossiping about it. Their betrothal has fallen apart. I've never heard of such a thing happening so quickly. It's highly unusual, isn't it?

"This is who he is. A shortsighted, greedy man. I fully expect he will ruin all his chances for an advantageous marriage. The oaf will return to York with his tail between his legs, believing everyone has wronged him."

She shook her head and sighed. "I hope he stays up there, and I never have to see him again. In truth, I'm more worried about Stoke's daughter, Lady Melinda. I fear her situation is impossible. Now that I am about to be so happily married–"

"Within the hour, I hope."

She cast him an indulgent smile, for he was like a dog with a bone and unwilling to give it up. "Yes, my love. Now, where was I? Oh, yes. Poor Melinda. Loving you so deeply makes me sad to think she will never know this joy for herself."

He reached for her hand. "Then, for her sake, I hope she is not experiencing true love. I would not wish that pain on her. We shall see what unfolds."

Dahlia nodded. "Hopefully, nothing before the budget vote. I'll send a note to her in the morning explaining that I am newly married and cannot start on the redecoration of her father's study until after

Christmas."

"Right, you will be too busy engaging in hot, wild monkey sex with your new husband."

She burst out laughing. "Ronan!"

"Teasing you, Queen Pea. But don't think for a moment this isn't foremost on my mind. I'll just have to figure out how to accomplish it without putting myself in a coma." Ronan finished slathering the unguent on his chest. He wiped his hands on the damp cloth Dahlia handed him and then set it aside on the night table. It irked him that he had to remain in bed like an old man, his feeble body propped against the pillows.

Dahlia sat beside him. "I can't wait until I am permitted to stretch out beside you and talk to you, wife to husband. I look forward to closing the door behind me and nestling close to the handsomest man in existence."

"I assume you are referring to me. You still find me handsome?"

She cast him a tender smile. "Exceptionally."

"Lord, I'm in agony. I'm not sure I will last another hour without touching you."

"Getting you properly healed is most important. Anyway, we won't have much privacy until we are in your new home."

"*Our* new home. Whatever I possess is yours, Queen Pea. My rib cage should be nicely healed by then. I haven't spoken to Finn about the status of the purchase yet, but I'm sure the indenture deed has been drawn up and is merely awaiting Lady Wellbrook's signature. I've been giving him such a hard time about obtaining the special license and the minister, that I think he will toss me out the window if I ask him anything else."

"Would Miranda mind if we stayed with her until the new house is yours? It might help ease her into dealing with her own soon to be empty home."

"I think she would enjoy having you with her. It will give her the chance to get to know you better. But no more talk of mothers and houses and forlorn duke's daughters."

"All right. I shall only think of you. Honestly, Ronan, even though we've read *The Book of Love* together, I still have so much to learn."

"We'll learn it together, Queen Pea."

She nodded. "I'm still in disbelief we are getting married."

"I'm not." He spoke with surprising conviction. "We were meant to find each other and fall in love. It was going to happen with or without that book. Perhaps we would have hit more bumps along the way, made more mistakes. I know we would have moved slower toward this end. But I don't regret our taking this leap. Will you give the book to Heather now?"

"I will, but not right away. She has a little more growing up to do, I think. She's a young eighteen-year-old. Do you know what I mean? Robbie calls her a pixie, and I think it is apt because she is still a little girl in some ways. Not that I am one to judge. I was hardly a good example for her to follow. I think–"

Ronan suddenly pulled her forward and threw himself over her as something smashed through the window, sending shards of glass hurtling toward them. Most of the shards landed in a spray beside the window. But several sailed farther, landing dangerously close to the bed. "Queen Pea, are you all right?"

"What just happened?" she asked in a shaky breath.

"Someone tossed a rock through the window." Under normal circumstances, he would have been on his feet, pistol drawn, and ready to chase after the culprit. But he couldn't move. His lungs felt as though they were about to burst, and pain was shooting up both sides of his body. "Bollocks, I've ruined your gown."

He was atop her, probably crushing her with his weight. They were chest to chest, and her bodice was smeared with the foul substance he had just applied to his wound.

She scrambled out from under him as he rolled off her with a grunt. "Ronan, are you all right? Can you breathe?"

"Yes, Queen Pea." *Bollocks.* He lay on his back, seeing stars as pain continued to course through him.

"Dear heaven! I've never seen anyone move as fast as you did just now. How are you able to do this? And injured, no less? Don't worry about my gown. Let me run down and get help."

She ran out before he could stop her. He barely had time to wrap the sheet around himself before his brothers and Robbie tore into the room. Glass crunched beneath their boots as they hurried to the window.

A cold wind blew in through the broken panes. But he was still in a sweat and struggling to quell the fire in his chest, so he felt none of the chill.

"Whoever the blackguard was, he must have run off by now," Robbie said. "We were just on our way out to fetch the minister, but...I'll look around and see if I can find anyone still lurking suspiciously. Snow's on the ground. There may be some tracks to follow."

"I'm coming with you," Tynan said.

Joshua ran a hand roughly through his hair. "Me, too."

Finn stopped him. "I'll go, Josh. This is your house. You'll need to have the window repaired as soon as possible, and the shards of glass cleaned up. Who do you think did this?"

Joshua shook his head in dismay. "Hell if I know. It wasn't aimed at me or Holly. Lord knows we've had our own headaches. This had to be someone angry with Ronan. Why else toss the rock through an upper floor window instead of into the parlor where we were all standing?"

"Or someone who is angry with Dahlia," Finn mused, now frowning. "After all, until yesterday, this was her guest chamber."

Unfortunately, Dahlia returned in time to hear these last comments.

"Me?" She put a hand to her throat, and her face went ashen. "Who would want to hurt me?"

Chapter Seventeen

DAHLIA FELT COMPLETELY drained. It could not have been more than an hour before the window was replaced, the glass swept away, and Ronan safely settled back in bed, but it felt like an eternity to her.

Ronan was in pain. In typical fashion, he was too stubborn to admit to it. Fortunately, his breathing did not appear strained, nor did he appear to be in any worse discomfort than he'd been in before the rock was hurled at them.

Who had thrown it, and why?

She had no enemies.

In truth, Ronan had none either. Everyone was hailing him as a hero. Except perhaps Lord Peckham, but he did not seem the sort to hire a ruffian to cause overt destruction. Men like him were political weasels, sneaking behind an opponent's back within the halls of Parliament to undermine that opponent's power by duplicitous deal-making and snide innuendo.

What hurt most was this prank had ruined the gown she had chosen to wear for her wedding. Perhaps it was petty of her to feel this way, but she could not help it. Ronan was hurt, their wedding plans were rushed, and the beautiful gown she had intended to wear for the ceremony was covered in slime because Ronan had almost killed himself tossing his body over hers to protect her.

The members of their families, all of whom had been cheered to learn he was on the mend and that wedding plans were moving forward, were now quietly seated downstairs, too overset by what had happened to even crack a smile.

Dahlia, with Heather's help, took a moment to change into another gown before returning to Ronan's side. She knocked softly before entering his room while her sister went downstairs to join the others.

"Queen Pea," he said, his eyes still etched with pain. "I'm so sorry. I'll make it up to you."

She shook her head. "This wasn't your fault. Ronan, are we about to make a huge mistake? Perhaps we ought to put off our plans to marry."

Is this what *The Book of Love* was warning them about?

He reached out to caress her cheek when she sat beside his bed. "Taking you as my wife is the best decision I've ever made," he insisted. "If you were the target, then I'm more determined than ever to get the ceremony performed immediately. I want the right to remain beside you, to protect you night and day. I don't care if I have to break a thousand ribs to do it."

Her eyes rounded in horror. "Oh, Ronan! What if you did break another one while lunging to protect me?"

"I didn't. Believe me, I would have felt it."

Could she trust him to tell her the truth about his injuries? He was intent on exchanging vows with her today. What if he was holding on by sheer force of stubbornness and determination?

Her eyes began to tear, and her chin wobbled.

He groaned. "Don't cry, Queen Pea. I couldn't bear it if you did."

"Promise me, nothing else is broken."

"I would be howling if it were," he said, cupping her chin. "I promise you, I'm in the same mangled condition as I was before the rock was thrown. We'll figure out who did this. Joshua's already contacted Homer Barrow, the Bow Street runner who was so helpful to your cousins in Oxford and again to Holly when she was in danger.

Anyway, I've been giving it thought, and I have my suspicions about the identity of the culprit."

She stared at him, trying to remain sensible and not to melt in response to his touch. But his words startled her. "You do? Who do you think did this?"

"Wainscott."

Was he speaking out of jealousy, or was there substance to the claim? "Why? What possible motive could he have?"

"Lady Alexandra and her parents live right next door. Or have you forgotten already?"

She blushed. "I had put it out of my mind. It merely… I wasn't thinking of Gerald or them any longer."

"I'm glad. But I suspect Alexandra's father tore up their betrothal contract in front of Wainscott shortly before that rock came flying through this window. It is also likely Lord Balliwick threatened to have him shot if he ever came near his daughter again. Wainscott must have stormed out angrily."

"But he's already seduced a duke's daughter if the gossip rags are to be believed. And when my sisters and cousins were fussing over me earlier in Heather's room, my cousin, Honey, confirmed it was true."

"Did she now?"

"Yes. Honey said that she saw Lady Withnall earlier today, and Lady Withnall confirmed Gerald was trying to worm his way into this duke's family by seducing his daughter. He actually had this poor girl in a carriage on their way to Gretna Green, but the duke caught up to them in time and foiled his plans. Lady Withnall wouldn't tell Honey who the poor girl was."

Ronan began to laugh.

"What's so funny?"

"Queen Pea, you are making my head spin with all these details. I'm still trying to figure out how I'm going to put my breeches on for our wedding."

Despite their situation, she couldn't help but join him in a chuckle. "Must you? Am I complaining about you lying naked in this bed? I think you look perfect as you are." She leaned closer, eager to learn more about why he thought her former beau was the culprit. "Why would Gerald ever bother with me? I'm the nobody he originally tossed over for Balliwick's daughter."

"You're an angel, and he's a fool for ever giving you up." Ronan frowned as he took her hand and entwined his fingers with hers. "I've told you before. Wainscott will end up with nothing. He has overplayed his hand. Sheer greed did him in. He had an earl's daughter – a bird in the hand – but he wanted more. He went after this mysterious duke's daughter and got caught. Now that Lord Balliwick has learned of it, all hope of Wainscott's ever patching things up with Lady Alexandra is destroyed."

"What if this duke's daughter is now with child? I know he tried this with Lady Alexandra…having seen them first hand when I caught them in the act."

"This duke is now going to do everything he can to suppress the scandal. He'll buy off everyone who might talk and will never allow Wainscott within a hundred miles of his daughter. I know it is harsh, but if there is a babe…assuming it survives to term…it will be given over to a family or to an orphanage. If the babe is fortunate, the duke will provide for him or her. But that's the best to be hoped for."

Her heart lurched in dismay. "That's awful. It would tear me apart to give up a child."

"Another reason why I love you. I have no doubt you would fight with all your heart and soul to protect our children. But the point I am trying to make is about Wainscott. As he left Alexandra's house, he must have known he'd just lost everything. Then he saw our families gathered in the parlor, perhaps heard that you and I were planning to marry today, and so he hurled that rock."

"Out of spite?"

Ronan shrugged. "Or out of frustration. Anger. Yes, spite."

"It seems farfetched. How would he know to hit this exact window?"

"He may have known you and Heather were staying here and been watching you all along. I don't know. But it's a place to start the investigation. I'd go next door myself and ask questions, but…" He glanced down at himself. "I doubt the Earl of Balliwick will appreciate a naked sea captain knocking at his door just now."

In spite of her misery, Dahlia managed a smile. "Perhaps Joshua can walk over there later."

"I'll ask him. If it's any consolation, I doubt Wainscott will bother you again. If he has any sense, he's riding out of London as we speak. Surely, he has to know the Braydens will come after him if he remains in town."

She nodded. "I think there is something I must do now."

He arched an eyebrow. "What, Queen Pea?"

"Our families need to be reassured. I've been crying on and off this past hour, questioning whether we ought to go through with this rushed farce of a wedding. But loving you is no farce. I don't want anyone doubting my love for you."

"Or mine for *you*."

She rose and eased her hand out of his grasp. "I'll be back in a little while. Are you hungry? I'll bring up some broth and fish for you."

"Sounds delicious. Just one thing," he said as she was about to leave.

"What is it?"

He cast her a rakish grin. "Whatever you do, *don't* smile."

She walked out, laughing and shaking her head. Of course, this is how he always teased her. She couldn't stop herself from smiling, and that smile stayed on her lips while she told her family how much she loved Ronan and thanked them for being with them despite the chaos of the day. "Once we are settled in our new home, we will have a proper party. Ronan will be wearing clothes, I promise you."

Everyone laughed.

"He already has his suspicions about who threw that rock. Joshua, he'll talk to you about it later. He believes it is not something likely to happen again. In any event, nothing can lessen our love for each other. Ronan is on the mend, and this is a happy day. Please do not walk on eggshells around us. And now I must feed that gorgeous wildebeest before he melts away to nothing. We are getting married as soon as Robbie and Finn return with the minister."

She felt good when everyone began to cheer.

Heather ran over and hugged her. "You and Holly are both so brave. She with that deranged man who was stalking her, and now you with a rock-hurling fiend. I wish I was as brave as both of you. But I'm not. I just hope my wedding will be dull and uneventful."

Dahlia groaned inwardly as her sister began to sniffle. "Heather, don't start crying. I won't allow it."

"I can't help it. I'm going to miss you and Holly so much. You'll be marrying Ronan, and then I'll be all alone."

Dahlia had gone out of her way to be cheerful. Yes, her sister needed a little more time to come into her own. "Our family is too large. You will never be on your own."

"It isn't the same. You'll both have husbands, and I won't."

Oh, heavens! Was Heather bent on making the same mistake she almost made with Gerald? "Don't talk like that." She cast her Aunt Sophie a pleading glance.

Her aunt came over and took Heather in hand. "My dear, you'll know when the time is right for you. Don't rush into anything because you are eager to be a bride. You don't even have a beau yet."

"But Lady Withnall said I've already met the man I'm going to marry."

Dahlia tried not to lose patience with her sister. "Yes, but he hasn't made his feelings known to you. In the meanwhile, you'll have a line of gentlemen eager to pursue you. Enjoy your season. Take time to sort out your feelings."

"And read that book. I will get it next, won't I?"

"Yes. Heather, please. Don't leap into marriage because Holly and I will be married. I haven't even had my wedding ceremony yet." She shook her head and sighed. "We'll talk about it later. All right? Just let me get through this day."

"Oh, I'm so horrid! Of course." She allowed Aunt Sophie to scoot her away.

After issuing another quick thank you to everyone for their concern, Dahlia returned upstairs. Ronan must have found *The Book of Love* in the drawer of the night table, because he was reading it as she walked in.

He shut it and smiled at her. "I was bored. Probably not the right thing to say to the young woman I'm about to marry. But you were downstairs, and my mind was still racing. I thought I would read it again while you were gone."

"Better put it away before Heather comes up here. She's feeling as though she's just lost her two sisters and is taking it hard. I don't want her rushing into marriage simply because she does not wish to be left out. I want her to have the book…"

"But?"

"Something is holding me back. I don't know, perhaps it is just my muddled head. I'll think more clearly after we're married."

He cleared his throat. "I have a suggestion."

She was eager to hear it. "About Heather and the book?"

He nodded. "Robbie wants to read it, too. He's levelheaded and experienced."

"A little too experienced," she said with a frown.

"He's honorable, Queen Pea. He would never take advantage of Heather. I'll have his word on it, and he will never break that oath. You're worried that she'll be distracted by the wrong man, aren't you?"

"Yes, it is my greatest fear. I don't want her to lie to herself and force a love match where no love exists. I did this with Gerald, and I'm so afraid she learned nothing from my experience."

"All the more reason to have her read the book with Robbie. He'll watch over her and protect her from making a mistake."

"Ronan, do you hear yourself? If they read it together, he's going to fall in love with her. Isn't this what happened to us? Not to mention, Holly and Joshua and Violet and Romulus. Same for Belle and Finn. Need I go on? We all fell in love over this book. Are you purposely matchmaking?"

"No, I'll leave that plotting to you ladies. But you've just told me Heather is young and impressionable. She wants to leap into marriage because her two sisters will be married. Do you or do you not wish to stop her?"

"I do. How can I convince her the consequences will be disastrous?"

"She has to figure it out on her own. And while she does, Robbie will be there to protect her if she's about to make a mistake. He's an excellent judge of character. He will know to chase away the bounders and only allow the worthy men near. He will be vigilant and diligent, and no one will do a better job of looking out for her."

Dahlia had to admit the idea had merit. "Having them read it together may not be such a bad idea. If she reads it on her own, she will miss the entire point of the book."

He smiled at her. "So? What's your verdict?"

"Robbie it is."

A few minutes later, the very man in question strode in. "We found the minister. Are ye two lovebirds ready to get married?"

They both stared at him.

Robbie arched a wary eyebrow.

They continued to stare at him.

"What's wrong with ye?" He glanced down at himself and checked his uniform. "Why are ye grinning at me like a pair of hyenas?"

CHAPTER EIGHTEEN

RONAN WAS CONCERNED Dahlia would be disappointed by their wedding ceremony, but to his surprise, she wasn't. In truth, she appeared to be relishing his scandalous nakedness – no matter that he was wearing a banyan borrowed from Joshua and his vitals parts were securely covered.

Still, he wore nothing underneath that itchy robe.

It took him a moment to realize the source of her glee. She was looking forward to claiming the title of Most Shocking Farthingale Wedding.

Finally, at the appointed hour, and with much logistical planning, the immediate family members were permitted into his bedchamber. His mother, his brothers, their wives, and Dahlia's sisters. Also permitted were Sophie and John Farthingale and Robbie. It took a bit of doing to fit them all in and leave space for Dahlia to make her grand entrance as the bride on the arm of her Uncle John.

The quiet affair had spun out of control, but it was to be expected considering the nature of their families. They were fourteen in all up in his room. More were downstairs. Cousins and their spouses who had stopped by out of concern for his injuries. But now they were staying to celebrate their wedding.

He supposed this was how their lives would be from now on. They each had large families with close bonds, and it was not unusual to have relations come by with regularity. "Ready, Queen Pea?"

The minister was horrified to find Ronan standing before him in bare feet and a black silk robe. Ronan did not know what the man had to complain about. He had shaved and wiped the unguent off his chest so the odor would not overpower everyone in the tightly packed room.

He'd reapply it later.

He had also authorized Finn to promise the minister a king's ransom to perform the bedside ceremony, so it was going to get done no matter how much this man of the cloth disapproved. Of course, knowing Finn, he'd bartered the man down to nothing. "This is most irregular."

Ronan did not care. "Is it lawful?"

"Why, yes," the minister said with an indignant huff.

"Then get on with it."

Dahlia's smile and the look of love she cast him whenever glancing up at him, stole his breath away. He'd ruined her first gown, but this one was just as lovely, a pale lilac which brought out the violet swirls within the beautiful ocean colors of her eyes. Her hair was as she'd first styled it, drawn off her face and left to tumble in a silky waterfall down her back.

His heart swelled with the knowledge she would soon be his, just as he was permanently and irrevocably hers.

The minister had a dull, droning voice.

Ronan struggled to pay attention, and more than once had to stifle a yawn. But he snapped to attention as the end approached. "Captain Brayden, do you take Dahlia Farthingale to be your lawfully wedded wife…"

Ronan took Dahlia's hand. "I do."

The minister asked the same of Dahlia, and she responded with an "I do."

The cheers were deafening as the minister proclaimed them husband and wife. Everyone straggled out of the room shortly afterward to join the rest of the family downstairs. "Most odd," the minister grumbled on his way out.

Tynan grinned at him. "We're giving you five minutes alone with your lovely wife, then we'll be back to put you properly into bed. George will have our hides if you take a tumble and crack more ribs."

"And ye'll need that unguent back on yer chest," Robbie remarked, wincing as he turned to Dahlia. "Yer uncle's orders."

"I know." She blushed. "I've already been admonished not to…well, I'm to keep away from him for the next two days and perhaps more."

Ronan groaned. "All right. Everyone out. Not you, Queen Pea. I want you in my arms."

His brothers and Robbie hurried out, shutting the door behind them.

He and Dahlia stood a moment, facing each other in silence.

From the laughter, the clink of glasses, and clatter of china downstairs, Ronan realized their families were about to partake of the wedding meal Holly's cook had hurriedly prepared for the occasion. It felt odd not to be there with them, but there had been nothing normal about this past week or this day.

Dahlia must have understood what he was thinking. "Don't you dare apologize to me about this wedding. I've married my hero. This is the happiest day of my life."

"Mine, too, Queen Pea." He held out his arms to her. "Care to share a kiss with your new husband?"

"I had better take advantage before you stink like moldy cheese again."

She came into his arms, feeling so soft and sweet against him.

He ignored his aching rib cage and the fire in his chest.

He ignored his unsteady legs and the pain searing through his body merely for standing.

While he could not make love to her yet, there was nothing wrong with his lips, and he meant to use them to full advantage. His mouth captured hers, and he kissed her with all his heart, soul, and happiness.

He also kissed her with barely leashed passion and all the love a husband ought to hold for his wife.

The innocent ardor of her response affected him deeply. In the past, his kisses were meant for seduction. But this one was all about promise for their future, for the bonds of love that would strengthen between them over time. Of course, he still wanted to seduce her, to hear her soft, breathy moans of pleasure. But he also wanted to fall asleep holding her in his arms and wake to her warm body pressed to his.

"I love you, Queen Pea," he said upon ending the kiss, for he no longer trusted his legs to hold him up. He released her and sat heavily on the bed.

"Oh, Ronan!" Her eyes reflected her concern. "You have beads of sweat along your forehead. Oh, I knew it. You're in pain again."

"No, love. You take away my pain."

"Says the man now struggling for breath." She rolled her eyes. "Let me help you lie back down."

He shook his head. "I have to take off this robe first. Turn around."

She refused, smirking instead. "And miss the sight of your body? I can do this now. I am your wife. You are my husband. Doesn't it sound wonderful?"

He was not keen on showing himself off when he could do nothing productive with his given attributes. But he was glad she was no shy miss who would need coaxing into his bed when the time came. *Two days.* He would not be healed yet, but sufficiently along not to do himself too much damage when he finally claimed her.

Besides, there were ways to minimize the strain on his ribs.

He did not have to be the one on top.

A knock at the door took him out of his thoughts and relieved him of the need to refuse Dahlia's offer of assistance. "That will be my brothers and Robbie come to help me back in bed."

She looked disappointed but said nothing as she walked to the door to open it. "Come in."

"Ye need yer laudanum," Robbie said, heading to the bureau to prepare it for him.

"And your unguent," Tynan said, looking none too pleased as he picked up the pot and a clean washcloth.

Finn and Joshua helped him out of the robe and eased him back against the pillows and under the sheets.

Dahlia was lost amid these men who were attending to him with the precision of a military drill.

The strain of standing for the wedding and then taking the laudanum proved too much. Despite his stubborn struggles, he fell asleep within minutes.

"What time is it?" he asked when he awoke, still groggy from the laudanum and inhaling the putrid scent of the unguent on his chest. He wasn't even sure anyone was in the room with him. Night had fallen, and the house was quiet. Then he noticed one lonely figure seated in a chair beside the hearth, staring into the golden blaze of flames. "Queen Pea?"

She turned to him. "It's almost midnight. You slept soundly. I knew this day was too much for you."

He struggled to a sitting position.

"Ronan, don't!" She rose and hurried to his side. "You'll hurt yourself."

"You're still dressed. Do you have a nightrail with you?"

She nodded. "Yes. One of those flimsy, silk things. But I wasn't sure…"

He smiled. "Let me help you out of your gown and into that flimsy garment. However, I intend to have it off you in short order, so you needn't put it on for my sake."

"So you think I ought to stay with you tonight?"

"Hell, yes. Where else would you be?" He realized his chest was coated with that slimy substance. "Blast. Perhaps you are better off with Heather. I can't blame you for not wanting to get near me."

"It isn't that. My nose has adjusted to the odor. And it isn't *you* who smells bad, it's just that poultice. I could use your help with these stays and laces."

"Are you sure?"

She nodded. "If you're all right with it."

He groaned. "I'm more than all right having you in bed with me. If your nose can take it, then hop in." But he silently cursed his injury as he watched her slip the gown off her body and carefully set it over the chair. She then sat in the chair to take off her shoes and stockings.

He was the one who ought to be doing this for her, who ought to be sliding his hands along her body, holding her and kissing every delectable inch of her.

When she rose to remove her chemise, his breath caught. She stood outlined in the fire's glow, the fabric so delicately thin, he could see the dark patch at the junction of her thighs and the dark rose tips of her breasts.

He closed his eyes and quietly shuddered, trying to quell his low-brain frenzy.

He knew she'd be beautiful.

Watching her undress was a thing of splendor.

It did not matter that she had moved to hide behind the chair while trying to quickly slip off the chemise and don her equally thin nightrail. It was a skimpy, silken thing that hugged her body and showed more of her nicely endowed chest than it hid.

Whoever designed this garment, knew what they were doing.

Those glimpses of her skin had him excited, he would admit. But it was those parts strategically hidden that had his eyes bulging and his brain working double time. He *needed* to see what lay beneath.

He'd read about this effect in the book. It wasn't a matter of curiosity or even urgency. It was a primal urge that sprang from the depths of his soul, the first thing his primal brain sought, and the first thing his eyes went to. *Her breasts.* The source of life for his offspring.

The source of pleasure and desire for him.

She climbed into bed beside him, slipping under the covers so that the only barrier between them was her soon to be discarded nightrail.

Next, he had to figure out how to pleasure her without sliming her or the bedcovers…or puncturing his lung again. He gave it considerable thought as she wrapped her lovely body against his arm and nestled close.

In truth, he knew just how to accomplish it. However, Dahlia would need some convincing because this was not something one sprang on one's innocent wife.

Although she was not shy about assuming her wifely duties, this one was too much to ask of her this first time out.

She was not going to hop atop him and start dancing with abandon on his private parts.

He lay in the dark for a while longer before finally turning to her. "Queen Pea…"

She gave a little snuffle in response, then her breaths became smooth and even.

He glanced up at the ceiling and quietly groaned.

She had fallen asleep.

He brought her hand to his lips and kissed her soft palm. "I love you," he whispered and fell back to sleep himself.

Chapter Nineteen

RONAN HAD DUTIFULLY remained in bed, following Dr. Farthingale's instructions to the letter for the past week, which meant he had not been allowed to return to his parliamentary duties on Monday or any other day, and he had not yet claimed Dahlia properly as his wife. Today, he was going to take care of these two important matters.

The first was to attend the Parliament session on the navy budget vote. The Lord Admiral had done his best to retain the support previously secured, but Ronan had been the linchpin during these negotiations and knew his absence had hurt their position. He needed to be there today to herd these lords back in the proper direction.

The second important matter was to finally consummate his marriage to Dahlia. Nothing was going to stop him from this undertaking. No revolting unguent. No raw, aching bones.

Not even doctor's orders.

He was going to bed his wife tonight and had no intention of shirking that duty.

He had just stepped out of the tub and wrapped a towel around his waist when Dahlia came in. "Oh, my heavens." Her eyes rounded, and she gaped at him.

"Is something wrong, Queen Pea?"

She laughed. "Other than my rattled brain? I thought you'd be dressed by now. But my goodness, I'm glad you're not. I am very much enjoying the sight of you."

He shook his head in dismay. "I'm moving a little slow this morning. It's to be my first day outside of this bedchamber."

"Let me help you, my love. Joshua's carriage is already out front. He's eager to be on his way. Yours is not the only budget the House of Lords will be voting on."

"It will take me only a minute to dress."

"Nonsense. It will take you an hour at the speed you are moving." She teasingly sighed. "It is a tragic shame to cover up that splendid body of yours. The sacrifices a wife must make for her country."

They were still in Joshua's home since Dr. Farthingale had admonished them not to move him yet. But this forced idleness had done wonders for him. The burning in his chest had subsided. His ribs ached only the littlest bit. His head no longer felt as though elephants were stomping on it, and his eyes no longer blurred whenever he turned too quickly.

As soon as he was dressed and had donned his boots, he pulled Dahlia onto his lap. "You look beautiful, Queen Pea." He kissed her tenderly, his lips seeking hers as he drew her body against his, always loving the way she felt against him and the cinnamon scent of her skin.

Her lips molded to his, and she clung to his shoulders with sweet urgency. "Ronan," she whispered, her eyes still closed as she absorbed the lingering sensation of his touch after he ended the kiss, "we had better go downstairs, or Joshua and Holly will leave without us."

"Right." He sighed and allowed her to slip out of his arms. "You really do look beautiful."

She was wearing a dark blue gown, once again, nothing fancy. Just elegant and subtly catching to the eye. He watched as she put on her hat, a pretty thing in a dark blue fabric to match her gown and a small feather sticking out of the top. She set it on her head so that it jauntily tipped to one side and somehow made her eyes look bigger.

Gorgeous eyes.

Her hair was done up in a loose twist so that he could see the highlights of gold and copper peeking out from beneath her hat.

She looked breathtaking.

He felt a surge of pride that he would be the one escorting her into the halls of Parliament.

"About time you got down here," Joshua muttered but made certain to help him into the carriage.

Ronan fell heavily against the squabs, irritated that the slight effort of climbing in had sent pain shooting up his sides and across his chest. Dahlia settled beside him, her eyes filled with concern. "I'll be fine in a moment," he assured her.

She curled her arm in his and clung to him as the carriage rolled through the busy London streets. They did not have far to go, but even this short ride badly jostled his ribs. Dahlia knew it. Joshua and Holly knew it. But his expression must have been fierce, for none of them dared to utter a word about his discomfort.

It would have been pointless.

He would have denied it.

He was going to be present for the vote even if it killed him…as it well might, he decided when the carriage bounced over a particularly large rut. "Bollocks, how much did you pay for this cheap contraption?"

Joshua shot him a look that was somewhere between a smirk and a glower. "You're the problem, not the carriage. Behave yourself, you arse, or I'll toss you out and leave you to walk to Parliament on your own."

He closed his eyes. "Fine. I'll shut up. I suppose I owe you for saving my life." He felt Dahlia shudder beside him. "Sweetheart, I'm just being surly. All's well."

Which it wasn't, and they all knew it.

But he only needed to hold himself together for another hour at the most. His three earl cousins, Tynan, James, and Marcus, were standing out front, obviously awaiting their carriage. He should have known they would be here, for this was typical wildebeest behavior, the stronger ones coming to the rescue of their weakest, gathering around him to protect him.

"I'll punch the first one of you who dares carry me inside," he warned, appreciating their concern, but not wanting them to overdo it.

"Fine," Marcus said, "but we're sticking close. Miranda will kick us to Bedfordshire and back if any harm comes to her baby boy."

He groaned. "Is she here yet?"

"No, thank goodness," Tynan muttered.

Ronan turned to James, Earl of Exmoor, and the eldest of the eight wildebeests. "How are you feeling today?" He glanced at his cousin's mangled leg, suddenly feeling ashamed for behaving like a petulant and infantile tyrant. James had been wounded badly in the war, his face and body scarred, and his leg so badly injured, were it not for George Farthingale's miraculous treatment, the leg would have been amputated.

James nodded. "I'm fine. Sophie came along with me today. She knew Holly and Dahlia would be here and wanted to join them. She's already seated in the spectator gallery, holding their two seats."

Dahlia smiled. "Excellent, shall we join her now?"

"No," James said. "Not you, Dahlia. You see, Ronan is England's hero at the moment. He needs to play it up to the hilt. This means making his entrance with you by his side. The newspapers and their readership will devour it. A wounded hero in love with his beautiful, new bride."

He turned to Ronan. "Here, take my cane. Use it to walk in. You can give it back to me later."

Ronan did not immediately reach for it.

James frowned at him. "Don't be a prideful arse. Do you want your budget to pass?"

"But what about you? Don't you need it?" The last thing he wanted was for James to fall. Nothing was worth seeing him helpless on the floor and humiliated.

"Marcus and Tynan will stay close to me. Dahlia, do you think you can pretend to love my stubborn cousin? Cast him an adoring glance or two?"

She laughed. "I shall try. How's this?"

"Irresistible." Ronan groaned. "I'm going to carry you off to a dark corner and have my way with you."

James clapped him on the shoulder. "Cavort naked in the Thames, if you like. I hear you enjoy taking plunges into icy waters. But not before the vote. Come on. Let's go in."

The wildebeests peeled back to allow Ronan the undivided attention. To his surprise, the Duke of Stoke immediately approached them. He bowed gallantly over Dahlia's hand, obviously pleased to see her. "I have my daughter back, and I owe it all to you."

When the duke left their side, Dahlia turned to him in a fret. "Oh, Ronan. I hope this is true. But I'm so worried disaster is about to strike."

"Let's hope not. Perhaps Lady Melinda will fall in love with someone new. And it sounds like this Dawson character has a good head on his shoulders. He's likely to put her off so that she'll give up and seek a real marquess this time, instead of the fake marquess she's been going on about."

Dahlia nodded pensively. "I wonder if he is fake, after all. What if her marquess actually does exist?"

"Fret about it later. Cheer up, Queen Pea. Everyone will believe you're tired of me already."

She shook her head and laughed. "That will never happen. I love you, Ronan."

"Love you, too."

The Duke of Edgeware came up to them, similarly bowing over

Dahlia's hand and casting her a grin. "Dillie says I am not allowed home if your husband's budget does not pass. I'm rather fond of my wife. Rather enjoy sharing our cozy home with her. So don't fail me, Brayden. That budget had better pass."

Dahlia smiled, knowing Edgeware's cozy home was one of the finest houses in London. But she had no doubt it was filled with happiness and warmth because he and Dillie truly loved each other. "Give my cousin a hug for me. Your Grace, I sincerely hope all will be successful, and you shall return victorious to her open arms."

This is how they made their way onto the floor of the House of Lords, constantly stopped by well-wishers and taking a moment to respond with good cheer. The Lord Admiral greeted them but quickly stepped aside to allow others to approach them. Ronan received congratulations from many of the lords, not only for his rescue of The Invictus but also for his marriage to his obviously beautiful and adoring bride.

They only had a moment before the Earl of Wycke stepped forward to escort Dahlia to the spectator gallery. But that brief moment, and the love shining in her eyes as she bid him farewell, was enough to have every newspaper sketch artist suddenly pulling out their pads and furiously drawing Dahlia, intent on capturing her perfect expression of love.

Ronan's gaze did not leave her as she was led out of the hall.

His were not the only eyes following her, nor was his heart the only one sad to see her leave. There was something enchanting about Dahlia, a natural beauty and grace that captivated more than a few old lords and several younger ones as well.

Joshua lightly nudged him. "Session's about to be brought to order. Wipe that besotted grin off your face, or these peers will make mincemeat out of you."

Reluctantly, Ronan returned his attention to the business at hand. If not for today's vote, neither he, Joshua, nor Robbie would have been permitted to remain in the main chamber of the House of Lords once the Lord Chancellor opened the session. But this was the special day they'd all been working hard toward these many months.

His budget was brought up first. Despite scowls and grumbling from Lord Peckham, who made a feeble attempt to fault him for The Invictus incident, it easily passed.

Since the lords and the public had also heard of Joshua's feats of heroism in saving Ronan, it was no surprise that the army budget also passed with little objection.

Usually, he and Joshua would have left the floor once their presence was no longer necessary, but they remained in a show of support for Robbie and the Scottish military forces.

It suddenly struck Ronan that his friend, despite having hordes of women in the spectator gallery swooning over him, was quite alone.

Of course, Robbie would flirt with these women afterward. But right now, his concentration was on the peers, and he did not glance up even once at the ladies. Was there not one among them who had captured his interest?

Ronan knew it would take a very special young lady to claim this tough Scot's heart.

He was also sad to note there were very few Scottish lords present to support Robbie. Not even his grandfather, the Earl of Caithness, was in attendance. That old fox was among the sixteen Scottish peers permitted to sit in the House of Lords. But most of them were already on their way north because they could not be present to cast their votes and also make it up to Scotland in time for their Hogmanay celebrations.

Indeed, Robbie was alone, the burden of obtaining sufficient funds for the Highlands regiments falling upon his lone shoulders.

As for the holidays, Robbie would be included in all the Brayden festivities, of course. Likely the Earl of Wycke would have him over as well since Wycke's sister was married to Robbie's brother. But it wasn't the same as sharing the holidays with family.

Well, the big Scott was about to get a dose of love once he got his hands on *The Book of Love.*

Ronan wasn't sure the book would work on Robbie the way it had on the other men who had fallen prey to its supposed power. In truth, he did not believe the book could make any man fall in love. At best, it helped that reluctant male understand what he was already feeling toward the one woman who would capture his heart.

But Robbie?

If he wanted to raise his prospects, marry into a family of rank and consequence, then Heather was not the girl for him. Nor would Robbie suit Heather's purposes, not if she wanted a peer of the realm.

He dismissed thoughts of them and the book, and returned his attention to the budget vote, thumping Robbie on the back when his funding also passed. As soon as the session was adjourned, the three of them headed to the spectator gallery. Ronan knew his next action would be frowned upon, but he was newly wed and in love with his wife. Surely, no one would complain when he cupped her face in his hands and gently kissed her on the lips.

To his surprise, a sketch of him doing this began circulating in the newspapers by the afternoon. Several papers had put out a special edition on the 'hero of Tilbury' as he was now known. He should have been angry they'd included a sketch of their kiss, but it was his fault for the display of affection. The artists present had captured the moment beautifully and with all due respect.

Dahlia was smiling and sighing over it, as were all the women in the family. He supposed it was all right then. But he silently chided himself and vowed to leave these displays for the bedchamber from now on.

They had only been back at Joshua's home for about an hour when Finn came by. "Congratulations to both of you. I heard the army and navy budgets passed unscathed. I have something for you,

Ronan."

He held out some papers and several sets of keys. "The house is yours. Lady Wellbrook has moved out and is on her way to Bath as we speak. Her furniture is loaded in wagons and will eventually reach her new home, although it will be rough going in this weather. Will you see the house today or wait until tomorrow?"

Dahlia's eyes widened in delight. "What do you think, Ronan? It isn't very far from here."

He chuckled. "Since I doubt I can hold you back, sure. Why not?"

Joshua nodded. "My coachman will have the carriage readied again."

"That is very kind of you," Dahlia said. "Would you like to join us in touring the house? And you, Finn? We cannot thank you enough for taking care of this matter."

"I'll pass," Finn said. "Belle will expect me home soon. We'll stop by one day next week. I'm sure you'll be there every day to oversee its decoration."

Holly and Joshua also declined as well. "You should walk through it just the two of you. Besides, Heather will be back soon. She went to Lady Dayne's tea with Aunt Sophie. It should be ending about now, and I would rather not have her return to an empty house. Besides, she'll be excited to hear how the Parliament vote went."

He and Dahlia left shortly afterward.

Climbing into the carriage proved easier than it had this morning. Although he'd already been on his feet far longer than Dr. Farthingale had recommended, there was something uplifting about this day that gave him renewed strength. He might feel the aches tomorrow, but he wouldn't care then.

In truth, the wonder in Dahlia's eyes was worth any amount of discomfort. She was so obviously happy, it made his own heart soar. "We'll just explore these main rooms," she said, her brow furrowed in concern about his climbing the stairs. "No need to inspect the bedchambers yet. We can do that tomorrow at our leisure."

She'd brought along her pencils and a sketchbook, and immediately began to make rough drawings of each room. The guest salon, the family parlor, the dining room, the study, the library. But once done with the library sketch, she closed her pad. "We've done enough for one day."

He did not object.

Standing around was far more tiring than walking, and he'd probably done too much of both.

Holly had supper ready for all of them by the time they returned. Heather was back, and he was not surprised to find Robbie seated in the parlor, drink in hand, as he and Joshua discussed the successes of the day.

It was to be just the six of them for supper this evening. Holly's cook had prepared a hearty stew that the women seemed to peck at, and the men devoured like jungle beasts. Dahlia laughed when he glanced at her questioningly. "If I ate like you, my stomach would explode," she said with a grin. "I am amazed at the amount of food you are able to shovel inside of you."

He realized then how different setting up a household with one's wife would be from living with brothers and a drill sergeant for a mother. A loving mother, of course. But he did not think Dahlia would be smacking him on the head whenever he did something foolish. She would either hold it in or she would spill quiet tears that would rip his heart worse than any smack to the head.

He was still thinking of this a short while later as they retired to their bedchamber. He'd only been thinking of claiming her, not how to go about it. But as she stood by the fire's glow, removing her pelisse and then sitting on a chair to take off her shoes and stockings, he knelt by her side. "Let me do that for you, Queen Pea."

She watched, wide-eyed and blushing, as he knelt before her and took off her shoes, setting each one aside.

She eeped as he slipped his hands beneath her gown and slowly slid one stocking off and then the other, also setting each one aside.

"I'll help you out of your gown," he said, his voice aching and raw as he lifted to his feet and drew her up along with him. She was still blushing, but he knew she was curious and excited. Her breaths were coming faster now, noticeable by the slight heave of her breasts.

He turned her around and bent to plant light kisses on her neck as he slowly undid the fastenings of her gown, taking his time to trace his fingers over the swells and curves of her body and caress her as he nudged the gown ever lower until it fell in a pool at her feet. "Oh, goodness. My legs are soft as pudding."

"Ah, then I have done my job." He lifted her in his arms and carried her to bed.

She gasped. "Ronan, your ribs!"

They didn't hurt.

Nor did it bother him that his heart was thundering. The molten heat of his desire numbed him to any pain. He set her down in the center of the bed, leaving her still clad in her chemise while he stepped back to peel off his jacket and shirt. But he could not manage his boots on his own. *Bollocks.* He should have thought of that first. Dahlia realized his difficulty and scrambled off the bed to help him.

Ah, so much for prowess.

He clutched his ribs as the effort of tugging off his boots shot bolts of pain up his sides, and stars burst in his eyes. When his vision cleared, he saw her look of concern. "Ronan, perhaps we ought to wait–"

"Hell, no. I'm fine, Queen Pea. Truly." He rose and took her in his arms, staving off further protest by claiming her mouth in a torrid kiss that did wonders to stir her heart and arouse her body. He felt her every slight change and knew she was responding to him with a heightened awareness of pleasure.

She pressed herself against him so that he could feel the pounding of her heart against his own. Her breasts, those beautiful, plump mounds he was determined to explore quite thoroughly, molded to the hard planes of his chest. The rope burns he'd suffered had yet to fully heal. Would his skin's rough texture bother her? She did not appear to mind it.

He breathed her in, lost himself in the cinnamon and apple scent of her skin.

He unpinned her hair and ran his fingers through the silken length, then removed her chemise and tossed it to the foot of their bed, not caring where it landed. This angel was in his arms, lost in his hot kisses, and he was lost in the splendor of her body, the perfect way she fit against him and how right she was for him in so many other ways.

Then somehow, they were on the bed again, atop the covers, and she was beneath his body. He cupped one full breast and began to tease it with his thumb. She gasped when he brought his mouth to the taut bud and began to gently suckle it.

He moved to the other and did the same, his tongue flicking over it, laving it, and loving Dahlia's response, the honesty of her soft, breathy sighs and whispered moans. "Ronan, I never knew it could be like this."

"Always, with us. I love you, Queen Pea." He moved back up to kiss her throat, her face, and at the same time, his hand moved down her body, caressing and stroking, and finally coming to rest between her thighs.

She gazed at him, questioning what came next but also eager to find out if her steamy look of confusion was any indication. He parted her legs slightly and began to stroke her intimately, watching her response as she closed her eyes and gave herself over to these new sensations of passion.

He loved her expressions, the way she nibbled her lower lip, her sighs, and the way her body responded to his touch. She clung to his shoulders and gave herself over to his touch with so much trust, he felt a boundless love for her.

When he felt she was ready, he entered her slowly and carefully, knowing this experience was new to her and not wanting her to feel any pain.

She wrapped her arms around him as he broke through her maiden barrier, clinging to him as he led her toward fulfillment of this timeless act. His thrusts were cautious at first, but grew bolder as her body adjusted to him. She was slick for him. Hot for him. She was his mate. His love. Forever his.

He took her breathy moans into his mouth, kissing her while he thrust inside her, watching her passion build, knowing just how to make it build. He felt her on the precipice of rapture, wrapped his arms around her, and held her in his embrace as she fell over the edge to experience a woman's pleasure for the first time.

She whispered his name. "Ronan. *Ronan.*" And clung to him tightly. Sweetly.

He followed soon after, spilling himself inside her, lost in his own surge of pleasure.

Heat roared through him.

Hunger and craving for his Queen Pea fired his blood, as he knew it always would. Their coupling had changed him, for he was no longer merely himself but a part of her as well, bound to her in body and heart.

Once they both began to calm, he smiled down at her and kissed her with a gentle longing.

Now spent, he carefully pulled out of her and fell onto his back, drawing her atop him and closing his arms around her.

She had the most incredibly beautiful body.

And the loveliest mouth, now curved in a wondrous smile.

He arched an eyebrow and grinned. "What are you thinking, Queen Pea?"

"I'm not thinking at all. My brain and body have completely

turned to pudding. But I can still feel, and there is so much feeling gushing out of me. I love you, Ronan. I'm so grateful to have you in my life. I don't know what I've ever done to deserve the gift of you."

"Mutual, sweetheart. But you're the gift. Hell, I have no idea what I've ever done to deserve you. But never doubt that I shall always treasure you."

"Who would ever have thought, even a month ago, that we would be married and end up like this?"

He stroked her hair, brushing back her soft curls. "I hoped for it. So many times, I wanted to say something to you. When I pulled the bean out of that Twelfth Night cake, it seemed to pulse in my hands. I knew you would be the one to pull out the pea. You had to be. No one else could ever be my queen. And no one else ever will be. You are the only one who will ever claim my heart."

"As you will only ever be my King Bean. I think I must find a wallpaper of beans and peas and hang it in our bedchamber, what do you think?"

He knew she was teasing. "Do whatever you please, so long as you share my bed and fall asleep in my arms. And always love me."

"Loving you always is the easy part. Perhaps we won't need that wallpaper. Maybe just a small painting on the dining room wall of a pea and a bean and a Twelfth Night cake." She curled herself around his arm, as she'd taken to doing these past nights when every other part of him was covered in that unguent. "You are the best Christmas gift I ever had."

"Mutual, Queen Pea. Sweet dreams, my love."

Chapter Twenty

London, England
May 1821

DAHLIA STOOD BESIDE Ronan in the entry hall of their now decorated home, delighted to be hosting their first party, an afternoon tea. The day was bright and pleasant for what Dahlia hoped would be a casual gathering of friends and family. She was so proud of the work she'd done to bring out the beautiful features of the house and restore it to its original glory.

Adding to the festive air was the fact that so many of her cousins and even her sister, Holly, were sporting telltale tummy bulges that boded of new little Farthingales and Braydens soon to come along. "Your Uncle George is going to have his hands full come summer," Ronan murmured against her ear.

She was delighted for Holly, and her cousins, Honey, Violet, and Belle. Not to mention Dillie and Daisy were also expecting. But what brought tears to her eyes was the news that Ronan's cousin, James, and his Sophie, were going to have their first child. After all their years of marriage, they had almost given up hope. "We dared not say anything to anyone until now," Sophie confided, "but I am four months along. We're still afraid to talk about it, for this is our miracle baby, isn't it? However, we wanted the family to know."

"Congratulations. Have you told Uncle John and Aunt Sophie?" Dahlia did not get a response before their families flocked around

Sophie and James, carrying them off into the parlor. But she expected her aunt and uncle had been the first ones told, probably weeks ago. They were the two Sophies – Sophie Farthingale and Sophie Brayden, who was also known as Lady Exmoor – and they had grown to be very close friends.

A few minutes later, Heather came up to her. "Is he here yet?"

Dahlia wasn't certain who she meant, and then the realization dawned on her. "You're here with the Marquess of Tilbury. You are betrothed and about to marry him. Who else would you be looking for?"

Her sister tipped her chin up. "Why didn't you tell me Robbie had resigned his position as Parliament liaison and was returning to Caithness for good? Is this why he disappeared three months ago without a word to me? And now he's back to wind up his affairs in London and then be gone forever."

"Why are you overset? I assumed you knew. I gave you *The Book of Love* shortly after the new year. Have you not read it with him?"

"No."

Dahlia's eyes widened in dismay. "You promised you would. Oh, Heather! You *promised*."

"Hell," Ronan said softly. "Why didn't you, Heather?"

"Because I… Lord Tilbury was courting me, and I saw no need. But I gave the book to Robbie, and I was always available to him if he wanted to discuss any particularly confusing passages." She clasped her hands and began to wring them. "What's wrong with the two of you? Why are you frowning at me?"

"You broke your word." Dahlia wanted to grab her sister by the shoulders and shake her. "Have you read any of the book?"

"Me? Well, no."

Dahlia wasn't certain why she was now getting distressed over her sister's actions. Or rather, inaction. But her stomach was twisted in knots, and she could not shake the feeling that something was terribly wrong. She wasn't certain why she felt this way. After all, the Marquess of Tilbury was a very good man. "You must read it with Robbie. You have to do it before he leaves."

Ronan put an arm around her waist. "Dahlia, love. It doesn't matter. Your sister is marrying Tilbury in a few weeks."

"No, it does. It matters very much. You lied to me, Heather. You promised me you would. *You promised.*"

Tears sprang in her sister's eyes. "Don't be angry with me. I couldn't bear it if you were. I love you, Dahlia."

"And I love you. This is why you have to read the book with Robbie."

"Don't make me do it. Please, don't." Tears were now trailing down Heather's cheeks. "I'll fall in love with him if I do, and then I'll never marry my marquess. And why would you wish me on Robbie? Shouldn't he have the right to reach for the moon and stars? An earl's daughter? Or the daughter of a duke? Why would you foist a Yorkshire merchant's daughter on him?"

She understood her sister's fears, but her own feelings were powerful, and she was only looking after her sister's happiness. "The book won't make you feel anything you don't already feel, Heather. It isn't about tricking you into falling in love with the wrong man. It's about having you understand what true love is all about and finding the *right* man."

Dahlia glanced at Ronan, now worried she had overstepped and was breaking her sister's heart. After all, with Heather's wedding almost upon them, it was too late for her to break things off with the Marquess of Tilbury.

"The *right* man? Are you suggesting I haven't found him? I don't want to hear another word." With a sob, Heather turned and fled the house.

Now Dahlia wanted to cry. "Oh, Ronan. We ought to go after her."

"No, love. She won't go far. She'll probably head for the garden in the square and sulk there for a little while. Give her a moment to herself. I'll go fetch her if she isn't back in ten minutes."

Dahlia laughed mirthlessly. "Is it ten minutes yet?"

"Not even ten seconds, Queen Pea." His arm was still around her waist, now resting there protectively. He knew she was overset, and being Ronan, he was going to protect her even if he thought she was in the wrong.

He must have read her thoughts. "You have the right of it. She broke her promise. But it wasn't out of immaturity or malice. She broke her oath because she's desperately afraid of her feelings for Robbie."

Dahlia looked up at him, loving him more than she could ever convey. "I shouldn't have said anything. What if I've forced her and Robbie together and it turns out Robbie doesn't want her? I have to find her and apologize."

"I'll come with you, love. We both owe her the apology."

But they had yet to take a step before there was a commotion at the door, and their butler was knocked aside. "Grimsby, what…"

Robbie strode in, carrying an injured Heather in his arms.

Dahlia swooned and would have collapsed if Ronan had not still been holding her.

"Robbie, bloody hell! What happened?"

"Och, Ronan. I'm not sure. The pixie ran straight into the street and almost got run down by a passing carriage."

"Run down!" Dahlia was going to faint. "This is all my fault. I'll never forgive myself."

"She's fine. No harm done," Robbie quickly assured, obviously noting Dahlia's pallor. "I pulled her to safety, but I think she might have twisted her ankle. Why was she running off in tears? What happened to overset her?"

Dahlia swallowed hard. "I scolded her. I shouldn't have. Please,

Robbie. Carry her upstairs to one of the guest bedchambers while I find Uncle George. My poor uncle. We never give him a moment's rest." She placed a hand gently on Heather's arm. "I'll tell Lord Tilbury you've–"

Heather inhaled sharply. "No! I don't want him to see me like this. Robbie, please take me upstairs. He'll think I'm a ninny and will never want to marry me."

Robbie appeared to lose patience with her. "He's already committed to marrying ye. He canno' back out of it now. Dry yer tears, Heather. Ye'll be a marchioness before the month is out."

Dahlia watched him stomp upstairs with Heather in his arms.

Ronan ran a hand through his hair. "Hell, Robbie's hurting, too."

Dahlia did not think she could feel any worse than she did now. "Is he in love with her?"

"I honestly don't know. But he's a Scot, and when a Scot loses his heart, it's forever. Even a hound like Robbie."

She nodded, now feeling quite miserable. "Let me fetch Uncle George."

Ronan held onto her a moment longer. "I love you, Queen Pea. Please don't be sad. Your sister has to make her own choices and live with her own decisions. You cannot live her life for her or force her to follow your advice. Put it out of your head for now. You need to put on a smile and dazzle our newly arrived guests."

He tipped her chin up when he saw she was nibbling her lip, a sign of her fretting. "Queen Pea, it rips me apart to see you hurting."

She reached up and kissed him. "I know, my love. I'll be all right in a moment. I suppose there's little I can do about Heather now. She and Robbie are together again…not under the best circumstances, but I have faith that whatever is meant to happen, will happen."

She tucked her arm in his as they walked into their newly decorated parlor together. It was a beautiful room, done in soft tones with a splash of floral in the pillows and curtains. She considered saying a word to the Marquess of Tilbury, for he would surely have noticed Heather's absence by now. But he appeared engaged in deep conversation with the Duke of Stoke and Lady Melinda.

A shiver ran up her spine.

Ronan frowned. "Love, are you certain you're all right?"

"Yes. Let's find Uncle George. Oh, there he is, talking to Rupert."

She left the party a moment to lead her uncle upstairs. When they reached the guest bedchamber, they found Heather lying on the bed, her shoes and the stocking on her injured foot removed. Her foot was resting on a pillow, and she had a damp cloth across her brow.

"Thank you, Robbie," Dahlia said, realizing it could only have been him tending to Heather.

George arched an eyebrow. "You've done most of the work, MacLauren. Left little for me to do but bind her ankle. Is it broken?"

"No, just a mild sprain." He had been standing on the opposite side of the room, his back to all of them as he peered out the window onto the street below. But he turned to face them now. "I'll be going. Ye dinna need me here."

Heather gasped and sat up. "Robbie, please. Stay."

He did not look at all delighted with the request. "Why?"

"Because I need you to read *The Book of Love* with me. I promised my sister I would. I broke my oath to her, and I'm so ashamed. I'll be off my foot for a few days. Won't I, Uncle George?"

Their uncle sighed and rolled his eyes. "Yes, two days for certain."

"See, Robbie." Heather cast him a pleading look that he ignored, refusing to even look at her. "I mean to make things right."

"Och, pixie. Ye're too late for that. I'll return the book to ye before the week is out. Read it all ye like. Read it with yer marquess, for all I care." He stormed out of the room.

Heather's chin wobbled, and her eyes turned watery. "Oh, Dahlia! What have I done?"

Dahlia sat on the bed beside her sister and wrapped her arms around her. "Nothing that wasn't meant to happen." She fervently hoped so. "Just listen to your heart. The magic will happen."

It had to happen, didn't it?

Whether or not Heather ever read the book with Robbie.

Ronan walked in just then. "I was worried about you."

Heather believed he was talking about her. "Only an ankle sprain," she said. "I'll be fine in a day or two, right Uncle George?"

"Yes, Heather."

Dahlia kissed her sister. "I had better return to my guests. I'll send a maid up to take care of you."

She walked out with Ronan and turned to him just before they made their way downstairs. "Ronan, I love you."

He arched an eyebrow. "What brought that on?"

"Other than you are wildly handsome, and I cannot keep my hands off you."

He stroked her cheek affectionately. "I'm going to remind you of your words as I lure you into my bed tonight."

"You cannot lure me if I'm determined to go willingly. Desperately. Eagerly."

He grinned. "Fine. And by the way, feel free to explore my body to your heart's content. I won't stop you." He nodded toward their bedchamber. "I'm sure no one will miss us. Care to…"

She threw her arms around him and hugged him fiercely, knowing she must have surprised him by her actions. "Oh, Ronan! I feel so off-balance. Every little thing seems to make me cry. I must have been insufferable this past week. And now Heather is overset, and it's all my fault."

"It isn't. She knew what she was doing…or avoiding. Robbie's back now, and I expect these next few weeks are not going to be dull. They are going to do whatever they are meant to do, and hearts will win out in the end. As for you…" He laughed softly. "How are you feeling?"

"Wretched. You know I am. I've been so worked up over this party and now Heather. My stomach is in a constant roil. I haven't been able to hold down my food all week. Why are you laughing?"

He kissed her with aching sweetness. "Because, my love, I strongly suspect that *roil* you are feeling is my son or daughter."

She looked up at him, gaping. "What? How can you be sure?"

He held out his hands, cupping them in the air and glancing at her breasts. "I know your body. You used to fill the cups of my hands, and now you spill over–"

"Ronan! That is not scientific at all."

"But I'll wager it is just as accurate. Dry your tears, my beautiful Queen Pea. I think I shall be a father by Christmas, and you shall be the most beautiful mother in the world."

Also by Meara Platt

FARTHINGALE SERIES
My Fair Lily
The Duke I'm Going To Marry
Rules For Reforming A Rake
A Midsummer's Kiss
The Viscount's Rose
Earl Of Hearts
If You Wished For Me
Never Dare A Duke
Capturing The Heart Of A Cameron

BOOK OF LOVE SERIES
The Look of Love
The Touch of Love
The Taste of Love
The Song of Love
The Scent of Love
The Kiss of Love
The Chance of Love
The Gift of Love
The Heart of Love
The Hope of Love (novella)

DARK GARDENS SERIES
Garden of Shadows
Garden of Light
Garden of Dragons

Garden of Destiny

THE BRAYDENS

A Match Made In Duty

Earl of Westcliff

Fortune's Dragon

Earl of Kinross

Pearls of Fire*

(*also in Pirates of Britannia series)

Aislin

Gennalyn

DeWOLFE PACK ANGELS SERIES

Nobody's Angel

Kiss An Angel

Bhrodi's Angel

About the Author

Meara Platt is an award winning, USA TODAY bestselling author and an Amazon UK All-Star. Her favorite place in all the world is England's Lake District, which may not come as a surprise since many of her stories are set in that idyllic landscape, including her paranormal romance Dark Gardens series. Learn more about the Dark Gardens and Meara's lighthearted and humorous Regency romances in her Farthingale series and Book of Love series, or her warmhearted Regency romances in her Braydens series by visiting her website at www.mearaplatt.com.

Made in the USA
Columbia, SC
19 June 2025